986549 $24.00

FICTION
MORGAN   Morgan, Charlotte,
          One August day

One August Day

One August Day

A Novel

by
Charlotte Morgan

VAN NESTE BOOKS
Midlothian, VA

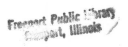

Library of Congress Cataloging-in-Publication Data

Morgan, Charlotte.
   One August Day / Charlotte Morgan—1st ed.
      p.   cm.
   ISBN 0-9657639-1-9 (alk. paper)
   1. Hurricane Camille, 1969--Fiction.
   2. Hurricanes--Virginia--Nelson County--History--
   20th century--Fiction. 3. Hurricanes--Virginia--
   Richmond--History--20th century--Fiction.
   I. Title.
   PS3563.0824505   1998
   813'.54--dc21   97-23020
                                                        CIP
This novel is a work of fiction. While the flood is an historical fact, the characters are invented, and their resemblance, if any, to real-life people is coincidental.

First edition: September 1998

Manufactured in the United States of America

VAN NESTE BOOKS
12836 Ashtree Road
Midlothian, VA 23113

For John
and, especially, for the eight

The rain ceases, and a bird's clear song suddenly announces the difference between Heaven and hell.

Thomas Merton—*The Sacred Land*

Remember me as you walk by
For as you are, so once was I
And as I am, so you will be;
Remember me.

Anonymous Headstone
Tombstone, Arizona

On the evening of August 19, 1969, and early morning of August 20, during a five-hour period, rain in excess of twenty-five inches fell on Nelson County, Virginia. This rainfall still holds the world record.

Stirring to her son's restless sleep sounds, Helen Jansky roused from her own deep slumber. Shaking herself awake, forcing herself up onto her elbows, she had no inkling as she looked toward the hands on the softly-lit face of the bedside clock that she wouldn't be lying back down in her warm bed again. The time: 4:19. She groaned.

Stevie's moaning, his insistent "Uh, uh, nunh-unh," interrupted the sole calm and quiet Helen usually experienced in a day. Easing her heavy warm body from her side of the bed so as not to bother Joe, her mommy-antenna fully alert now, she felt her way out the dark room, down the hallway to her son's half-shut door. He was the only one of the five of them who had a room to himself; she breathed a silent thank goodness for that small advantage. The others might not hear.

"Unhh, unhh, uh-uh," he kept whimpering, louder and louder, thrashing the air in front of him with his hands, kicking the top sheet down around his feet.

Helen moved toward the sound, touched her oldest child's shoulder soft and easy, said in a whisper, "Stevie, honey, you're all right, Stevie."

He sat up, rigid. While Helen couldn't see his facial features, she sensed the shocked-animal fear in his stiff shoulders and chest.

"Mama's here, Stevie," she assured him, barely touching his thin shoulder again.

He turned toward her. "Mama? Go back to bed, Mama. Please. Don't wake him up." His voice, too, was no more than a hurried, faint murmur, as though a lurking intruder might hear him, might figure out where he was and come for him.

Helen moved closer to her son, tried to smoothe his

sweat-damp hair. "What were you dreaming, Stevie? Tell me."

He shook her hand away, lying back down. "Pleeease. Go back to bed, Mama."

"You sure you're okay?"

"I'm sure."

"All right. Love you." She tiptoed to the hall, stopped outside the door to listen until she could hear his steady back-to-sleep breathing. What in the world were Stevie's nightmares about? He wouldn't tell her, insisted each time he was fine; he didn't want her to come to him. Still, she hated not being able to comfort him like she had when he was little and woke in the dark needing to go to the bathroom or get a drink of water. What in heaven's name did he dream about that frightened him so?

The bad-dream nights had only started this summer. The first few times she'd been uneasy, but told herself it was only the heat and the humidity that caused him to be restless. This city could be brutal in July; they all had a hard time getting settled. But the nightmares kept on, night after night, and the noises he made sounded like someone terrified beyond all reason. In daylight, Stevie refused to talk about the dreams, even to her, begged her please not to mention them.

Helen ran her fingers through her thick dark hair, feeling helpless. Stevie was asleep again already, probably exhausted, but she was fully awake. Might as well tiptoe back to the room, shut off the alarm, get going on the day, she decided. Usually she was up at five fifteen anyway. She could sort the clothes she'd brought in from the line late yesterday, start breakfast. Creamed chipped beef and biscuits. Joe liked that, but it'd been too hot even first thing in the morning lately to cook anything in the oven. Still, he insisted on a big breakfast, said a man couldn't be expected to do a day's work on cereal. That's what she'd do, fix creamed chip beef and biscuits. Weekend food. Stevie would like that, too, though she'd have to leave it on the stove for him and the girls to reheat, since she'd be at work before they got up.

Quiet as a cat, Helen made her way down the dark hall toward her bedroom. If she tried to go back to sleep now, she'd only fidget in bed, maybe wake Joe. No, she'd best leave him be. She paused at her daughters' doorway. The faint aura from Aimee's seashell night light made her two sleeping girls look soft, hazy, like the dreamy children in picture books. Neither stirred; apparently the others hadn't heard Stevie. For an instant Helen had the illusion all was well. Grateful for the moment, for the peaceful, settled feel of the house, she padded to her bedside, guided by the clock's faint bluish-green glow. Not needing to see what she was doing, with that ease of familiarity, Helen pushed down the alarm button. Time to start the day.

Davis Creek,
Nelson County, Virginia
7:35 a.m.

The clock. I didn't hear Daddy's clock chime seven. I can't remember waking up in the morning in my entire life without hearing that clock. I'd bet a bundle Ora forgot to wind it. As many times as I've told her. Maybe it's not seven yet. It's not too bright out, but with the weather we've had these last few days it's hard to tell. Been cold some this week off and on. Then so blamed hot I can hardly get my breath. Funny weather, even for August. I'll lie here a few more minutes and listen, see if I hear the ticking. So blessed quiet in this house, I can hear it ticking if I listen. I don't know why I pulled this quilt up. It's about to smother me. It's so warm already, even a sheet would be stifling. Must be close to eight.

She didn't wind it, I'm sure of it. And she promised Daddy she'd take care of that clock just like he did, and it's certain he never went a Sunday night without tending to it. He was one for habits, anybody would say the same. He made a ritual of winding that clock. Even after he stopped going into town to tend to his office he still got up every morning and shaved and dressed and put on his tie and coat. He was about the handsomest man that ever lived. If Henry Trice had possessed half of Daddy's looks and a particle of his charm I might have let him marry me. Might have.

She didn't wind it because she didn't come Sunday. She told me she was going to that revival down in Tyro. Still, it's her job. I recall now. She told me to wind it. Well it's not mine to do, it's hers. All that carrying on she does about Jesus is downright bad taste. It's not right to make such a display of yourself, not proper at all. If I've told her once I've told her a dozen times, but she will insist on going to those hollerin revivals. I can't even remember the time I saw one, but I must have. I can see it as clear in my head. Practically smell it, it's that real. Ironed starchy clothes, fresh perspiration, talcum powder heavy in the air, like a dozen roses. Or a Sunday afternoon baptism, that fresh water and fried fish scent mixing with the leafy green smell. Yes I do. Certainly never went to one of them heathen things with my daddy, that's for sure. Must've come upon it, out riding or walking, that's all. Mind's a funny thing, plays tricks when you get up in age. Goodness, my stomach's roaring; I'm hungry enough to eat half a ham. Where in the world is that Ora anyway?

I know: Daddy and I were at Nelson County Day when one of those holy-roller meetings was going on in the field right next to the fairground. I must have been seventeen, 'cause I had that yellow parasol he'd given me for Valentine's Day, and Mama'd been dead a few years. He pointed to those people screaming and sweating over in the field, said they looked more like hogs squealing around in the pen before feedin time. Not a bit like civilized people. Which they weren't. Ora ought to have a higher opinion of herself.

I'm hungry as a field hand. It's bound to be close to eight. She ought to be here. She's supposed to have my breakfast ready by now. She knows I can't stand to wait.

Gives me the nervous stomach, and then I can't enjoy my food. I intend to let her have a piece of my mind concerning that clock, I surely do. She told me she wasn't coming yesterday, but still it's her job, not mine.

She's been a regular know-it-all lately. Downright bossy at times. Who does she think she is I'd like to know. I won't have her staring at me like it's my fault. Doesn't matter one bit she's been with me so long. Let me see, for more than fifty years now; I hate to think how long it's been. Yes indeed, she came stepping up the hill, calm as you please, no more than a day or two after Mama died. Not that I had a thing to do with it. Nobody acted like I should've had a say, even though I was thirteen and already knew my own mind. I certainly did. Daddy and I could've gotten along just fine. All we needed was somebody to cook and clean. Cinchy kept to herself. She did fine by herself. Last thing we needed was a busybody. Aunt Lucy and Aunt Bunny were the ones who talked him into it, convinced him I had to have a companion, what with all the hired men around; more like a watchdog, if you ask me.

Still there's no call for her to act so familiar. I've got to talk to her about those smart-alecky ways of hers. Daddy would, he certainly would. "Don't beat around the bush," he'd say; "speak your mind." Didn't he make her promise when he died that she'd stick by me? Leaving her money and all, like she was one of the family. I wish he'd told me how much, but Mr. Gamble insisted I wasn't to know. Said that was Daddy's express wish. And she promised to do what he asked. He wrote it out and she put her name, and she repeated out loud so I could hear. Right there at his bedside. Those mahogany posters pointing up to the sky, like witnesses. Course I was so beside myself all that week after Doctor Elliot put him to bed with his heart I hardly remember a thing, but I do remember that. I couldn't forget it if I wanted to. That was his one worry, for me to be taken care of properly. For me to have no worries.

My ankles certainly are swelled up. Feels like my skin's about to split. I'll have to take care to stay off my feet today. Keep them propped. It's this heat. August is just about unbearable anymore. Seems worse than when I was a girl. I never remember so much as thinking about the heat. What's that racket?

"That you, Ora? Come up here right this minute. What time is it? I hear you clattering around down there, so don't act like you don't hear me. I heard the door slam clear as thunder. I want to talk to you. Come on up here right this minute, you hear? Don't bother stokin up that stove."

I guess I'd better get up out of this bed. These old bones are moving slow as sorghum today. It's so hot already. I better put my teeth in. I'm so hungry. I want a big breakfast. Get my strength up.

"Ora. Ora. I mean it."

Hot as it is, maybe I will try those bermudas Ora bought for me at the IGA. I dare her to say a word. They do feel good, considerably cooler than a slip and dress. Let me see. They must be here in this chifferobe. I don't think I could bear a slip and dress today. I have the whitest skin. Those ankles are swelled about as swelled as I've ever seen them. Yes, these green bermudas will do just fine.

Daddy would be shocked to see a lady going around the place in shorts. But like it or not, Daddy, times have changed. That's a fact. I'd love to see the expression on Aunt Lucy's face if she saw me in these Bermudas. I can just hear her now, "Bunny, do you see what Charlotte's got on? Well, I declare. If that don't beat all." I don't remember it being this hot when I was young. Especially first thing in the morning. Mornings were cool. Fresh. Like lemonade. Even in the summer Daddy would have on a white starched shirt and a dark jacket. He never seemed to notice the heat. "Horses sweat, gentlemen perspire, and ladies glow." I remember him saying that just as clear as well water. But since I've put on all this weight I can't bear the heat. Even that baby talcum she gets down at Massie's Store doesn't do a thing to keep me cool in such heat. Now if I was expecting anyone to call I'd find a light summer dress, maybe that pale yellow one that always did show off my coloring to advantage. When was the last time I saw that dress? Whatever happened to it? And some cologne. I can't remember the last time I did that. With just me and Ora there's no sense going to the trouble. I'll put in my teeth and put up my hair. A lady's always conscious of her hair. Mine's just as fine as ever, even if it is mostly white. Fine and lovely. A strong feature of mine, if I do say so myself.

Didn't Henry Trice say in that last letter, "Hair like a fairy-tale princess," or something close to that? He should never have taken such liberties. I had no choice but to throw him off the place. That's what I told Mr. Gamble when he called looking for him at the first of the month that same October. Said they had some business to talk over, said it wasn't like Henry to leave loose ends. I'll have to look up the year on that last disgusting letter he sent.

This brassiere is just too blamed tight. Ora better get the right size next time. It shouldn't be so much trouble to hook. It pretty near wears me out, trying to hook them all. I want that button necklace she gave me. That's the very thing to go with that loose blue plaid shirt. I don't think I could stand another thing against my skin. I'll be sweating like a peach picker if it gets much hotter. Where in the world is it? I could've sworn I left it on my dresser, in that cut glass notions box right next to my silver brush set. How'm I supposed to be able to find anything when she's always up here moving my belongings around, meddlin. Woo, my underclothes are sticking to me already. Here she comes, I can hear her trudging up those steps, slow as if she was going to her own funeral. Better just step out in the hall a minute. Let her see I'm up and around, even without the clock.

Nigras seem to have more get up and go first thing in the morning. Don't know why Ora's grabbing onto that rail so hard. She doesn't carry the weight I carry. She ought to be more spry. That brown face of hers looks almost pale this morning. Hope she didn't get up on the wrong side of the bed. Hope she took her medicine.

"Well what in the world is going on this morning, Ora? When I opened my eyes I thought for a minute I'd died and gone to heaven. The clock didn't chime."

"Morning, Miss Lottie. Sorry I'm a little past time, but James Earl was up most of the night, and I just couldn't seem to step too lively this morning. Well, my, my, you look right smart in those Bermuda shorts; I should say so. Yes indeed. What have you got in mind for breakfast? I've got some nice tomatoes from the garden."

"Didn't you hear what I said? I'm out of sorts this morning, Ora, and it's all on your account. And the last thing in this world I need is one of your excuses, what with the clock stopped. How in heaven's name am I supposed to know what time it is since you didn't wind the clock Sunday evening? I knew it, I knew yesterday afternoon something wasn't right. I could feel it. That clock was losing time all day long, and some time in the night it just stopped. Now what do you have to say about that?" I'll not lower my eyes, even if she does stop dead in her tracks and look at me with that wounded-cow look of hers. She needn't think she can put the blame off on me. Put my hands on my hips. Show her I mean business. Don't bother me a bit when she crosses her arms like that. We both know who's boss.

"Now, Miss Lottie, you know good and well I reminded you to wind that clock at least a dozen times before I left here on Saturday. That was the last thing I said when I walked out the back door. I said, 'Be sure you wind the clock now, Miss Lottie.' You told me you would. You've got no call blaming that on me."

Pout all you want. Don't make a whit of difference to me. "All the same it's your responsibility. Didn't you promise Daddy on his death bed? Doesn't that mean a thing to you?"

"Now don't get riled. Your daddy's got nothing to do with this and you know it. I'll see to it when I go down, I certainly will, but I can't be sure just exactly what time it is, Miss Lottie. It can't be more than half past eight, 'cause I left the house a little before eight myself. I'll do my best to set it, but you've got no cause to go blaming me. Now what do you want to eat? The day's getting away from me."

"Fix me a few slices of bacon and biscuits and some of those tomatoes. And a boiled egg, but don't leave it set too long. I can't stand an egg that's set too long and gotten stiff."

"Don't I know that? Reckon I do. I'll get your breakfast on, then I guess I'd better see to the wash before it gets too hot to be hanging out clothes."

"Have you seen that blue-checked shirt you got for me this spring?"

She acted like she didn't hear that, and her no more than three feet from my face. I know she heard me. Just 'cause she turned her back. Likes to pretend she's losing her hearing. She can hear what she wants to hear, that's for sure. Look at her going down those steps like she's got the cross of Almighty Jesus on her shoulders. She has no right to reproach me. She knows it, too. I could see it in her eyes just as plain as day. Well, it was her fault.

Need to go on back in here and finish my toilette. What did I do with my twenty-dollar gold piece? I want to wear it with the button necklace. It's been a while since I've had it on. They look right becoming together. I know Ora wishes she had them both around her fat brown neck. I can see it in her eyes when she looks at me. One day I'm just going to look her in the eye and say, "Thou shalt not covet." I'd like to see the look on her righteous face then.

When Daddy gave me that gold piece for my eighteenth birthday I cried and cried. There's no end to how good he was to me. I can see it as if he'd just walked out the door no more than a minute ago. He put it right around my neck while I was sitting at the breakfast table and he said, "Just a meager token of my love to my one true treasure." And he kissed me on the cheek. Leaned over from behind me. I can just about smell his shaving soap.

Where did I put it? I could've sworn it was right here in my button box on top of this dresser. I remember I moved it to a new hiding place so Ora wouldn't see it. Time was I'd leave it right out on my vanity with my combs and brushes, but the last few years she's stared at it so I'm sure she'd take it if I gave her half a chance. Better just to hide it. "Get thee behind me, Satan."

She acts so holier-than-thou, spouting Jesus all the time, singing that "Blessed Assurance" till I could scream. But she's not fooling me. I know she's been taking my money. I'm sure of it. I think I took it into Daddy's room. She'd never think to go in there without me. I'd just have to shoot her if I ever caught her in there without me. Find that pistol Henry Trice brought me the day I fired all the help. It's around here somewhere. He showed me how to shoot it. Said I was a natural shot, too.

I remember now. I put my gold necklace in Daddy's humidor, right there beside his bed. She'd never think to look there even if she did go into the room. She wouldn't dare.

"Miss Lottie, I'm putting the bacon on now."

"I can hear you. No need to holler so." You'd think she was deaf the way she hollers. I've told her time and again it's not proper manners. She should come to the door, wait to be acknowledged. Daddy always did say, "Breeding will out."

Sometimes when I come in here in his room it seems to me like Daddy's right behind me, and I could look back at the door and see his shadow ahead of him. I can feel him in here, I truly can. Reminds me of that book we used to read out loud together, *Can the Living Talk to the Dead?* He would laugh so. I can about hear him. I'll have to read some later. All the parts. Here's my necklace, right where I left it. This gold piece feels so good in my hand, like it's alive. If Ora ever dared to put it on I bet it would burn a circle right into her skin. Her brown dirty-looking skin.

I can smell that bacon all the way up here. That bacon smells good. I need to build up my stamina. Maybe today I'll walk down to the creek and look for gentians. Daddy said my eyes are just the color of gentians. He had the most beautiful blue eyes I've ever seen. Wise and kind and generous. The steps are a nuisance when my feet are in this shape. I don't know, what with my feet so swelled up, if I ought to try to walk far today. My stomach's starting to growl. It's all her fault for not winding that clock. There she is at the foot of the steps, looking put out already and the day just getting started good.

"The biscuits will be done in a few minutes, Miss Lottie. Do you want me to bring up this checkered shirt I washed out yesterday?"

"That'll do fine; bring it to the top of the stairs." Here she comes. I don't want her to see me in Daddy's room. She might figure out about the gold piece. "That blue shirt is about the color of my button necklace, Ora. Do you remember when you gave that to me?"

"Reckon I do. Here's the shirt. You just laughed, said it wasn't hardly fit for a lady. Notice you kept it though."

"That was the year after you came, the year after Mama died. You made it in that Vacation Bible School, the one the Baptists put on. I remember thinking it was the funniest looking piece of jewelry I'd ever seen. And when I wore it to supper one night, Daddy just laughed, asked if I was fixing to run away with the Gypsies."

"I heard him say that. I should've told you, Give it back to me, Miss Lottie, if you think you're too good for it, but I held my tongue. I see you're wearing it today. I expect I'd better check my biscuits."

"I'll put my combs in and be right there. If we've got any more of those damson preserves you put up last summer set them out, too. I've got a taste for something sweet. Are you looking for rain today? I thought I might walk down beside the creek in a little bit to cool off. Maybe pick some gentians for the table."

"I asked James Earl what the weather was gonna be like today, sensitive as he is to weather. He just rolled his eyes to the sky and made his moaning sound. He had a terrible restless night. With all the rain we've had lately I suspect it won't rain any more today, though. Maybe we'll get a bit of heat lightning around dusk. The rain hasn't done a thing to cool things off this morning. Can't imagine it being this hot this early. Don't seem right. I would like to get a wash on the line, just in case."

"Get on in there and put my food on the table before I faint. I'll be right there." Ora will ramble on about the most meaningless things. I'll pick some of those gentians and walk to Daddy's grave, that's what I'll do. After breakfast. I haven't been up there all this week 'cause of the cold and rain, and I feel an urge to go.

Davis Creek, Virginia
7:55 a.m.

"Behold, he is coming in the clouds! Behold, he is coming in the clouds!"

Clarence Winston quoted Revelations, his favorite book of the New Testament, as he walked down Route 29 toward the turn-off for Saunders Orchards. Most mornings he was there by now, had already picked an hour in the cooler early air. But today he hadn't gotten up on time, hadn't even taken five minutes to wash in the creek. He was dirt grubby. That wasn't a thing like him; he was one for clean habits. With all the rain lately, he'd been forced to move his camp-site. His sleep had been disturbed, his routine had gotten disrupted. He didn't like that edgy off-balance feeling one bit. He tilted his bushy head so he could see the blue-grey sky above the brim of his USHER cap. "Behold, he is coming in the clouds!"

Ain't enough clouds today, he thought. Some. Not enough. Air's already heavy and prickly, like one of them scratchy blankets they give you on the inside. Heat like this'll make them pickers go slow, them sissy split-tail pickers that work in twos. They probably squat to pee. Hell, I can go faster than any pair of them; working alone I'll have more peaches by the end of the day, even getting a late start, than any pair of them pussies.

"Behold, he is coming in the clouds!" His boots clacked

on the asphalt in time to his words. Today wasn't the day of the second coming, he could see that. But maybe he'd baptize Diane tonight, purify her in the eyes of her maker. Maybe this was the day the Lord had made for that particular holy task.

Clarence Winston hustled to the orchard, anxious to get his day's picking behind him, looking ahead to going to McGritz and watching Diane. "Behold, he is coming in the clouds!"

Richmond, Virginia
8:15 a.m.

" . . . always get what you wa-ant;
You can't always get what you wa-ant,
You can't always get what you wa-ant . . ."

The Stones blasted from the clock radio.

Judy Marsh, still half asleep, her eyes closed against the morning sun coming through bare windows, fumbled around by the bed, unable at first to find the radio because it was on the floor. Finally her fingers found the source of the music, and she felt the familiar knobs and buttons until she came to the one she recognized as the snooze alarm. She hit it, but the song continued, "But if you try some time, you just might find . . ." Singing along in her head she thought, I'll just give the damn piece of junk to the Goodwill when they come.

She sat straight up. It's today. Today's the day, she thought. Doggone. How could I forget? She threw the sheet back and sat on the edge of the single bed, running her fingers through her long brown hair, suddenly wide awake. She looked down at the clock face. 8:15. The men from Goodwill are coming in a few minutes. At least they said they'd be here first thing, around nine. I've got to get a

21

move on. The sooner I get started, the sooner I'll be in Lexington. With Drew.

She stood and put both hands on her hips, arching her back and shoulders, looking around the almost-empty bedroom. Where's my list? Where did I leave my clothes? None of her furniture was where it usually was, except for the bed. Boxes of things left over from the yard sale were stacked all over the room. The men would come and take those and the last few pieces of furniture and odds and ends scattered throughout the apartment, and she'd be on her way. All that was left were the things she hadn't been able to sell at the sale, and the things Mrs. Calabash didn't want. And the bed. She'd needed that last night. But she wouldn't be needing it any more. No more sleeping alone.

Walking over to the window she looked out as the song tailed off and the voice of the weatherman came on. Gonna be another scorcher like yesterday, she thought as she stared out at the dry grass and brown-tipped rose bushes in the back yard. By tonight I'll be in the mountains and it won't matter, though. Her cotton shortie gown felt sticky against her skin. Where did I leave my clothes?

". . . and headed toward western Virginia, the tail-end of Camille, luckily with little more than rain left from the fury that did so much damage to the coast of Mississippi. People in the valley will appreciate the rainfall after the last few dry weeks of record-breaking high temperatures. Locally, no rain in the forecast today or tomorrow. More highs in the upper eighties, with late night temperatures in the low seventies . . ."

The cat rubbed against her bare ankles. "You hungry, Sophie girl? Or just worried about all the commotion?" She reached down and picked up the orange Persian, rubbing between the cat's ears with her fingernails the way she liked. "Let's get some food, what do you say? I kept your dishes out. Cat chow for you, coffee for me. That's all she wrote, I'm afraid. No treats till we get to Lexington."

Carrying the cat tucked under one arm like a morning paper, Judy walked down the hall toward the kitchen, which was almost empty except for a red metal stepstool and a few pots and pans and dishes on the counter. She put Sophie down on the cool green tile floor and ran tap water into an aluminum pot, opening one of the cabinets and taking down a jar of instant coffee from the barren shelves at the same time. The floor felt good on her bare feet. "You can't always get what you wa-ant, You can't always get what you wa-ant," she was singing, while the water ran into the pot and the cat rubbed against her ankles.

"You in there, Judy?"

Judy turned to the back door, and could see Mrs. Calabash standing there through the window in the top half. She could barely hear her, though. "No, I'm on the moon with Neil Armstrong," she said as she cut the water off and looked around for something to dry her hands. "Just a minute."

That was just like her landlady. She wouldn't want to knock and bother her, but she'd come over as soon as she heard the alarm or the faucet. When Judy told her a couple of weeks ago that she'd be moving, Mrs. C. almost cried; her whole face drooped. She reminded Judy of a day-old jelly doughnut—kind of caved in, shoulders rounded, breasts and tummy sagging. Ever since Judy had given her notice Mrs. Calabash had been itching to know her plans, had been popping over with any excuse to sniff around for information. Judy had been just as determined to keep it to herself, though she was far too polite to tell her neighbor to mind her own business. Mrs. C. had been a pretty good landlady, even if she stuck her nose in a bit too much for Judy's liking. About once a week she'd bring over home-made brownies, goodies from the bakery, half a pie left over from Sunday dinner. And she always got the repairman in right away if something broke. But she was a nosy-posy, no doubt about it.

She'd hung around the backyard sale all the past week-end with cheese doodles and lemonade, prowling the tables, despite the fact that Judy gave her first choice of the things she was getting rid of before she had the sale on Saturday and Sunday. "Where'd you get this candy dish, Judy? I never saw it before. One of your mama's?" And Judy had let her take her pick of the leftovers for free after it was all over, before the Goodwill was scheduled to come and haul away the remnants of her life there. She found a roll of paper towels under the sink, dried her hands, walked over to the door and opened it.

"Morning, Judy. I got some melt-away pastries at the bakery—your favorites, right? And the coffee's perking, so you can put that instant away." She wrinkled her nose in disapproval, gave the little jar on the counter a disdainful glare. Mrs. Calabash was big on homemade. Anything instant or packaged was automatically b-a-d. "Mind if I take one more look around? I'd hate for the Goodwill to get something I could use." Smiling, she stepped into the kitchen.

"Come on in. Help yourself. Let me get dressed, okay? Look around all you want."

Sophie rubbed her head against the door. "Don't let the cat out, okay? I've got to keep her in so I can give her that pill later. Her knock-out drops. I don't want her running off." Judy went down the hall while Mrs. Calabash wandered toward the living room. She knew her landlady was hanging around because she didn't want her to go. She'd been the perfect tenant in Mrs. C's eyes. Quiet. Paid the rent on time. Didn't have men over to spend the night. Minded her own business. Mrs. C. told Judy when she'd come to see the apartment, "Lord, it'd be such a load off my mind to have someone in their thirties, somebody who isn't likely to have hippies over for sex and drugs and ungodly loud music. Not like that younger generation." She'd rolled her eyes, "Since Mr. Calabash has been gone, this place has been nothing but a worry for me. It'd be a blessing to have a professional woman next door." Judy smiled again, remembering that conversation. Everything was making her smile today. She saw her cut-offs and yellow tank top on top of a pile of towels on the bathroom floor. She pulled the shortie gown over her head, strapped on a bra from the pile, then the shirt.

"How about this owl, Judy? Did you say you were keeping that? It's right cute. I'll take it if you're getting rid of it. Sorta reminds me of Mr. C." Mrs. Calabash was calling from the living room.

"That goes with me. Remember? I told you about one of my students making it for me? A few years ago?" She stepped into the jeans, tossed the nightie on top of the pile and walked back down the hall, brushing her hair. "Mr. Huffman. One of the men in that first night class I taught."

The two-foot-tall wooden owl, carved out of a tree stump, grinned at her. No matter where she moved she'd never leave that behind.

"Maybe you did. I guess so. Let me just take a look in the bedroom, okay?"

Judy remembered the night she'd gotten the owl. Mr. Harold Huffman, day laborer, brought it to her after class one evening, the first year she'd been in Richmond. With time on her hands, she had volunteered to teach adults who hadn't finished high school two nights a week. Mr. Huffman lingered after class, and after everyone had gone he said he had a little something for her out in his truck. He was tall and thin and hardly said a word in class. In fact, his pale blue eyes were so scared-looking that she didn't think twice about it when he asked her to come with him out to the parking lot. Leaning against the tailgate he said, "I was looking at the paper this weekend, just like always, looking at the pictures. And all of a sudden I called to my wife, Gladys, 'Come in here, Gladys. Listen to this.' And I read out loud to her: 'Gunsmoke will not be on tonight due to the Grammy Awards.' I could actually read it." Those pale eyes were bright. "And I've got you to thank for that, Miss Marsh," he said, picking up this bundle tied in a drop cloth on the front seat of his truck. He had carved this owl for her—that's what he did in his spare time, wood carving.

She couldn't believe how heavy it was when she carried it to the living room from the car. She'd set it down by the sofa and bawled. Mr. Harold Huffman had learned to read, and she was learning to stand on her own two feet. That had been quite a night. Nope, she wouldn't get rid of that owl for love nor money.

"What about this floor lamp in here, Judy? This black one with the three places for bulbs? You keeping that?"

Judy followed her into the room. "Nope. I thought for sure somebody would buy it. You're welcome to it."

"It'd be just the thing in my den, beside that blue plaid chair I read in. You sure you don't want me to pay you for it?"

"It's yours. Do you see a piece of notebook paper anywhere? I made a list of what I need to do today, and everything's such a wreck I can't remember where I put it."

"That it over there in the windowsill? I'll just take this lamp on to the house. You come on over for some coffee whenever you're ready. What time the men coming for the stuff?"

Judy picked up the piece of folded paper from the sill. "Thanks, Mrs. Calabash. Around nine, I think. Let me just brush my teeth and fix my hair and I'll be over, okay? See anything else you want?"

"No. Thanks, Judy." Stooped over, carrying the pole lamp and dragging the cord behind, her grey-haired neighbor eased down the hall and through the kitchen. "Come on pretty quick. Don't dawdle. Coffee ought to be ready by now."

"Thanks. I will." Judy walked back to her room and sat on the bed and looked over the list. She guessed she'd become a compulsive list-maker when she started teaching school, back before she met Allen.

> Stuff to Goodwill (truck comes around 9)
> Scrub kitchen cabinets
> Clean fridge (food to Mrs. C.)
> Scrub kitchen floor
> Vacuum and wax living room, bedroom, and hall
> Wash windows inside
> Scrub bathroom
> Key to Mrs. C. (get deposit)
> Pack car
> Trash out

Plenty to do, but she couldn't really get started till the place was cleared out. She'd just go for a quick breakfast next door. Keep Mrs. C. company for a few minutes. She couldn't help but be fond of her. By then the truck should have arrived. She could start cleaning after they left. With luck and a lot of hustle she should be finished by around four, ready to get her shower and get on the road. The cat jumped up in her lap.

"You're not going to like it a bit, but I'm going to put you in the closet before those men get here. They might scare you. Or let you out." She petted Sophie's soft fur, talked to her quietly. She wasn't used to having a pet yet, but they were getting along pretty well so far for two set-in-their-ways females. Judy picked the cat up, cradled her in her arms the way she'd seen her mother hold her a million times. "Come on, I've made you a bed. I'll leave the door cracked. You wouldn't like these big old men, anyway." She set the cat down on a worn wool sweater on the floor of her closet. "I'll bring you some water, okay?"

Judy walked into the bathroom to brush her teeth. The week had been hectic, but she wasn't tired at all, now that she was up and moving around. In fact, she felt energized, ready to tackle whatever came her way. After she had made up her mind to marry Drew, she'd rushed around canceling the utilities, letting the principal know she wouldn't be coming back in the fall after all, stopping the mail, closing out her checking and savings at the bank, paying her bill off at Miller & Rhoads and closing her account, getting ready for the yard sale, settling things with Mrs. Calabash, getting the car checked and tuned. Phew! Starting over wasn't easy. She'd done everything in person, too; she'd never been so grateful for the summer time off from teaching.

The man at the post office acted personally offended when she wouldn't leave a forwarding address, tried to talk her into it. "Well, ma'am. There's nothing the post office can do but return your mail, you know, if you don't leave a forwarding address. Or send it to the dead letter file if it doesn't have a return address." He'd looked horrified at the idea. Tough luck, buck-o, she had thought. I'm way beyond letting people push me around. Judy Marsh wouldn't exist in a few more days, anyway; she'd be Judy Carter, or Mrs. Drew Carter to those old-line Virginians at W & L who couldn't get used to calling a woman by her own name instead of her husband's. She'd been thrilled to get rid of Allen's name, after the divorce was final; now she couldn't wait to claim Drew's. So let the letters rot. She couldn't think of a single reason anybody would need to get in touch with her once she drove off, anyway. Or a single person she would want to hear from. She'd run around like a chicken with its head cut off to get everything done, so she could start a new life. Why leave a forwarding address from the old one?

She looked around the counter for the transistor radio she kept in the bathroom, before she remembered she'd stacked it by the front door the night before with the things she needed to pack in the car. It was funny to be in there without any music on. Music was one of her passions; for a long time she thought it might be the only passion in her life, after her divorce from Allen. Now it was part of the air she and Drew shared. When she looked back on it, it wasn't all that surprising that they had met at the symphony. She had given herself season tickets for her birthday a few years earlier. They meant a lot to her. Something she loved, just for her. And Drew's ticket was beside her. At first they merely said polite hellos, recognizing they were seat neighbors for the season. Then they began talking about the selections during intermissions. He'd taken his glasses off that first time, turning to her, "Excuse me, do you have a tissue? Seems like my glasses are steamed." She'd fumbled around in her pocketbook. "That particular Beethoven Larghetto always gets the best of me. He wrote it when he knew he was going deaf."

"It's the first time I've ever heard it," she'd answered, finding a crumpled tissue in her coat pocket. "This is my first season. Don't worry; it's clean. The tissue, I mean." They'd laughed together.

He told her the background of the piece, and they exchanged fragments of their own lives. He drove in from Lexington, where he taught music and music appreciation at Washington & Lee. After that first connection he would lean over during breaks, give her on-the-spot reviews of the performances, tidbits of background information about the composers. It made her smile; he made it sound like the gossip of classical music. She noticed he sat forward in his seat during a piece he especially wanted to hear. After about three concerts they started looking for one another, talking as if they were old friends. He offered to buy her champagne during the intermissions, then asked her out to dinner afterwards. They ate Greek food at the Athens Taverna, and she drank Retsina for the first time in her life and got this warm feeling from the inside out. She found herself looking forward to seeing him more than listening to the music. Eventually, she started going out with him because she wanted him in her life, not because she needed him. Not a thing like when she married Allen.

She brushed her thick hair. Geez, it's too hot to wear it down today. It would feel like a rug on my neck. Maybe I'll put it in a pony tail. She found a hairholder at the bottom of her make-up kit, put her hair up, went back into her room to find her sandals. Where in the heck are they? God, it'll be a relief to be settled again she thought as she looked under her bed, found the red sandals, and sat on the bed to put them on. She'd kept them out to wear with her red sundress later.

Judy picked up the framed picture on the floor by the bed. It wasn't one of those posed studio things. It was one she took herself a few months ago, after she and Drew had been up half the night drinking Asti Spumante and singing every Elvis song they could think of. It was Drew playing guitar, sitting on a rock at Goshen Pass, head thrown back, big grin on his face. Drew was as different from her first husband as water is from dirt. Allen would probably call him a pansy or a loser or one of the other sneery words he used to describe any man who didn't spend every waking minute making money or looking at sports on television. Drew loved baseball, followed the Orioles like a star-struck kid. This July fourth they'd driven up to Memorial Stadium together for a double-header and had a blast. But he'd never played himself—a definite strike against him by Allen's standards. Drew was a man who'd rather go to a symphony instead of a pro hockey game. A music professor who played the flute, for heaven's sake, and went on picnics and walks and had two cats instead of a golden retriever. A man who wore glasses instead of contact lenses, and corduroy sports coats instead of three-piece suits. A guy who hadn't pegged every girl he'd gone out with since he was sixteen. Judy had no trouble imagining Allen's disdain. Allen considered himself the supreme male: former college baseball star; much-in-demand corporate lawyer; a go-getter, whether it came to money or women or people he wanted to impress. It made her sick to think of him. Now, she saw through him. But when he and Judy had gotten engaged nobody could believe she'd "caught" him, especially her father. Drew she didn't catch; Drew she got to know. And he got to know her. And they were in love.

Four days earlier, when she'd made up her mind to marry Drew, after that terrible period of doubt when she wondered if she dared marry anybody after the fiasco with Allen, she'd gone into high gear. She wanted to surprise Drew in a good way, after she'd stunned him with that letter putting everything on hold for a month. Now she didn't want to keep him waiting a day longer than she had to. She thought, maybe we can go away to the beach for a long weekend. We both love the ocean. Swim. Lie on the beach. Soak up the sun. Sleep in. Make love any time of day or night. Wasn't that the way things went; just when she'd filed away everything in the past and was dying to get going, she had to hang around one last day and clean up. Come on, Judy, she prodded; aren't you the queen of patience?

It had taken a long time and a lot of work after the

divorce, after she got out of the hospital, before she could think about herself without feeling like a failure. She hardly recognized the needy person she'd been for most of her life. That person was buried inside her, for good, along with the memories of Allen and her family. Like photographs in an album at the bottom of an old chest pushed way back to the attic wall. Photographs she wouldn't be looking at again. Not like this photograph.

These last four years, in this apartment, had been good. She'd quit trying to be Allen's wife or Daddy's daughter or anybody's anything. When she got out of the hospital, she rented this duplex and got a job teaching in Richmond. Her mother had been offended and hurt. "Doesn't make a bit of sense, you paying to live in Richmond when you could live here with me, for free. In your own home. What in the world would your father think of you wasting money like that, rest his soul? You're all I've got left. Seems like you would want to live with your own mother, help out around the house." Her daddy had been dead a couple of years; died of a heart attack, his first, right in the middle of drinking a beer and looking at television; the New York Giants versus the Redskins, her mother had said. But she'd held out, scared as she was, and moved into the apartment alone. Wouldn't even take any of the family furniture. Instead, she'd started going to the Salvation Army and yard sales, picking things she liked instead of things people told her she ought to like. Her place was quiet, sparse; she never even got a TV. Just a stereo. And an album collection along the way. Classical. Show tunes. Rockabilly. They became her friends. She had signed up for evening classes at RPI, thinking that would help the nights pass. At first that was all she had wanted, just to get through each night alone. She'd enrolled in a course of study for remedial reading teachers, thinking she'd like to do some volunteer work, she had so much time on her hands. That was when she had started working with adults who couldn't read, and she'd been good at it. She'd made a rich life for herself. People, not things. When she had met Drew, she wasn't even looking for him.

Early in the summer, her mother died in her sleep after going into the hospital with chest pains. She had some weird form of arthritis Judy had never heard of, pulmonary arthritis. Her lungs hardened up, gradually, until finally she couldn't breathe. Suffocated, the doctor said. A horrible way to go. Those last years, after her father's death, her mother had her church and clubs and money, but her life always seemed lonely and empty to Judy despite the full daily schedule attached to the refrigerator with a Dr. Pepper magnet. She never felt like she knew anything about her, though she visited every couple of months and at Christmas. They talked, but whenever she left she had the feeling she'd been talking to Ann Landers or Dr. Joyce Brothers or Paul Harvey. She could recite a dozen of her sayings without taking a breath, but still she had no idea what her mother thought about at night when she was lying awake in bed. Judy cried as much for that as for her dying. When she went to clean out the house, she made herself listen to the echoes she'd heard there ever since she was a child. Listen, and let them fade. By the time the furnishings were auctioned she could walk through without hearing a single voice. She kept the juice glasses but sold the good china, crystal and silver. Those four juice glasses that were on the table every day of her childhood. The ones that held the whispers for so many years.

"Meredith, sit down and eat your French toast."

"Motherith, I'm in a rush. No can do."

"Let her be, Ruth. She's in a hurry. Drink your juice, honey. You need your vitamin C."

"Thanks, Dad." And Merry would pick up her juice glass, down its contents, kiss her daddy on the forehead, and bounce out the back door, blond hair blazing. Judy would sit there, her hand on her own glass, feeling the ridges of red, yellow and green encircling it. Waiting for her daddy to notice her.

Her mother's voice: "You go ahead and eat your breakfast, Judy, even if nobody else is going to around here. No sense letting good food go to waste." And she'd eat. Every bite. Her mother would clear plates. Her father would read the paper. She'd drink her juice. Invisible.

She'd kept the glasses. That was all. They were like her family: Mommy, Daddy, Merry, Judy. Motherith, Fatherith, Meredith, Judith, as her sister used to tease. In some abstract sense, Judy realized that's all the family that had ever existed. Those four glasses in the same place every single morning. She knew she'd probably never unpack them from the box marked "Fragile," but she'd wanted them, anyway. Her room had been gone for years. Her daddy converted it to an office at home right after she'd married Allen. Whenever they came to visit they'd slept in there, on a pull-out sofa, clearly guests in the guest room. Meredith's room was like it had been twenty-four years earlier, right down to the lavender ruffled bedspread and tester. Judy gave everything in that room to the Goodwill, even her sister's old love notes and diaries and souvenirs tacked on the corkboard. She hadn't wanted to throw away anything, hadn't been able to sell her clothes and things, didn't want the money from them. Funny how her daddy had spent his whole life making money selling houses to other people, buying that house, and she didn't want it. She cried for her sister and mother and father, cried for herself as a child, buried her mother, and went back to Richmond. To her new life with Drew.

And then she'd gotten cold feet. Called it off. Asked for a month to think it over. What an idiot.

". . . and Senator Kennedy's staff contends he did nothing improper during what they deem an unfortunate . . . BUZZZZZZZZZ"

Judy jumped at the sound of the alarm going off, dropping Drew's photograph on the floor. The snooze. She hit the button, "Damn. I don't know if Goodwill will even want this piece of junk. Damn thing's possessed." She reached down and unplugged the clock radio. The picture was broken. A crack ran diagonally across the middle of the glass. Picking it up she thought, it doesn't matter. I can replace it. And I won't need this photograph after today, anyway. I'll be sleeping with the real thing.

She stood up, put the picture on the unmade bed—got to get those sheets off before the men get here, she thought—

and headed for the kitchen. I'll go next door for a cup of coffee, then get a move on. That's all behind me. I've got my own mess to clean up today, my own life to live. With Drew.

Massie's Mill, Virginia
9:00 a.m.

Daniel wasn't one to complain, but he was hot and thirsty and tired all over. Seemed like he'd been up in the tree picking at least two hours. It was bound to be time for a break, he thought. He was glad for the work, glad to be outdoors and on his own. And nothing could make him go back to Norfolk. Still, he was mighty thirsty.

Out of sorts, he started muttering to himself. "Won't that way. Won't that way at all. But didn't nobody believe me. For no reason. No reason at all. Daddy wouldn't listen, either. Had his mind made up about how it happened. Didn't leave me no choice. Didn't leave me a bit of choice in this world."

Daniel Alexander was talking under his breath while he picked peaches and handed them down to a skinny blond boy about fourteen standing directly beneath him, who set them on a slatted wooden flat beside his ankles. The younger guy on the ground wasn't paying any attention to Daniel's gibberish. He was used to the way the boy in the tree would talk to himself every now and then. They'd been partners a couple of weeks, since the beginning of the picking season. The two of them could've been machine parts.

"Hold up a minute down there. I gotta wipe my face. Can't hardly see what I'm doing." Daniel raised his voice to speak, and the kid below him, called Pauley-B, stopped reaching up and stood still. Using his right forearm to wipe the sweat from his forehead and the gnats from his eyes, Daniel started chewing one of the fingernails on his other

34

hand in spite of the fact that he hated the bitter taste of the peach fuzz. The muscles in his thin face were taut, his blue eyes alert as he looked up at the hazy sky. Wonder why them birds been flying over all morning, he thought. A city boy, from Norfolk, he wasn't used to the racket birds could make. Still, he'd never seen as many as this morning. Steady streams of them, the ugly brownish-black ones Miz Malory called grackles. He looked up and down the rows. Peach trees as far as he could see, each one exactly like this one: a picker, a handler, a flat. Nobody was paying any attention to him and Pauley.

He was always looking over his shoulder these days, expecting somebody to be pointing a finger saying, "There he is! That's the one," like on TV shows. He'd been trying to grow a moustache, trying to look different, trying to look older so people would show him some respect. Even though he was sixteen, almost seventeen, he didn't look a day older than the kid at the base of the tree. Took after his mama, his daddy used to tell him, his daddy who was big as a tank. The blond fuzz above his upper lip refused to take shape; he still didn't have to shave more than every three or four days, and the hair was more like chick fur than an actual beard. He was skinny, too, but not as skinny as he'd been before he started staying at Miz Malory's rooming house. He smiled, remembering that first night he knocked on the door when she said, "Just call me Miz Malory; rhymes with glory." He could tell she was a nice lady. He chewed fast; he was an expert at chewing his nails. "Okay, here ya go." He handed down another peach. The nail on his left pointer finger was bloody, chewed to the quick. "Hotter'n blazes up here today. Wish we'd get some rain."

"Not until we get the peaches in." The boy on the ground didn't change expressions. Just kept moving his arm up and down.

"Yeah. Gotta get our hours in. Wish I had a hat, though. Keep the sweat from rolling down in my eyes."

"He got a hat."

Daniel didn't need to ask Pauley-B who he was talking about. The dark one. The one who wore the Navy blue baseball hat with USHER in big dingy white letters where it oughta name the team. The one who looked exactly like one of them Hell's Angels. The one who never talked to anybody, acted like he was so high and mighty, him no more than a peach picker like the rest of them. Never even sat and talked while they ate. Went off by himself, like he was too good. Ate, leaned up against a tree and took a nap. Least he seemed to be taking a nap. Kept his eyes closed, stayed as still as a snake sunning on a rock. Sometimes read from a Bible. Didn't bring that too often, though. Pickers steal you blind. Think nothing of stealing a Bible. Still, Daniel couldn't imagine anybody working up the nerve to steal something from him. He looked like he'd just as soon hit you as look at you. High and mighty. Holier than thou. Daniel didn't like him, and he liked most everybody. He couldn't see him at the moment, but he knew he was there somewhere in the row. He could feel the snap in the air, the way he made everybody jumpy around him. If he were Saunders he wouldn't keep him on. What did Saunders know, though? The pickers never even saw him. Just the field boss, Campbell. And he wasn't about to get rid of a strong picker who minded his own business. Even if he did look like the missing link, like he ate the heads off chickens for fun.

Daniel scrunched up his nose like he smelled something bad, but the other boy wasn't looking up. "Wouldn't want his old greasy hat anyway. Probably got cooties. I ain't never had no bugs like some of these guys. I get a bath every night. Miz Malory's got all the hot water you could want. Not like the cabins. Hell, no, don't have no bugs of any sort. He's probably crawling, though. I wouldn't put that hat on my head on a bet. Rather sweat."

Pauley-B below switched arms, started reaching with his left hand, as Daniel passed down the ripe fruit. "Bet he'd give us the time of day if that damned USHER hat of his was to disappear. Bet he would. Be riled something fierce. I'd like to see that."

"I wouldn't want to have nothing to do with making him blow a gasket. Not unless I was a glutton for punishment."

More to himself Daniel added, "Man, I never was into beating people up. Too likely to get it myself. Sure as hell wouldn't take on a guy like that. Wouldn't think about it. Wouldn't beat up some old bed-ridden man, either. Daddy should've known I wouldn't have nothing to do with that. Believed the police instead of his own son. Anybody in a uniform, he'll take their word in a minute. Take anybody's word over mine."

"What'd you say, Danny? Can't hear you."

"Nothing. Nothing about nothing. Just said I didn't want to get that guy mad at me. Wouldn't want his damned filthy hat anyway."

"Ain't a matter of wanting his hat. It's a matter of him acting like he thinks he's a big shot. Better than the rest of us. Take him down a peg or two."

Daniel could've laughed at that one if it hadn't been so dumb. The idea of a scrawny kid like either one of them messing with the dark guy was about as stupid as sticking your head in a engine to see if it was running right. Still, Daniel knew what he meant. The guy did make everybody on edge, made them all feel like they had to speak up for themselves, even though he never said a word. He'd only been working a little over a week, but he'd made it clear on that first day that he didn't want nobody to mess with him. And Daniel wasn't one to mess with anybody anyway. Kept out of the way of trouble. Least that's what he tried to do.

The cowbell sounded for break. All around the orchard men and boys jumped from the trees and walked in the direction of an enormous oil drum, cut in half and filled with water. The bare earth around it sent up puffs of dust as the men trudged up. Trucks went down the row, black men stacking the loaded flats onto the truck beds while the pickers got drinks, then found shady spots near the water tank to rest for fifteen minutes.

"You gonna go up in the tree next, or you want me to stay?" Daniel splashed water from a paper cup onto his face, neck, his sweaty brown hair. He hadn't had it cut in a couple of months. Not since he'd left home.

"Don't mind if I stay on the ground, if it's all the same to you."

Daniel knew the kid hated to climb the trees. Most of the teams switched at break. But the kid had this thing about being off the ground. Said it spooked him. So Daniel didn't make him switch. They made a good team. Probably if the kid worked with one of the men he wouldn't have lasted, Daniel thought. And he knew he needed the money. They all needed the money. Daniel took out a blue bandana from the back pocket of his jeans, wiped his face, took off his T-shirt and turned it inside out. He headed for the lean-to set up as a rest area for the workers. The dark one wasn't around, as usual. Daniel could see him off underneath one of the peach trees with his hat beside him, smoking a cigarette.

Daniel nodded his head toward the far end of the shed. "Come over here a minute, Pauley. I want to tell you something."

The two thin boys walked to the end of the shelter, squatted down close to one another. Daniel leaned toward the kid. "I'm going to the hatchery after we get off today. I'm gonna try to get on permanent. You want to come?"

"Ain't you gonna finish out the season? We got a couple of weeks, for sure, before all the peaches are in." Pauley-B looked directly into Daniel's face for the first time. The right cheek muscle was twitching.

"Course I am. Less they want me to come right away. But I'm gonna try to stay on here in Massie's Mill when the season's up."

"Why's that? Ain't nothing here but peaches. Soon's they're in, this place will be deader than a possum putting on."

"Miz Malory thinks they might take me on at the hatchery. And I can keep on boarding at her place. Says she'll give me supper regular if I do the heavy work around the house and yard. Says she won't go up on the rate, either."

"If I was you I'd keep moving on, Danny. Ain't you gonna be drafted if you stick in one place long enough for people to start asking questions?"

Daniel chewed the middle finger on his left hand. "Hell, I ain't near old enough. Besides, I don't have nothing to do with that Vietnam mess. Ain't nothing to do with me. It's a bummer all right, though. People look at you like you're dirt if you got long hair. Like you're one of them draft dodgers. You're right about that." He shook his head.

"What about your daddy? Didn't you say he'd be after you till the day one of you died? Norfolk ain't that far, you know. You stay here, ain't it likely he'll track you down for sure?"

"Far as I know my daddy ain't never heard of Nelson County. Why in the world would he think to look in a podunk place like this? He thinks I'm a J.D. Thinks I do drugs, run with the freaks. Just cause the guys I hung with didn't have crew cuts and wear khakis. He'll be looking for me in Richmond or Norfolk or maybe even D.C. He'd never think of sending the fuzz looking in a hick place like this." Daniel's voice was getting louder as he spoke. A couple of the men looked in their direction. Their heads moved almost in slow motion. Most of them were smoking, making one cigarette last the entire break, too tired in the heat to take the energy to even flick the ashes. They looked toward Daniel and the kid almost as though they were dogs barking.

"Keep it down, Danny. Anybody find out about you running away, might try to call the police, collect some kind of reward."

Daniel laughed. "My daddy's so tight he wouldn't pay two pennies to get me back. He'll just let the juvenile authorities or the social services do the work, keep pestering them. He don't give a diddly damn about me. Just don't want me giving him a bad name. Might get back to the almighty Navy. Man. He is such a drag about the damned Navy."

The kid smiled for the first time, showing yellow teeth pitted with black. "I know why you want to stick here. You ain't fooling me. I got your number. Thinking 'bout that girl, ain't ya?"

"I saw her again last night." Daniel kept on chewing his fingernail while he talked through his teeth.

"Yeah? You hang out at the school?"

"Band was practicing again. Guess they're practicing just about every night now, getting ready for school to start. Football season. She didn't see me, though."

"How you know? How you so sure she ain't watching you same as you watching her? She leave with anybody?"

"Just another couple girls. The short fat one I told you about. The blond with the big nose. One they call Carol. They took off together. Bet they went to the Dairy De-Lite before they went home." Daniel sat back on the ground, Indian style his kindergarten teacher called it, letting his hands hang down between his crossed legs. All of his fingernails were chewed, the skin around the nails raw. "Why would she be checking me out? Somebody like her?"

The kid grinned so all his nasty teeth showed. "Never can tell. Never know unless you try."

"You ought to go with me one night. Maybe tonight. You want to meet me in front of the school later?" He leaned forward. "They'll probably be practicing. You ought to see her. I swear, she's prettier than the girls in those skin magazines. Way prettier. That long hair hanging down her back. Never seen hair like that. All the girls back home kept theirs sprayed and teased and looking like shit. Never seen hair like that." He started chewing the nail on his right middle finger.

"Hell, no. I ain't getting no closer to a school than I have to. Give that up for good when I started following crops. Not even for a girl. Shoot some pool, though. Want to go play some pool?"

"Nah. Gotta save my money for some wheels. Gotta get me a car before I can even think about asking somebody out. Specially somebody like her."

"Not me, man. Girls just cost money. I want a Honda, one of them sweet little bikes. Me and the road. Who needs a girl?"

"You seen one of them new GTO's? Man, are they something. Guy brought one to the station one day, let us look under the hood. That is one hot car."

"Nuh-uh. Rather have a bike any day."

"Can't take no class girl out on a bike. Gotta have wheels. You oughta come see the girls with me tonight. Listen to the band. That might change your tune. Ever go to a parade?"

"You kidding? Only parade I ever seen is the trucks taking the workers to the next crop."

"My daddy used to make me go to the base all the time to parades. Seemed like every other day. Made me wash for hours to get ready, put on Sunday shoes and all that shit. Just to watch a bunch of friggin Navy guys marching around. Never made a bit of sense. He'd make me stand there with him, him in his uniform, acting like it was so godalmighty great. He'd say, 'Now ain't that a sight in this world, Danny-boy?' And I'd have to say, 'Yes, sir. Yes it is, sir' Got so I couldn't stand the idea of a parade. But this is different. Girls and guys. They march all around and make the school letters about as big as four Mac trucks: NCHS. Man, I don't know. It's just different. Out of sight."

"You just got your eye on that Audrey girl. That's the thing that's got you all steamed up. Got nothing to do with the damn marching band." Pauley-B leaned forward and punched Daniel on his shoulder. They both grinned.

The cowbell sounded again, and Daniel and the kid stood. The pickers around them stood, too, shoulders slumped. Slowly they stretched, stomped out cigarette butts. The men and boys all turned with a single motion, headed back toward the trees and empty flats. Nobody dawdled. Didn't get peaches in by dawdling.

Back up the tree, handing down peaches without even noticing what he was doing, Daniel couldn't get the picture of the high school girl they called Audrey out of his head. He could see her just as clear in his mind's eyes, exactly like in a regular sleeping dream. "That hair probably don't feel like no hair I ever touched. Probably feels soft as all-get-out, like a little kid's hair. That way she throws her head back when she's marching, throws all that hair off to one side. Marches along playing her flute with that hair flapping around, prettiest sight I've ever seen."

"Say what? You talking to me?" Pauley-B didn't usually ask, Daniel talked to himself so much.

"Huh? I was just thinking out loud." He handed down a peach. "You ever steal anything?"

"What'd you say?"

"You ever steal anything?"

Placing the peach on the flat, looking up and down the row, Pauley-B reached up again, answered, "What kind of question is that?"

"Just wondering, that's all. Girl like Audrey, she probably never stole anything in her life. Probably think somebody who did was scum, you reckon?"

"What she don't know can't hurt her."

"Girls don't steal that much anyway."

"You gotta be kidding, Danny-boy. My junior high school, girls steal your lunch while they were looking right at you. Think nothing about it. Man, some of the girls I knew were about as mean as snakes. Rob anybody. Do anything."

"Guess I never knew that many girls back home. Never hung out with girls. Just a few guys." The rhythm of their arms continued as they talked. Neither seemed aware of the activity they were performing. Once, Pauley-B switched arms by taking a small step to one side, but his movement did nothing to break the beat.

"All that bullshit about stealing being a sin don't make no sense to me." For the first time, Danny's voice changed tone, went from sounding like he could've been talking to the guys to like he was telling somebody to get off his property. "Lots worse shit than stealing if you ask me."

They worked without talking a few minutes. Both boys had sweat rings under their arms, across the backs of their T-shirts, on their foreheads. The August heat, even this early in the morning, was stifling, would've kept dogs under porches and cats stretched out on cool floors inside somewhere. The orchard was so quiet that the bee noises seemed like they were on a loudspeaker. Daniel could hear their wings making little scratchy sounds all around him in the tree. They never bothered him, though. He didn't put any of that sweet-smellin' stuff on, either. Why would they bother him when they had acres of peaches to suck on? Thinking about stealing, about his father, made him irritable again.

"I used to steal plenty. And I ain't sorry I did, neither. Not a bit sorry."

"That a fact?"

"Me and two other guys, we had this regular thing. Car radios, stuff like that. Nothing big."

"Yeah, I stole some jumper cables once."

"Buzzy, he was the oldest, he knew where to sell the stuff. I never knew anything about that part. He'd just give me some cash every week or so. It was neat, you know? We'd go out late. People leave their cars unlocked. Ain't no big deal. Don't hurt nobody. See, they get a new radio. From the insurance people. And we get money. That's the system, man. That's what Buzzy used to say."

"How come your daddy let you go out late like that all the time? I thought you said he was a hard-ass."

"Wasn't a matter of him letting me do anything. He wasn't home most of the time. I did as I pleased. 'Cept when he was there. That was a different story altogether. Most of the time I just came and went as I pleased."

"Sounds cool to me."

"You don't know what you're talking about. Man, I couldn't even listen to my Stones or Dylan albums when he was home. He'd blast his Patsy Cline all hours of day and night, though."

"That a fact? Wish I had me one of them transistor radios we could listen to."

"Hold up a minute, O.K.?" Danny shifted to the next branch over, wiping his face with the bandana from his pocket. Pauley-B shifted a couple of steps to position himself under him. "Don't do for a man to raise a kid, least not my dad. He didn't give a shit about anything but the almighty Navy."

Pauley-B couldn't tell if that last remark was for him or if Danny was muttering to himself again. "That why you ran off?"

"Hell, no. I'd a gone a lot sooner if that was it. Won't it at all. I was tight with Buzzy and Jake. We'd spend a lot of time doing stuff, you know. Not just lifting stuff. And I didn't mind school that much. My auto mechanics teacher was all right. That and woodshop were all right." He was passing peaches down as fast as Pauley-B could handle them. The new spot was loaded. "I was gonna finish up, get a job at one of the gas stations—there's about a million in Norfolk, I swear there are—and get my own place. Maybe move in with Buzzy first. Then he got in this thing about hitting a house, messing up an old guy."

For a few minutes Danny didn't say anything, just passed peaches down to the hand beneath him. When he spoke again, his voice was agitated. "It won't the way they said it was. Said two guys were with Buzzy, and everybody said since we hung out all the time I was bound to be one of them. The old guy couldn't see good. Pointed me out from a school picture. I never hurt nobody in my life. But my daddy was ready to turn me over, man, just like that." He threw a peach into the ground, hard.

"You gotta be kidding." Reaching for the next peach, Pauley-B looked up. Danny's face was fiery red, like he'd been running a race or working on the roof.

"That's how he is, man. Don't never listen to what I have to say. Never has. Don't want the goddamn Navy to know his business, think he's got any troubles at home, you know. I was just one big goddamn problem to him. He'd a probably hired a band if they put me away."

"Didn't your mama speak up for you?"

For the first time Danny laughed. He laughed like somebody who's just told a joke, and nobody else laughs, so he laughs himself. Even though it isn't funny. "I never had no mama. I've never even seen a picture of my mama."

"That right? That's the pits."

"Don't that beat all? My daddy never even showed me a picture. I don't know if he even has one. Used to tell me, when I was little, that I was scrawny like my mama. Made me tell people the Germans killed her if they asked how come I didn't have a mama. You know what I found out from a neighbor? She died of measles. German measles. Don't that beat all?" Pauley-B shook his head, didn't answer. "And you know what else he used to tell me? Used to say it was a wonder the Germans didn't get me, too. Used to give me nightmares, thinking about it."

The two boys continued their work in silence. Daniel didn't like thinking about the nightmares. Soldiers, all as big as his daddy, talking loud in some way he couldn't understand, surrounding his bed, grabbing for him with meaty hands the size of shovels. Sometimes he started breathing hard just remembering them. He didn't want to do that out here where the men might notice him, think he was some kind of sissy. He was hungry, his stomach was growling, so he started thinking about what Miz Malory was fixing for supper. That was one of the bad parts of not having a mama. Everybody else got regular meals cooked at home. He got sandwiches or frozen dinners or pizza and subs from Antonio's down the block. Funny thing was, his daddy was Chief Petty Officer in the Bakery Division at Norfolk Naval Base, and he never cooked a single solitary thing at home. The only leftover Daniel ever had, before he came to Miz Malory's, was leftover cold pizza.

When he was little, before he could stay home alone, the baby-sitter fixed him peanut butter and jelly sandwiches and canned fruit cocktail every single meal. He'd starve before he'd ever put those in his mouth again.

Miz Malory, she cooked like a mama ought to cook. Like she stirred up some of herself in whatever she was fixing. Funny thing was she'd never even been married, never had any kids of her own. Daniel's favorite dish was that casserole she made, the one she called "Hot Cheesy Dog." Said she got it off a Velveeta box. At first he didn't want any. His daddy always left him Velveeta in the refrigerator, and whenever he was by himself and he got hungry he'd cut off a hunk. So he didn't have much of a taste for Velveeta. But this had cut-up hot dogs and noodles and peas and crunched-up potato chips on top, besides the cheese, and he could eat the whole Pyrex dish at one meal. His mouth was watering, just thinking about it. When he was getting ready to go that morning, while she was frying his eggs, Miz Malory had told him she was fixing "Hot Cheesy Dog" for supper. She knew how much he liked it. He couldn't wait.

"Yo, Pauley-B, you know what cripples are?"

"Of course I do. You must think I'm ignorant as dog piss." The kid grabbed the peach Danny was handing down and faked like he was going to throw it at Daniel's head before he put it on the flat and reached for the next one.

"Not cripples like people; cripples like food, dummy."

"Huh? Guess I . . . maybe I don't know what you're talking about."

"That's what they call the stuff they mess up in a bakery. Cripples. Like if the pie crust gets crumbled around the edges, or the cake falls on one side. See? That's what my daddy used to bring home all the time. The cripples. Got to be a drag. I got so I couldn't stand sweets."

"Sounds good to me. We just had Twinkies and stuff."

"Miz Malory makes the best peach pies. I didn't think I'd ever want to eat pie again after all those cripples, but she makes this thing she calls deep dish, you know? It's not even round. And she puts a big scoop of vanilla ice cream on top while it's still hot. I could eat a boat-load of that right now, I can tell you that. Hey, remind me to take her some of the windfalls tonight, okay? If I get that job maybe she'll make me a pie."

"You really going to the hatchery this afternoon?"

"Yep, soon as I get a shower. When I get off here I'm gonna go back to Miz Malory's, wash up and change, get this peach grit off, and go right over there. Miz Malory told me who to ask for. Said she'd give me a reference if I needed one. That way I can get steady work, not worry about moving on with the pickers, you know?" Daniel stopped for a minute and sat still on the branch. "I sure don't want to have to leave. I like it here. Beats the hell out of Norfolk."

Pauley-B looked up at him. "Pickin's better money."

"That ain't it. I like being outside and all. And I like the money. And the hatchery probably stinks like all-get-out. But I want to stay on here. Miz Malory says I can take a test and maybe get my high school diploma. And she'll give me supper, regular, if I work around the place on weekends, do the stuff she can't do herself so she don't have to hire people to do it. Maybe I can get some wheels one of these days."

"Hand me a peach, will ya, before Campbell sees us," Pauley-B said. Danny started the picking/handing-down motion again. "I know what you're planning." He smiled up at Danny. "You're planning on taking that Audrey girl out, ain't you?"

"Maybe I am. Maybe one day. Once I get settled and can buy some clothes and stuff. You think you smell like fish at the end of the day, working at the hatchery?"

"Damned if I know. Damned if I'd want to go around smelling like a can of tuna fish, though. It's enough to gag a maggot if you ask me."

"Ain't nothing else around here but the IGA. And they're full. I already asked. Miz Malory says the hatchery always needs people. That they'll take just about anybody. Maybe I can change later on, once I take that test and get my diploma, you know? You never can tell."

"That's a fact. You never can tell." Pauley-B put the peach in his hand on the flat, noticed it was full. "Hey, hold up. Let me get another flat. O.K.?"

Daniel leaned down from the branch, tapped Pauley on the shoulder. "Guess what I did last night."

"What?"

"I left her a note. On her car." His eyes were like two brown peach pits.

"No shit. What'd you say? You ask her out?" The kid's voice squeaked on the "out."

"Hell, no. I didn't even sign my name. I just left it on her windshield. All I said was, 'You have the most beautiful hair I have ever seen. Your secret admirer.'"

Pauley-B grinned. "No shit." He bent down, stretched his arms as wide as they'd go, picked up the loaded flat and headed for the closest truck.

Daniel sat listening to the bees, smelling the greenish-smell of fresh peaches, staring up at the hot blue sky. He shut his eyes, tried to see Audrey's face in his mind. For some reason his father's face appeared, looking purply with the veins standing out in his forehead like he was hopping mad. "He shoulda known I wouldn't hurt nobody. Taking stuff's one thing. Ain't half of what comes out of Vietnam stolen? Everybody takes stuff. But hurting somebody, especially an old scrawny man in his bed, that's another thing altogether. Daddy shoulda known. He just couldn't stand the idea of me running with my friends. Wouldn't take my word. That was it. Still, you never can tell. Maybe it was just as well. I like it here. I like it a lot." Before he ran away Daniel had gotten so he'd crawl in windows for Buzzy, hand out radios and portable TV's and stuff like that. But Buzzy always checked the place out first, made sure nobody was home. Daniel couldn't get the idea of that scrawny old man out of his head. He wouldn't hurt anybody. He hadn't thought Buzzy would either. Damned if he'd whip up on some old guy. Made him think of that wacky old lady Miz Malory told him about.

Pauley-B walked over with the empty wooden flat, set it under the tree, reached up for a peach.

"Pauley, you ever hear about that old crazy lady in the haunted house up on Davis Creek?"

"I don't believe in that haunted house shit, I don't care where it is. Ain't no such thing as a haunted house."

"Miz Malory said this crazy old lady lived in this big old house, bigger than the Lovingston Inn. About like Graceland. Said she was crazier than a March hare, and rich as Croesus, whatever that means. I got the clear impression she had a fortune hidden away up there."

"That ain't haunted. Shit, what's that got to do with haunted?" Heat waves rose from the trees. Pauley-B's voice sounded irritated, like Daniel was trying to put one over on him, like with the cripples. Arms getting sore, both boys were slowing down.

"She's probably dead by now. Nobody's seen her in years. Miz Malory said she used to park up there when she was about my age. They'd drive up and park back behind

her old dried up peach trees. She even found a little cemetery back in the woods. Said all the kids used to do it for
fun. But everybody got spooked. The old lady started coming out in her nightgown and shooting at the cars, trying to
shoot out the headlights, stuff like that. Miz Malory said
none of them would tell their parents 'cause they weren't
supposed to go up there in the first place. Said she would-
n't go back up there for love nor money after the shooting
started, but a few others still did. Just for the thrill, you
know. Then the road washed out and people stopped going
up there altogether. Started making up stories like the old
lady ate little children, crazy mess like that."

"You don't believe stuff like that, do you?"

"I believe Miz Malory when she says she went up there.
And she says it was so long ago that the lady is bound to be
dead, the house is bound to be caved in. You reckon relatives got the money? Or the silverware and stuff like that?
If it was a mansion there was bound to be a lot of valuable
stuff. Maybe even some diamond jewelry."

"Anything worth a nickel's probably long gone, if you
ask me. Especially if it was a mansion and all, like you
said."

"Yeah. You're probably right. Still, I wouldn't mind
trying to find it one day. You wanta go with me some
Saturday, see if we can find it?"

"Not particularly. Old places give me the creeps. I'd
rather shoot pool. Now if you wanta steal something, what
do you say we try to get that guy's hat while he's napping
after lunch? That sounds cool to me. See what he'd do if
he woke up and it was gone. He'd probably go ape."

The cowbell sounded for the next break. Daniel swung
down to the ground, looked at Pauley-B like he had just
announced he was running for president. "You'd have to be
out of your mind to mess with that guy." He walked ahead
of the kid, anxious to get some water and cool off. "If you
ask me that's just looking for trouble. As far as I'm concerned the last thing in this world I need is any more trouble."

When Helen Jansky left her office that morning to take her kids to the dentist to get their teeth cleaned and checked, and to Miller & Rhoads to get new school shoes, she had no idea she wouldn't be back. She told the manager Tom that she didn't know exactly when she'd return, but sometime early that afternoon. They were good about that at the paint store. They always gave her time off if the children were sick or if she had to take one of them to an appointment of some sort. And they didn't even dock her pay or take the hours off her vacation. Truth be known, they depended on her. She'd been there for twenty years. She'd seen six managers come and go. Her young boss always said, "What would we do without Helen?" And of course no one ever thought that one day she might not come back. She hadn't thought it, either.

This particular Monday Helen had asked Joe for money while they were drinking coffee at about six, before he left for his contracting office. He'd been reading the paper at the kitchen table and she'd been rinsing his breakfast dishes, sipping from her mug on the counter. "I'm going to need some money today, Joe. The kids have check-ups at Dr. Moss', and if I'm going to take off I might as well get their school shoes at the same time, don't you think? I can wait to get clothes at the sales. They don't have to go with me for that. But I need to take them with me to try on shoes."

"Un-huh. How much you need?" He kept his eyes on his paper.

"Well, I figured it out. The doctor will be twelve dollars each. And shoes ought to come to forty-five. So eighty-one dollars, give or take a few. That ought to do it."

He'd pushed back the metal kitchen chair and reached around to his back pocket for his wallet, without looking up. He counted some money and put it by the sugar bowl, then leaned forward so his belly touched the table and returned the worn leather wallet to its place, buttoning the single button to hold it in. He'd had that wallet since she'd known him. "Grocery money's in there, too," he said as he turned to sports. "And I want you to go by the high school today and find out when football practice starts. I want you to sign Stevie up. You hear me?"

"But, Joe . . ."

"No ifs, ands, or buts, Helen. Stop babying him. He's going to play football and that's that. No son of mine's gonna be a sissy mama's boy." He snapped the sports section closed.

She took a sip of her lukewarm coffee. No sense trying to change Joe's mind. No sense reminding him, again, that he'd never played sports in school. He'd just go into his routine about working construction since he was thirteen.

"Want anything in particular for supper tonight?"

"Don't matter. Just plenty of it." He picked up the business section of the paper. "And don't bother me about more money for the next coupla weeks. The kids don't have to have new stuff for school. You spoil 'em. Big auction coming up Saturday. I want to hold onto my cash."

They'd been married for nineteen years, and that's the way they'd always handled the money. Helen didn't like turning her check over to Joe one bit, but with his temper it was just as well not to make an issue of it. He usually gave her what she asked for. She'd complained a couple of times after they'd been married a few months, and he'd flown off the handle at her, swearing like a wild man, looking like he might hit her if she kept at it. "It's the man's place to handle the money. That's that." He'd glare at her, red-faced. And Joe hated to owe anybody, to be under obligation, as he put it. They didn't have a single charge account at any of the department stores in town; they paid cash for everything except the house. Lately, though, it seemed like the older and fatter he got, the tighter he got with money for her and the kids. And the more often he smacked her. So Helen had to be a good planner, and she was. She checked the sales every week in the Thursday paper, cut coupons, and called the stores to be certain they had the children's sizes in stock before she went shopping. She didn't waste much of anything.

She sold Avon, and Joe didn't ask for the money from that. Going door to door in the neighborhood, with her regular customers, she was able to put away a few dollars a month. She hated to set Joe off, now that the children were old enough to jump into it, so she just went along. He'd never hit one of them, never even hit her in front of them. "Keeping the peace," she called it. Besides, she had some "hide money" he didn't know about. She had her own little secret.

Helen dried her hands on a fresh linen towel, leaned over Joe's broad back, and picked up the money. She'd met Joe at the paint store. He came in to get some paint samples for a job, and they got to talking, and one thing led to another and he asked her out to lunch. Nothing romantic. Just sandwiches and coffee at Willy's counter. It was never romantic between them. He just happened to ask where she'd gone to school, and he found out she was in the same class as one of his younger brothers, and they knew a few of the same people, so they felt connected, somehow. That was over nineteen years ago. She'd been twenty-six and he was thirty at the time, and neither of them had been what people might call "a catch" in high school. Her plain face and unremarkable figure were nothing to write home about, and if anybody noticed her, they usually were asking to borrow notes. Joe looked like a person who'd always been old: a crew cut, Sunday trousers with a belt, white shirts his oldest sister ironed. Both of them came from enormous families and worked hard to "do better," so they fell in with one another in what seemed like a comfortable way at the time.

Joe was sure of himself and stable and a good provider; he'd majored in civil engineering in college, served his two years in the Army, and he started his own contracting business by the time he was twenty-eight. She checked his company's account and found out that he always paid on purchase. That impressed Helen, since her daddy was a spendthrift no-account. But her father told his kids stories at bedtime and got down on the rug and played with them; still, they never had enough of anything. She'd always worn hand-me-down clothes and carried peanut butter or bologna sandwiches for lunch, all through school. And when she got to be old enough to baby-sit, she'd sock the money away, to buy things for herself, but her daddy would go on a binge and beg her to give him some. She never did, though. So when Joe wanted to pay off her Chevrolet Biscayne instead of going on a honeymoon, she'd been taken with his money sense. She didn't find out about his temper until after they were married. She'd never expected him to be perfect. So she just made sure she didn't get him going.

That was Helen: Good Old Dependable Helen, as she snidely called herself. She was 45, but she looked 55. When she took Aimee to kindergarten her first day the fresh-out-of-college teacher said, "Are you Aimee's grand-mother? Why couldn't one of her parents come today?" Her face had aged fast since her marriage. Thin little lines around the corners of her mouth and eyes made them look pulled down in a worn way. The only thing young about her, still, was her hair. She had long brown wavy hair with-out a strand of grey in it. It was her vanity. She washed it and put conditioner on it every Saturday, and brushed it until it shone every night before she went to bed. She'd take both hands and fluff it around her shoulders when she was finished. But the way she wore it in the daytime pulled back in a low ponytail, on the back of her neck, only made her face look strained, older. Joe and the kids could surely see how beautiful her hair was. But they took it for granted, didn't notice when she was brushing it dry in the sun. Only Aimee would occasionally ask if she could brush it some, and say it looked pretty. The hair, not Helen.

Of course, her size didn't help. She'd put on weight after Stevie was born—only a few pounds, and she'd thought she had a handle on it then. At five-two she'd been tiny and roundish all her life. That's what her daddy called her: Tiny Tears, after the doll who cried. So when she went from 115 to 125 everybody said she looked good filled out. But she'd gained ten more pounds after Estelle, and about twelve after Aimee. And it seemed like every couple of years the scales tipped up another pound or two. She'd stopped worrying about it, though. When she fixed up to go out and sell Avon she looked real attractive, she thought, in a comfortable, well-groomed way. Her customers would give her compliments, at least.

Certainly she couldn't go to all that trouble every day for work, not with the time it took in the morning getting the kids ready for school and fixing Joe's breakfast. What difference would it make at the paint store, anyway? She just worked in a cubicle by herself most of the day. Besides, Joe's gut was as big around as a fifty-gallon barrel, so he didn't say too much about her fat unless he was in one of his fits. He'd stopped telling her to come sit by him on the sofa after Aimee was born. Instead he stretched out alone in his recliner. Said he couldn't settle on the sofa with her leaning up against him. But most of the time he didn't say a thing about her weight, and she didn't say a thing about his. In fact, they didn't say much of anything to one another, except what had to do with the day's business. It was better that way. Fewer arguments. Fewer slaps.

"Your dad will be glad none of you had cavities." Helen pulled out of the tiny parking lot onto the street, headed for downtown. All the windows were down, but still the heat was unbearable; only hot, humid air was blowing in on them. The weatherman was calling for rain. That'd be a relief, Helen thought, as she pushed back some damp stray hairs from her face. The station wagon didn't have air conditioning. Joe thought it was a waste of money all around: first the extra he'd have to pay to get it, then the extra all summer long because the car would use more gas with the air conditioning on. So they rode along in the Richmond mugginess. Helen pulled her skirt up over her knees and eased her thighs apart, hoping to get some breeze. They all sat still, trying to stay as cool as possible.

"Mama, can we go for ice cream?" Estelle asked. She was the one who always asked, thinking her Mom would say no. She seemed to expect the world to say no. Joe named her for his mother, Stella Janskowski. Helen wondered, often, if giving her the name caused her to be sour-faced, like her mother-in-law, or if it was just a coincidence.

"Let's get the shoes first. If we have any money left over, we'll go to The Clover Room for ice cream on the way home. Okay?" Estelle didn't answer, but then Helen didn't expect her to answer.

"I want Weejuns. That's what the other guys are wearing. If I can't get Weejuns I don't want any new shoes. I'll just wear my tennis shoes. That would be better than wearing some lace-up rubber-soled nerd shoes." Stevie blurted all this out in one big burst, seeming to be talking to the dashboard. Helen couldn't have been more startled; he rarely asked for anything, much less something he knew his dad wouldn't approve of. He sat in the front seat of the Ford wagon, tall and slim, with dark brown hair, like a young version of his daddy. Joe always said, when Stevie was little, "I can't blame this one on the mailman." This wasn't like Stevie at all, announcing something rather than making a request. Estelle, yes. Stevie, no.

"Hon, you know those shoes cost too much. Your daddy would never pay thirty dollars for school shoes. Just get some regular loafers. You can't tell the difference." Stevie was a loner. Asking for something so he could look like the guys was unusual for him, and she wished she could give him what he wanted, this once. But Helen knew Joe would never stand for some "fancy pants" brand in the house.

"*You* can't tell the difference. I can. I don't want any regular loafers." He just stared straight ahead.

"We'll see what we have left after the girls get theirs.

They don't care about any particular brand, do you girls?" Estelle pulled her mouth to one side. Helen could see her smirk clearly in the rearview mirror. Aimee didn't say anything. She rarely said anything when the other two were around. Some invisible shield, Helen thought. Probably inherited it from her. Watching her with Joe. Could kids inherit things like that?

"It doesn't matter what I wear. Mama will pick some ugly brown shoes with little holes all over the toes, like I was six years old. And I'll hate them, but I'll have to wear them. Nobody in my class will have shoes like that. But she'll say, 'Daddy wants me to get you all shoes that will last.' Which means ugly. Which means brown. So what difference does it make what I ask for?" Estelle rarely missed an opportunity to complain.

But the children almost never bickered with one another. They got up in the morning, fixed their own cereal just as quiet as could be, even Aimee, and looked at books or colored or did school work. Aimee played paper dolls by herself, hours on end. Or sorted Helen's Avon samples. She never asked to have anyone over. In fact, none of the kids ever had friends over. Or mentioned other kids. Joe left early, before they were up, but his presence ruled the house. Stevie stayed in his room a lot. Joe taunted him because he didn't play football, called him a "skinny britches" or "split tail." Helen hated it, but she knew better than to rise to the bait. And so Stevie stayed in his room sorting his baseball cards, or he rode his bike. They all stayed out of Joe's way, which was how he liked it.

Joe hadn't wanted children in the first place. Growing up, he had brothers and sisters and aunts and uncles and grandmothers all crowded into his house. He never had any privacy, and being in the Army only made him more determined to have things the way he wanted them. So when they got married, he told Helen he didn't want children. He really hadn't intended to get married, but he told Helen she seemed sensible and neat and quiet, and he missed the things the women did at home, even if he didn't miss the women. Helen hadn't minded; she thought the women in his family were all loud and overbearing, too. Besides, before Joe she'd pretty well reconciled herself to being single.

So she'd never expected to have children either. But after four or five years of marriage, after they'd bought the house and she'd furnished it, room by room, she was lonesome. She could work at her job and keep the house and sell Avon and still be lonesome. Joe agreed she could have two children, if she'd promise to go back to work at her old job, not ask him to act like a mama and change diapers and all that women's rights foolishness, and not keep him up at night when he had to get up early to go to work. First they had Stevie, and Helen was back to work six weeks after he was born. She kept her end of the bargain, never even suggesting he so much as hand her a bottle from the refrigerator. So he didn't complain much when she said it was time to try for a girl. Estelle came along. She was a solemn little thing, and Joe didn't pay a bit of attention to her, but Stevie adored her. Helen took the children to Mrs. Goodwin's early each morning, went to work, picked them up, gave them supper, washed them, read to them—she never had a minute to feel lonesome. In fact, she'd never been happier than when she had the babies.

Joe didn't have much to do with any of them and the rhythm of their lives was such that she was satisfied. Maybe she would've stayed satisfied, if not exactly happy, if Aimee hadn't come along. Joe kept to himself the whole time she was pregnant, even took to sleeping in front of the TV or on a daybed in his workroom. That's when the yelling and screaming turned into occasional smacking. And when she went into labor, Joe took her to the hospital and picked the two of them up three days later; he didn't visit her and the baby once. She'd called him to ask what he wanted to name the new baby. He said, "That's your problem," and went on to complain about what Mrs. Goodwin was charging to keep the other two while she wasn't home. Helen called Aimee a surprise; he called her an accident. Even though she got her tubes tied after the baby was born, while she was still in the hospital, Joe seemed to think she had tricked him. He never picked the baby up or asked about her; it was like she didn't exist for him. And he paid even less attention to Helen, if that was possible. But her mornings and evenings were busy, and she loved the kids, so she didn't really mind him and his ways all that much.

Helen pulled into the Park and Shop and the man in the booth took their keys. She took Aimee by the hand and crossed Grace Street. The other two walked behind about two feet, acting as if they were downtown by themselves and had never seen Aimee or Helen before in their lives. All four of them looked like flowers that hadn't been watered in a week. As Helen pushed the heavy glass door, the air inside the department store stunned her; it was almost like stepping into a deep freeze. She stood still just inside the double doors for a moment, thinking, Where am I? What am I doing here? Aimee pulled her by the hand over toward the information desk, and Estelle said, "Mom, come on." Helen shook her head and wondered at herself for such a lapse. It wasn't like her. Usually, she was efficient as a Timex.

They took the escalator up to the third floor; as they were being lifted along Helen noticed the huge clock above the information desk. 12:15. By the time she got the children's shoes and dropped them off at home it would be too late for her to take any time for lunch. Well, she could afford to miss a meal.

They got off at the third floor Children's Wear and headed for Children's Shoe World. Helen sat down and the two girls plopped on either side of her; Stevie stood over by one of the columns and looked in the other direction. They waited a few minutes without saying a word. Helen stood and walked around and picked up display shoes, showing them to the girls. Aimee nodded each time she held up a shoe, but Estelle made faces and wiggled around like she was sitting on a pin cushion.

"Can I help you?" A blue-haired lady in a grey striped suit spoke to Helen. She answered, "I'd like school shoes for my girls, please." She pointed to the styles she had in mind and the saleslady had them each take off their tennis shoes and stand while she measured their feet on a long metal contraption.

"Just one moment," she said as she disappeared into a back room.

Helen caught her son's eyes. He looked miserable. "Stevie, come on over here, please, and sit down."

"These are kids' shoes. I'm not a kid. Just don't buy me anything, all right? I'll save my own money. I'll use my yard-cutting money." He leaned against the column and spoke in a loud whisper, like he was being forced to visit some distant relative in the hospital.

The blue-haired lady returned and put three boxes down beside each girl. She fitted Aimee first, who chose a pair of navy-blue leather shoes that buckled in two places. Estelle tried all three pairs slowly, modelling each in front of a mirror on the floor, making disapproving faces. Finally she looked at Helen with pleading eyes. "Could I try some patent leathers? I'll be careful. I promise."

"We have to get something practical for school, Estelle. Maybe we'll get new dress shoes later. For Christmas or Easter."

"Sure. Later. Then can I get oxfords?"

"Who's going to polish them? You know your daddy won't let you go out of the house in dirty shoes, looking like an orphan."

"I'll polish them. At least let me have the oxfords. Please?" Estelle rarely begged; she complained a lot, but she almost never stooped to begging.

"All right. Wrap those two pair, please."

The saleslady picked up the boxes and headed for the cash register.

"Stevie, I won't be able to take off next week to go shopping again. Did you look around? Didn't you see any loafers you like? Your daddy wants you to get some shoes."

He turned his back to the post. "Is he gonna yell at you, Mom? I can't help it. I don't want any of these kid shoes. I'll buy my own. If I pay myself, what's it to him?"

Helen didn't know what to say. Stevie was stubborn like his dad, but he could read people like her, too. And he knew the price they'd all have to pay if he didn't follow the formula. Joe's life was regulated by a strict set of rules; after twenty years she knew all of them, one of them being, "My kids don't need fancy brand names to prove they're as good as anybody else." They all knew how to play "keep the peace," but at fourteen Stevie wasn't willing to go along all the time anymore. Not when he thought Joe was being unfair. Not when he thought he had a point. They'd been at one another's throats more and more lately, despite Helen's attempts to smooth things over. And those nightmares she couldn't ask about. It was all wearing her down.

"Would you like anything else? Some socks?" The saleslady was at Helen's elbow.

"Yes. Please. Give each of the girls five pair of white cotton socks, would you? And that will be it, I guess." She raised an eyebrow at Stevie, but he turned his head the other way.

After selecting socks from a bin, the clerk rang up the order. "That comes to thirty-five dollars, ma'am. Cash or charge?"

Helen was struck by that. Thirty-five dollars. Exactly. How many times could a person go into a store and have the bill come out to thirty-five dollars, exactly? She opened her purse and pulled out her wallet and gave the lady a twenty, a ten, and a five. All bills Joe had given her that morning.

The saleslady handed each of the girls a long M & R bag. "Hurry back." She smiled. Helen smiled back automatically.

Stevie slouched on ahead to the escalator, and the girls trailed along behind. Thirty-five dollars. Even. How peculiar. Helen wanted to tell someone. But she couldn't imagine who. What if she told Tom, at work, that her bill for the shoes and socks had come to thirty-five dollars, even. What would he say? "Well, isn't that something?" Or Joe? He'd probably look at her like she was an imbecile. Who could she tell? Stevie and Estelle wouldn't care, and Aimee wouldn't understand. Helen didn't really understand, herself, except that she didn't have anybody to tell. Nobody to say "How about that?" to.

And Stevie was right. Joe would yell at her because the boy didn't get any shoes. When she gave the fifteen dollars back he'd have to know why. And he'd be furious. "You spoil him. You've made him into a sissy. Letting him grow his hair long, like a girl. I can hardly stand the sight of him. So now he's too good to wear shoes like everybody else in this family, huh? So he's got to have expensive shoes? Mr. Fancy Pants. This is all your fault, Helen. It's the way you raised him. Where else would he have learned to throw money away? From me? Tell me that, Helen, from me?"

Ordinarily, Helen would just listen, not say a word, and get busy cooking supper or washing dishes or sorting clothes. She'd learned it was a waste of breath to argue with Joe. The argument just got louder and longer, his face got redder, and pretty soon he was swearing at her, calling her a whore and a fat slob and a no-account bitch, a pathetic excuse for a wife and mother. If she turned her mind off and waited, he'd go into his workroom and fiddle around with his Civil War relics or gun collection, or go into the family room and turn on TV and fall asleep in his La-z-boy. Helen thought, "Why do we call that the family room? Nobody goes in there in the evening, anymore, except Joe." The kids did their homework at the kitchen table and played in their rooms. They stayed out of his way, which seemed to suit him just fine. Today, though, she didn't think she could play dead and ignore what she was thinking and feeling. It struck her: she had no one to talk to, except her children. Back out in the heat, her head started to pound and she began to feel woozy.

Helen gave the man at the parking lot her claim ticket and the four of them went downstairs to wait for someone to bring the car around. She could hear the brakes screeching as the drivers brought cars down to the people in front of her. They drove so fast, so recklessly. In such a tight space. She'd never driven over fifty in her life. The children sat on a bench, staring at the cars as they came down the ramp, but she stood. Her children were so well-behaved. She waited thinking, "When was the last time I heard one of them laugh? What do they have to laugh about?" When her car came to a jolting stop in front of her and the young man with a front tooth missing handed her her keys, ("This your wagon, ma'am?"), Helen realized she'd been in a daze or a trance again. She grabbed the keys. "Thanks, yes. Come on, kids." They got up and went to their places in the car. They didn't even fight over who got to ride in the front. She could remember arguing constantly with her brothers and sisters over who got to ride shotgun. Why didn't Estelle fuss with Stevie about it? This heat. Should she have given that guy a tip? It must be the heat that was making her mind jump around so.

Helen started the engine and turned on the radio. Tom Jones' "It's Not Unusual" was ending. Seemed like that was all they played these days. "You deserve a break today, so get out and get away. . ." came over the speaker. Helen listened to the commercial for about the millionth time, but today for some reason she heard it, and it sunk in. She looked at Stevie, sitting next to her with his face so serious. What kind of break does he get? What kind of break did any of them get? Helen thought, I'll spend the fifteen dollars. I'll replace it with money from my hide fund. Joe won't like it that we've gone to lunch at a fast-food restaurant. The kids had to take packed lunches from home during the school year. On weekends they always ate at the house. He thought fast-food places were a rip-off, a waste of money. Well, she'd take them anyway. It would be air-conditioned inside. It wouldn't cost that much.

"Want to go to McDonald's?" Helen spoke loud enough so all three of them could hear over the radio.

Stevie turned to look at her, still not smiling, like she'd suggested they run away from home or something. When did such little things get to be such a big deal? How had she let this happen?

"You mean it, Mom? How will you pay?"

"Don't worry about that. How about you girls? What do you say?"

"Can I get a Big Mac? And a milkshake? And some fries?" Estelle was testing her, as usual.

"You can get what you want. What do you say, Aimee?"

"Sounds good to me." Helen could see her slight smile in the rearview mirror.

She thought, I'll call work. Tell Tom I'm not coming in for the rest of the afternoon. I've got the payroll to do, but I've got plenty of time. Nothing else on my desk has to go out today. He won't say anything. "Okay, let's go to the Boulevard. I think there's a McDonald's near Parker Field. Okay?"

The kids didn't say a thing, but their eyes were open wide. Alert. They sat still as statues, like if they made the wrong move she might change her mind. Why don't they look excited more often, Helen thought. Why do my kids look like robots most of the time? How have I let this happen? The radio announcer was saying something about the twin crises facing Nixon, the war in Vietnam and the inflation at home. Joe ranted in the evenings about inflation, how it was killing the contracting business. He hated Nixon with a passion, but he blamed the rising cost of everything on Johnson. Twin crises. War and inflation. Helen didn't feel touched at all by them. She felt touched by the faces of these three children in the car. They were hers, not Joe's. And she'd done this to them. She'd let him do this to them. His rules. His money. His house. His wife. His children. That was it. She was so busy tiptoeing around being his wife, protecting the children from him, she was so busy keeping them safe, that they never had any fun together, never learned what it was like to be happy, to laugh, to tease one another. Joe always went for the throat when he did his version of teasing. Calling Estelle "four eyes" when she hated her glasses so much; telling her any child with dirty blond hair couldn't be a child of his. He hardly spoke to her otherwise. That's the only way they knew about teasing.

And vacations. They were never fun. Again, Joe ruled the roost, made all the plans and decisions, chose what they would do according to what he wanted to do. He would take them camping near Civil War battlefields. They'd walk the battlefields, look at the slides in the information center, sleep in tents. She'd buy all the food ahead, and spend most of her time cleaning up after one meal and preparing the next one. Estelle would take her books, Aimee would take her paper dolls, and Stevie would help Joe look for relics. That was all they did together, look for and clean and mount and label Civil War relics. Stevie was good at it. Joe had taught him everything he knew, his rules for exactly how to handle their finds, and Stevie was a big help to him. They got along real well when they did that. Of course they didn't talk much, but Stevie always seemed satisfied when he pleased his dad.

Mornings, Joe would go off by himself to gun shows or auctions—he had to have his time alone—and she and the kids would stay at the campsite. They'd swim or hike. This would last a week, usually the first week school was out. That's all the vacation time Joe would ever take. Said he couldn't afford that, really, when the weather was good. But he'd take them. None of the children had ever been to sleep-over camp. He couldn't imagine why anybody would pay money to send their kids somewhere to sleep when they had beds and bikes and more than they needed right at home. Who'd want to sleep with a bunch of strangers, anyway, he'd ask.

Helen looked at her children. They didn't get in line to order. They stood in a clump, staring at the lists and pictures of sandwiches and drinks: all the choices. She walked up to them. "Get what you want. Go ahead. I'll come last and pay."

Estelle stepped up to a register. "I'd like a vanilla milkshake and an order of fries and a Big Mac, please." The clerk in the little yellow hat said, "Anything else?" and Estelle just stared at the board again. "Anything else?" The girl popped her gum impatiently.

Stevie spoke up. "I'll have the same thing."

"Me, too," whispered Aimee.

"Huh?" the gum-smacking girl said.

"I said me, too," Aimee repeated. She grabbed Stevie's hand.

Helen stepped up and ordered, "Coffee. No cream."

"Here or to go?"

Helen looked at the children. "Here, I think." She paid, and told the kids to pick a place to sit while she waited for the order. They walked off, shoulder to shoulder, not talking. Helen watched them and thought, "What happened to them?" Her hands shook as she lifted the crowded tray. "Thanks," she muttered to the waitress, who was already popping "Help you, please?" to the next person in line.

A birthday party was going on in the back of the dining room. About twelve kids close to Aimee's age were making enough noise to raise the dead, wearing those silly hats and blowing those rolled-up noisemakers, throwing french fries and wrapping paper and ribbon. Four mothers sat in a nearby booth, drinking coffee and talking, relaxed as you please, not paying any attention to the rowdy group of children.

Estelle was placing napkins and straws around at each place. Stevie and Aimee sat waiting for their food. They smiled when Helen walked up with the tray loaded down with paper-wrapped sandwiches and bags of fries and fat cups of milkshake. "Look at all that food," Stevie said. None of them reached for it. They waited while Helen passed out their orders.

"Aren't you going to eat anything, Mom? Do you want some of my french fries?" Aimee leaned over the table toward her, holding up her small bag of potatoes.

Helen felt like crying. Or screaming. Or picking up the food and throwing it. "No thanks, hon. I'm not hungry right this minute. I've got my lunch back at work. Enjoy them yourself."

The three children sat eating slowly. "Mom, this is really good. Thanks. Thanks a lot." Estelle smiled at her and sucked on the straw sticking up out of her cup. "This milkshake is supercal." No complaints.

Helen put her coffee cup down and put both hands on the table. It was cool in here. The cool air helped her think. "How would you all like to go on a little vacation? Just the four of us."

Three pairs of brown eyes stared at her face to see if she was teasing. Mom didn't tease. They knew that. They just gazed at Helen, without speaking, as if she were telling a joke of some kind. A crazy joke.

"We could go on a trip. Really. Daddy's too busy. He couldn't go. But we could. I have lots of vacation days built up at work. School doesn't start for a couple of weeks. What do you say we take off?"

Aimee squeezed her eyes closed as tight as she could. Stevie said, dumb-founded, "You mean it, don't you, Mom? You really mean it?"

Estelle broke in, "Dad would never let us do it. It would cost too much money. Besides, where would we go?"

"I want to go to the beach. I've never seen the beach. All the kids at school talk about it." Stevie looked at Stell, begging her to play along with Mom, just in case.

"What about the mountains? It would be so cool there. We could go to the mountains and eat out breakfast and go swimming every day. There's a park called Fairy Stone State Park. They say you can find stones in the shape of lit- tle crosses. Fairy tears. Maybe we could rent a cabin. Or we could get a motel room and have a TV all to ourselves. We could get one that's air-conditioned." She was falling in love with the ideas as she talked, falling in love with the expressions on her children's faces.

Aimee opened her eyes wide. "Do you really mean it, Mom? I'll go wherever you say." She stopped and put her thumb by her mouth. Her smile faded. "But Daddy would be mad. He wouldn't let us go. I know he wouldn't." Her eyes were wide and her eyebrows were raised, like some- thing had just frightened her. She stuck the thumb in.

"We won't tell Daddy. We'll leave him a note and take

off. What do you think about that? Who can pack a suit-case really fast?"

The three pairs of eyes stared, stunned.

"I can. And I can help Aimee." Estelle's eyes shone like new pennies, and her voice was more excited than Helen could remember.

Stevie looked uncertain, worried. "What'll he do when we come back, Mom? What'll he say? What if he sends the police after us? You know how he hates surprises. And wasting money. He won't go for this at all."

"Tell you what, Stevie. You let me worry about that. You all finish your food and I'll go call Tom and tell him I'm taking off. What's he going to do, fire me? He'll just have to do the payroll by himself this one time, that's all there is to it." Helen looked through her purse for a dime. "Hurry up and eat. We've got to get ready fast."

Estelle put the last of her burger on the tray and sat back against the booth. The sour look appeared on her face. "Where would we get the money, Mama? Tell me that. Some idea. Only problem is, we don't have any money." She smirked at the others' ignorance.

Stevie and Aimee stared at Helen. They looked like they wanted to believe her, still. Estelle hadn't squelched their happiness yet, but their faces looked like someone had just said, "Just possibly there's no Santa Claus. Or Tooth Fairy. Or Easter Bunny. Or Angels We Have Heard on High. Or even God." Helen felt like shaking Estelle, but she knew it wasn't her fault. That's all she'd heard all her life. "That would be a waste of money." Helen could hear it inside her head, too, right at that instant, and it made her want to scream. Instead, she reached over to Estelle and took her hand. "Mama's got some money, Stell. Plenty of money." And she left the table to call her boss.

Until Tom Graham came on the line she had no idea what she would say to him. "Hi, Helen, anything wrong?"

"No, nothing's wrong at all. I'm just not going to be back. That's all."

"You mean you're not coming back in this afternoon?

Anything wrong with one of the kids? Something happen at home?" His voice was concerned.

"Nothing like that. I'm just not coming back."

"What about the payroll? Will you have time to get that ready tomorrow morning first thing?" She could hear an edge of irritation.

"I won't be there tomorrow, Tom. It's all in a file folder on my desk. Goodbye." And she hung up, before she lost her nerve, before he asked her any more questions she couldn't answer. "Come on, kids. Let's hurry."

They jumped up from the table. Estelle started gathering up the trash, and Stevie said to Aimee, "You want me to wrap this up for you?" She was only half through with her food.

Aimee looked at Helen. "I don't think I can eat any more. Is that all right? Should I take it with me?"

Helen said, "Just throw it away. We'll get something else later, okay?" and smiled. Aimee skipped to catch up with Estelle, and all three of them ran out to the car. Helen watched as Stevie hugged Aimee before he climbed in the front seat.

"Everybody pack one suitcase, okay? That's all we'll have time for. I'll leave your dad a note." Helen started the engine. The steering wheel was so hot she could hardly stand to touch it, but she drove on, anyway. Now that she'd made up her mind she wanted to be on her way.

"Should I pack some sandwiches or something, Mama?" Estelle, practical, suspicious.

"Heck, no. We'll buy what we want when we get hungry. That suit you all right, your highness?"

"Sure thing, Mom. Sounds okay to me." Stevie looked at her like she'd grown a third foot right out of her forehead. She knew he still couldn't imagine they were going to go off like this, without Daddy. She wasn't too sure she could believe it, either.

"Hey, Stevie, maybe we'll get those shoes you want while we're gone. We'll see. And don't worry. I'll leave your dad a note. Don't worry about a thing. Girls, wear your new shoes if you want to, but pack your tennis shoes. And your bathing suits. And don't forget your toothbrushes. Aimee, you'll need Old Silky."

They pulled up in the driveway and the kids poured out of the car and up the back steps like they were playing hide and go seek, and someone had just started counting. Helen, hot and breathless, sat in the car a minute, looking at the house. A generic brick rancher. The swing set was in the back yard, unmoving in the heat. Her roses were wilting, needing water badly. The house's trim was white, fresh-painted this summer. Joe did that every three years without fail, complaining every second he had a brush in his hand. Said he hated it but he had to, it kept up the value of the property. The grass was cut—Stevie's job every Saturday morning in the summer—and a chain-link fence separated their yard from the neighbors on both sides. Joe didn't want their animals shitting in his yard, he'd said times without number. They'd never had a pet. Joe said he had plenty of mouths to feed as it was. She could see every room in her mind as she sat there, every ashtray in its place, every magazine stacked just so in the magazine rack. The beds were made, the dishes were in order on the shelves. The laundry was folded in the laundry room, waiting for her to sort it and put it away in the proper drawers after supper. She'd vacuumed that house how many times in eighteen years? How many times had she scrubbed the bathroom floors? How many meals had she cooked in that kitchen? How many lunches had she packed? How many times had Joe rolled over on top of her in their bed, no differently than the first time?

I'll get the kids' birth certificates, she thought. Maybe we won't come back at all. We'll see. What should I pack? It doesn't matter. It doesn't matter at all. I just need to get away from here before I lose my nerve. The sooner the better.

She slammed the car door and climbed the steps of the back stoop two at a time. Her hair was damp with perspiration; the back of her neck felt like prickly heat. Cool, she thought; we're going somewhere cool.

She headed straight for the linen closet in the hall bathroom. The one the children used. All her cleaning products were on the floor, in a plastic container. At the bottom of the container was a Tupperware celery crisper. And inside that was her money. Over eight thousand dollars. She'd counted it last Saturday when Joe was at an auction. She'd gone in to clean the bathroom and shut the door. She never even worried about Joe finding the money. He hadn't scrubbed a bathroom since she'd known him, not even when she'd just had the babies. He said he worked too hard to support them to have to get down on his knees and scrub a toilet. So she'd never worried about him finding it. Just cash. No interest. She could hear him on the topic. But she'd been afraid to open a savings account. Afraid he'd find out, or the IRS would find out. So she just stashed away her hide money every week. Twenty years' worth. Birthday and Christmas cash from her mama when she was alive, Avon money, leftover pocket money. Joe never knew she got a cash bonus every Christmas. Another secret. Part went for Santa Claus, part for the hide fund. She'd never really planned what she was hiding it for. She just knew she'd need it some day. And today was the day.

She took the green box with the white top into her bedroom and threw it on her bed and started opening drawers. She could hear the children in their bedrooms, like puppies in a box, scrambling around. When had they been this excited? Not even at Christmas, with Joe sitting there begrudging them every package. He insisted on useful presents, like pajamas and underwear, but Santa Claus always brought at least one surprise. Helen made sure of it. The children were excited, but never this excited. She felt, herself, like she'd been given an Emancipation Proclamation. Correction: like she'd given herself an Emancipation Proclamation. And it was so easy. But, then, she wasn't facing Joe. Not yet. Not for a while. Maybe never. It struck her that she hadn't looked forward to anything herself since right before Aimee was born. She was pulling open drawers, throwing underwear and nightgowns and shorts on the bed. She ran to the closet and got a sweater. She leaned back and yelled, "Yoo-hoo. Take a sweater and a jacket. It might be cold at night in the mountains. You never can tell. And jeans. Everybody take a pair of jeans."

Helen pulled her suitcase from the top of the closet, and Joe's duffel bag that he used for camping trips came tumbling down with it. She stared at it like it was a snake. Would he try to come after them? When they came back in a couple of weeks, what would he do to her? He wouldn't bother the children, but he'd be madder than hell at her. Probably madder than she'd ever seen him. He'd be furious about the money. That's what he'd be maddest about. He knew she had a little from Avon. But not enough to go away for two weeks. Not enough to go out on her own with the children. She kicked the duffel bag under the bed and started shoving her things into the suitcase. She was always so neat, but today she stuffed clothes in any which way. She reached into the green box and pulled out five twenties, shut it, and put it into her suitcase. Best place for it.

I won't take the car, she decided. It belongs to him. That's what he'll think. And he'd come after something that belonged to him. The children aren't his. He could care less about them. But he'd be in a rage if she took the car. I'll call a cab, she thought. That would be best. We'll go to the bus station. I'll need to stretch my money. But I won't skimp. Later, if it runs out, we'll come home and face the music. Or maybe I could find a job for a while. Sort things out. I'd better get those birth certificates.

Helen ran to her desk in the corner of the bedroom and began shuffling through files until she found the one marked "Children: Important Papers." She took the whole file and put it in her suitcase. Then she searched until she found her own birth certificate. Somehow she didn't want Joe to have that. She left the marriage certificate in the folder.

"Everybody about ready?" she called down the hall as she went into the bathroom she shared with Joe and began grabbing shampoo and toothpaste and her make-up bag.

She heard the girls answer, "Just a sec," and "I can't find my Mickey Mouse sweatshirt. Do you know where it is, Mom?" Their voices excited.

"I'm calling a taxi right now. Grab what you can. What you forget we'll have to do without. Or pick up along the way."

Stevie appeared in the doorway, unsmiling. She shut her suitcase and went up to him and hugged him around his skinny shoulders. He'd gotten so old she almost never got to give him a real hug; usually, these days, he'd just let her give him a quick squeeze on the shoulders.

"Mom, are you sure this'll work? I don't want him to get on you. You don't have to do this." Helen hugged him tighter.

"Stevie, we're going. I've made up my mind. We'll decide later whether to come back or not. Let's not talk to the girls about that. Let's just see what happens. One day at a time. Okay?" She touched his wavy dark hair with her hand. Patted it once.

"Okay." He put his arms around her thick waist and hugged her tight. When was the last time he'd done that?

"Now let me call the cab, or we'll never get out of here. Help the girls with their bags, okay? Make sure Aimee goes to the bathroom. And packs her Silky."

Stevie. The past few summers, when the three of them stayed home together, he'd managed to get along with his bossy sister and his baby sister, both, without taking sides or getting into arguments. Somehow he made Estelle feel like she was in charge enough to satisfy her, and he helped Aimee enough to convince her she was safe. The three of them were much happier staying at home; those years at Mrs. Goodwin's had been all right, but they liked being at home by themselves better. When Helen walked in the door from work every day, the dishes were all done, the beds were made, and sometimes Estelle had even set the kitchen table for supper. They were good children. Unusually good.

Helen went to the hallway that led to the bedrooms.

"The taxi's on its way, kids. It'll be here in about five minutes. Put your bags on the front porch. Girls, you can each carry one doll or stuffed toy. Stevie, get your baseball cards. Did everybody pack some books?" Helen pushed on her own blue suitcase to snap it shut. The suitcase she bought before she and Joe got married. And then they didn't take a trip. She looked around the bedroom. Blue sheers tied back, with shades to pull down to keep the sun out in the early morning. Joe hated the sun in his eyes or the neighbors' porch lights shining in the window at night. A dark blue quilted bedspread on the king-sized bed. Joe got the new bed about seven years ago; said they were both king-sized, now, and he couldn't sleep all cramped. Joe's dresser with some of his favorite relics—a bowl of grayish-white bullets and minié balls he'd found himself, and a Confederate belt buckle he kept shined. Nothing else was on the dresser, not even a picture. Helen didn't see another thing she wanted to take. She picked up the suitcase and walked down the narrow hall to the family room and set her bag down. She walked over to the shelf where she kept her coupon files and made her grocery lists. She wrote on the pad:

> Joe —
> The kids and I are taking a trip. Don't worry. I'm not using any of your money. The car keys are on the kitchen table. We plan to be gone two weeks. Maybe longer. I don't know. Depends on how things go. You can tell people I've gone to take care of my sister Jean in Boston, if anybody asks. I can't imagine who would want to know, except maybe Tom at work. Or tell him whatever you want. We'll be out of your hair for a while, anyway. Who knows, maybe forever.
>
> Helen

P.S. I never did get groceries today. Your
money is under the keys.

She picked up the note to put it on the kitchen table,
then grabbed another piece of stationery and an envelope.
She scribbled to her sister in Baltimore, the closest one to
her in age. She wasn't that close with any of her relatives,
especially since she'd been married to Joe. But she wanted
somebody besides Joe to know what she was doing. She
wrote:

Liz —
No matter what Joe says, don't worry
about me and the kids. We're better this
way. I don't know when I'll write or call. I
don't want him bothering you to find out
where we are. We'll be better off away from
him. Give my love to the others, okay?
Helen

The children stood in the doorway with their suitcases.
Stevie and Estelle were holding books. Aimee had her
Silky and shoebox of paper dolls. They all just stood there.
The phone started ringing. Helen knew it was Tom. Who
else would call at this time of day?

"Do you want me to answer it, Mama?" Estelle's face
looked worried.

"No, just let it ring. Come on out to the porch. Might
as well be ready when the cab gets here."

The four of them carried their suitcases to the front door.
Helen said, "Wait just a sec," and ran back into the kitchen
to leave the note and keys and money on the formica table.
She could hear a horn honking out front.

"Come on, Mom," Stevie yelled. She looked around the
kitchen one last time, and walked toward the front door,
swinging her pocketbook. She stepped out into the sunlight
and clipped the letter to Liz on the clothespin on the mail-
box. The mailman would be by before Joe got home from
work. By then they'd be long gone. She watched her chil-

dren put their bags in the trunk of the yellow taxi. "Ready or not, here we come," she yelled as she hurried down the driveway to join them.

Davis Creek
1:30 p.m.

"Ora, bring me that cedar candy box out here on the porch. I want to look over some of my correspondence while my dinner settles."

I can't remember the last time I did get any mail. It must have been 1953 or '54 when I told Ora to stop paying the rent on the box down in Massie's Mill. When Mr. Gamble passed on I wasn't expecting to hear from another living soul anyway. Aunt Bunny and Aunt Lucy went within a year of one another right there at the end of the war, and I never got a thing except a card every Christmas from Mr. Gamble. And it was right around then that I told Chatham Hall to stop sending me their magazines and nev-erending requests for money. I can't hardly believe they'd expect me to send money to a school that accepted a nigra girl as a student. To sit right there in classes alongside the white young ladies. That's what they always called us. Young ladies.

Aunt Bunny and Aunt Lucy were such busybodies, always wanting to know what I intended. As if I'd ever leave this place. They lived and died on Daddy's home place, two dried up old busybodies. Neither one of them ever had a grain of sense. Aunt Bunny seemed downright addle-brained at times. The idea of her leaving me her spin-ster ring. I put that right in my jewelry box. Never wore it a minute. What in the world would I want with a spinster ring? Nothing more than an ordinary amethyst at that. It was plain to see that Daddy got every bit of the looks and the brains in that family. I don't believe either one of them ever had a serious beau, much less a proposal of marriage. Except Daddy did say G. Whithers Moore came to court Aunt Bunny one fall when he was still at home, and he told Grandaddy that G. Whithers was no more interested in Bunny than he was in that knothole in the willow oak out front. No sir, he was after Bunny's position and future inheritance. And he never did come back again to call. Daddy could read people, he certainly could. I wonder what ever happened to G. Whithers Moore.

Daddy liked Henry Trice, spoke highly of him. Said for a common man without benefit of a decent education he had plenty of sense. Yankee ingenuity, whatever that is. Course Henry Trice never showed his true nature when Daddy was alive. He wouldn't have dared. Even though Daddy was an attorney, and spent nearly every day of his adult life upholding the law, I'm just as sure as I sit here that he'd have shot Henry Trice if he'd seen what he came to. Shot him right through the heart.

"Ora, did you hear me? I want that box."

"Hold your horses, Miss Lottie, I got flour all over my hands. I'm cutting up some of these peaches from the trees for a cobbler. I know how you love cobbler with fresh cream. And I thought I'd make one to take home, if it's all the same to you. You know James Earl's sweet tooth. And there's nothing in this world he favors so much as one of my cobblers. Here you are, here's your letter box."

She's carrying that box like it's a kitchen towel. What an unremitting oaf.

"Watch what you're doing with that. I don't want you to spill my letters. It's too hot to be crawling around on the porch floor. It's too hot to even think about food. Be sure you get those peels back on the compost heap right fast. I don't want flies and bees inside the house."

"Of course I will, Miss Lottie. Don't I always, even without you reminding me?"

"I see you shaking your head. Goodness knows what you'd forget if I didn't remind you. Like the clock."

She wasn't paying a bit of attention. That woman seems

76

to be in an everlasting pout these days. I hope she's been taking her blood pressure medicine regular. That time she ran out she ended up naked in the snow in the front yard, down on her knees just screaming to Almighty God. "Jeeee-sus," she'd holler like a banshee, with the brown flesh trembling on her arms and her shoulders rocking back and forth. "Jee-sus." I had to take Daddy's old housecoat out and wrap her up myself. I told her right then, when she'd calmed down enough to get dressed and go home, I said, "Don't you ever come back here without taking your medicine like you're supposed to, you hear." She gave me a look that afternoon I'll never forget. Seemed almost spiteful, like maybe she was thinking she wouldn't come back. She said the strangest thing, she said, "You know, Miss Charlotte, ain't nobody else on this earth would've put up with you and your mean ways like I have." I've never seen her so puffed up, before or since. I stood up to her, though, I told her, "Remember, you swore to take care of me in the name of the Lord, Ora. Don't be forgetting that. You swore on the holy Bible. And don't forget to get that prescription refilled this evening, either. You hear?"

Let me see. The letters from Henry ought to be right underneath this stack here that Daddy wrote me when I was at Chatham Hall. I wish he'd written to me more. I remember just aching to hear from him. They were such beautiful letters, each and every one. He certainly did have a way with words. A regular William Jennings Bryan. Course busy as he was with the office and the orchards it's a wonder he wrote to me at all. And every time he did he'd say how the place just wasn't the same without his own little Lottie around, especially in the evenings when he'd sit out on the front porch and smoke his pipe and talk about the peculiar clients he'd come in contact with that day. He said he missed having me to talk to then most of all. Of course Henry's letters were downright shoddy, held up to Daddy's. Still, he was a right clever man in his own way.

My dear Miss Fairchild,

Please accept my heartfelt condolences on the death of your father. He was an honest man, a hardworking man, and I consider myself fortunate to have managed his orchards and earned his trust and, I like to think, his respect.

If I can do anything to be of help to you, to ease the many necessary things you have to do at this time of distress, please let me know. You can count on me to keep up the orchards as your father would have wanted. He was pleased with the rainfall this year and looking ahead to a good crop. I will see to it. I will stay on as long as you would like to manage the men and the orchards. I mean no disrespect when I say I think he would want that.

If you would be so kind as to extend my condolences to your aunts I would greatly appreciate it.

Yours with all respect,
Henry Trice

I guess I should have known he was driving at something when I read that letter, but it never did occur to me at the time. Course it was right of him to send his condolences rather than come up to the house. Struck me he knew his place as one of the employees. Even "My Dear Miss Fairchild" struck me as his attempt to show some manners. Come to think of it, I was provoked, in a way, 'cause he was taking liberties describing my father's character. I remember thinking to myself, Who does he think he is, talking about Daddy's fine qualities? He's stepping over his bounds. But at the time I was just too overcome with grief to give him more than a passing thought.

July 15, 1920

My dear Miss Fairchild,

As you requested, I have informed Mr. Gamble that you would like to put the back twenty-five acres on the market once the peach crop is harvested. He says he will tend to it.

I have also informed him that the crop looks like a good one, and unless there is some freak of nature we can expect to have a good year.

He asked me to remind you that the regular workers always got a bonus from your father at the end of a good season. Of course the day laborers are only paid their hourly wage. He felt sure you would want to continue this custom of Mr. Fairchild's. I am sorry to bother you with matters of business, but you are the only one who can make such a decision. Since your father kept meticulous records, you could consult his farm ledgers for the past few years to help you decide what you want to do.

I hope you know you can depend on me to help you in any way I could be of service. If you don't mind my saying, I worry about you in that big house alone, with only Ora and Cinchy, now that your aunts have gone back home. If anything ever troubles you, I hope you will call on me. I'm certain Mr. Fairchild would want me to look out for your safety.

I remain, yours,
Henry Trice

He was no more mine than he was Ora's; I never even acknowledged his forward remarks in that last paragraph. Wouldn't have been right. Still, he wrote a fine hand for a foreman. Leave it to Daddy to hire somebody who could conduct business like a gentleman. But I started to notice him up around the house hammering or chopping this, twisting and scraping that. He'd tip his hat just as polite as you please, and I'd nod my head ever so slightly to let him know I was not in the least bit taken by any of his foolishness.

He was a striking man, though, with that hair about the color of pecans and his skin so dark from the sun he looked almost foreign. He kept himself neat as a pin. I noticed, when he started coming around to tend to the man's work about the house, that he never seemed to perspire, even in the middle of the hottest day in August.

August 15, 1920

My dear Miss Charlotte,

The crop continues to thrive, and you can look for an auction your father would have been proud of. I can't remember, in the seven years I've been here, a crop so fine.

I have passed along to Mr. Gamble your intention to pay only the set wage to the men at the end of the season. Of course I accept your decision, but I am worried that there will be talk and maybe even some unrest among the men. Be assured that I will attend to any problem that may occur. After you sell the back twenty-five there will not be any need to keep on so many full-time men, anyway.

Mr. Gamble has a number of bids for the property, so you can expect that to be tended to as soon as the crop is in.

Miss Charlotte, I know it is difficult

80

for a young woman to keep up a farm and a fine country home. Especially now you've let Cinchy go, and it's just Ora to help. I have been trying my best to maintain the buildings in the way your father would have wanted. I have tried to do as much as I can in the evenings. If there is any job you see that you would like taken care of you let me know, please, and I will do it myself or send some of the men.

I cannot help but notice that you sometimes walk about the place after dark. This causes me some worry, as some of the pickers are not from around here, and even though I have tried to be certain that they are reliable, we are short of regular local men since Mr. Fairchild passed away, and you can never be too safe. If you would like to walk in the evenings I would consider it an honor to accompany you.

As always, your faithful servant,
Henry Trice

It's as plain as the hair on my head he was trying to work his way into my affections. "My dear Miss Charlotte," right there. But I was such a ninny, twenty years old, fatherless, and it never entered my head that someone from his station would aspire to actually call on me. Daddy was no more than two months in the grave and here he was suggesting he walk with me in the evenings. Well, I just ignored his remarks and stopped walking after dark. What else was I to do?

But he kept on hanging around the house, working on polishing and greasing Daddy's car, tipping his hat and following me across the porch with his eyes. He kept his distance, though, and I couldn't help but notice he was always just as clean as if he'd stepped into his clothes right off the ironing board, even when he'd been working on the car or helping Ora plant the late garden. He was always wiping his hands on a fresh white cup towel. Ora had a fit, complained to beat the band, when she tried to get the grease out. And his nails were always clean. I remember thinking it was striking that day he drove me to town, that his nails were almost as white and trim as my own. Or Daddy's. Almost. He had fine looking hands for a laborer.

That fall was around the time that crazy young man claiming to be a shirttail cousin came to visit, and when Henry Trice realized he was a no-account phony he drove him off the place with his gun. What a sight that was, that pale, no-account boy whimpering at the sight of Henry Trice with a gun, running down the driveway without even going upstairs for his shaving set and extra shirt. Ora had it on the line. He couldn't have been a day over eighteen. What was his name? It was a mouthful: Rucker T. Fairchild the Third, I believe he said. Insisted he was Aunt Bunny and Aunt Lucy's second cousin's oldest boy, making him distant kin to me. But Aunt Lucy never wrote to introduce him, and when I finally wrote to her, she responded that she did seem to remember a cousin Rucker, from her mother's side, from over toward Scottsville, but she couldn't recall if he had any children or not. I figured he was just after my money.

Lucy was pretty well addled by then, even though she was no more than forty-five. I've always suspected she and Aunt Bunny indulged too much in peach brandy, especially after they were forced to accept the fact that they would have to live out their days in reduced circumstances.

Course I've always known they were both bitter because Daddy left them only a token in his will. Lucy more than Bunny, 'cause for some reason she considered she was Daddy's favorite. That just goes to show how off she was. But Grandaddy Fairchild had provided for them. There's no way in the world he could have known his investments would fail. He was a smart man, Daddy said, but he trusted the banks too much. Those two old dried-up spinsters weren't Daddy's to tend to. He had plenty, left me well provided for, but Aunt Lucy and Aunt Bunny always held it against me that he left them so little. Even though they had plenty on paper at the time. Just goes to show he was right not to trust them. He sure could read people. Daddy always said, trust yourself and trust the land, and anybody else you trust, trust with both eyes open.

"Ora, what are you up to in there? Are you asleep? Bring me a glass of water. I'm so thirsty I could drink the creek. Didn't I just hear the clock strike two?"

"Yes, you most surely did. I'm on my way, Miss Lottie, fast as these old bones can stir. Let me just finish tying off this thread."

They were forever jealous about the car. And neither one of them could drive. Every time they'd come to visit they'd make hints about the two of them needing some way to get about, being as they were getting up in age. And neither one yet over fifty at the time. Said I had no need of it, since I never went into town anyway, and Ora and Henry Trice could go for anything I might want. Said Henry could take the farm truck. What business was it of theirs?

"Thank you, Ora. Just put it down there on the table. And don't bother me anymore. Be sure you clean the globes for the lamps before you leave this evening; they seemed real smoky last night. I could barely see to go over my accounts. I'll do some reading later on. I think I'll rest my eyes in a few minutes, just as soon as I'm finished my correspondence."

"Sounds like a fine idea, Miss Lottie. Seems like you could use a nap."

I hate it when she makes remarks like that and rolls those eyes of hers. Thinks she's so clever.

September 18, 1920

My dear Miss Charlotte,

     The car is now in good working order. I have given it a going-over, inside and out. It's looking as good as new, and fit for you to ride in whenever you take a notion. Of course I would consider it an honor if you would let me drive you whenever you decide a decent time has passed and you would like to go into town.

I cannot tell you how outraged I was to find that the young man who visited recently and called himself your kin was an impostor come to take advantage of your innocence and isolation. I hope it was not too frightening for you when I was forced to take matters into my own hands to send him packing. I had hoped you would not be present, and I was embarrassed and regretful when I saw you standing there on the porch when the incident was over.

I have taken the liberty of purchasing a pistol for you in case, God forbid, there is ever another unfortunate situation in which someone else tries to bring you to harm and I am not close by to see to your safety. If it would meet with your approval, I would like to show you how to load and fire the pistol. I am sure your father would want to feel certain that you have the means of defending yourself from people like that preposterous young fraud. Harmless though he may have been, it's better to be safe, especially when someone young and unprotected like yourself is concerned, if you'll pardon me saying so.

I have turned over the season's accounts to Mr. Gamble, and he will be issuing final wages in the next few days. I have not informed the men that there will be no bonus. I would feel better if you had your pistol before the week is out, as some of them who have been with Mr. Fairchild's orchards for a number of years may react unpleasantly. I'd like to think not, but I'd rather err on the side of caution.

Mr. Gamble assures me that he has a buyer for the twenty-five acres who is only awaiting your approval of the price. He will drive out when he brings the wages to talk to you about the offer. I am sorry you have to be subjected to this legal and financial inconvenience. I wish there were some way I could help you even more.

Please let me know if you would like for me to drive you to town or to church or to visit your aunts.

With continuing admiration,
I remain your ever loyal,
Henry Trice

That Saturday, he did bring over the gun. It was the best day I'd had since before Daddy took ill. Henry wore a white shirt and a tie and a brown corduroy jacket, even though it was one of those warm September days that feels more like the middle of July. We walked down to the creek, quiet as two deer. The gentians were still in bloom. I do love gentians. When we got where it was shady and cool, Henry Trice found a shale bank across the creek and waded over and took a piece of lime and drew a circle.

When he came back, he took the bullets and showed me how to put them in the chamber, and how to cock the hammer, and it was all so simple and natural and he showed the greatest patience in explaining it. Come to think of it, he was almost courtly. He showed me how to stand, straddled-like, and aim, and take a bead. He seemed awful concerned about the noise, said that and the kick in my shoulder might be a bit too much for a small lady like me. It seemed only natural to me that he hit inside the circle when he shot; I just took it for granted that I would, too. When I did, the first time, he acted like he could hardly believe his eyes. He stared at the target and the gun and me without saying a word for at least a minute. He just carried on about it when he found his voice, told me to try again, and when the same thing happened the second time he seemed so proud and astonished, like I'd just given him a kiss or something. I felt like I'd been shooting that pistol all of my twenty years, and it was no harder for me than walking or biting a peach or combing my hair.

After a few more turns we walked back up toward the house, and when I stooped to pick some gentians and tripped he grabbed my elbow, real firm and strong. As soon as I righted myself he let his hand drop, like it had never even been there. But I felt the pressure all the way back to the house. At the back porch he tipped his hat and smiled, and that was the last good time I remember looking Henry Trice square in the eyes.

That afternoon is just as clear as anything in my mind. I told Ora I wanted a bath, and she brought the tub into the kitchen and I stripped down and got in. The water felt cool after I'd gotten so flushed out there in the woods. And I told her to bring me all fresh underwear, my mauve afternoon dress, and a pair of white silk stockings. And to go tell Henry Trice I needed him to drive me to town.

I know I was a sight for sore eyes that afternoon, with my pearls and gold-piece necklace and the lace gloves that came just to my wrists. Once, a long time ago, Mama told me that a lady never wore long gloves in the daytime. I put on Mama's white straw hat with the gauzy veil that covered my face and tied at the back of my neck. The only other time I'd worn a veil was at Daddy's funeral. Aunt Lucy said a veil required maturity. But my face was so ravaged at the funeral I had no choice. When I walked down the front steps Henry Trice just tipped his hat and held the car door and acted like he'd been my chauffeur for my entire life. He never drove me in the car but that one time. And when he said, formal like, "And where would you like to go, Miss Fairchild," I answered in my most serious voice, "Please drive me to Mr. Gamble's office in Lovingston." You couldn't tell we'd been in the woods shooting pistols just a few hours before.

Now that I think back over it, he never even said anything about it being Saturday afternoon, or that Mr. Gamble in all likelihood was at home instead of at his office. He just drove on in silence, me in the back with the windows up clutching my needlepoint purse, him sitting tall and formal-like in front. When he got to Mr. Gamble's office he said, "If you'll excuse me just one moment, I'll see if he's available," and walked up to the door right there on Main Street. Funny thing was my lawyer was there, as if we had scheduled an appointment, and Henry Trice spoke to him, though I couldn't tell from the car what he was saying. He came and held the doors for me and I walked in and told Mr. Gamble my final decision. His expression rarely changed in all the years I knew him, but his face was agitated as could be that day. Course he tried to change my mind one last time, tried to tell me Daddy wouldn't want it, to wait a while, that I had plenty of money without selling. But there wasn't a bit of use in that. I was bound and determined to do what I'd decided. What good was all that land to me? Daddy wouldn't have wanted me to fret over money. Mr. Gamble had handled it all as I had requested, of course, right down to getting the new owner to pay my taxes. In perpetuity, he called it. When I came back out to the car Henry Trice held the door—somehow, I felt as though he'd saluted, though of course he never did—and I rode back to Fairchild Acres in silence and pleasure. I had what I'd come for. I couldn't help but smile.

When he drove up to the house, Henry Trice stepped out quickly and opened my door. He never looked me in the eye that afternoon, like he had when he'd showed me how to shoot the pistol, and I felt free to look directly at him. I felt like I was full of Daddy's power that day, like he was speaking through me. "Have the men come to the front steps after supper. All of them. Tell them I have an important notice they all need to hear. Before dark."

Looking straight ahead he answered, "Yes, Miss Fairchild." But I could sense he wanted to know. I could almost feel the pressure of his hand on my elbow again. I walked up the front steps slow and careful, letting him know who was boss. I had the money in my purse, between the tan satin lining and my change purse, wrapped in a white lawn handkerchief. Nobody knew about it but me and Mr. Gamble. And I'd made him swear he wouldn't tell anyone about my intentions, though he'd tried to talk me out of them. All I could think at the time was, Daddy would be so impressed. He'd understand how I needed to do this. What did I know about running an orchard? He was so much smarter than the others.

To this day I can't comprehend how it turned out so bad. It's a puzzle to me. When they came up to the house, looking at me with those strange eyes, then not looking at me, holding their hats in their hands like naughty children, I knew how Daddy must have felt, being the boss of this whole place. They were in my power. I spoke fast, because nobody was saying a word. I don't even remember the crickets buzzing, though usually they raise a terrible racket that time of year. My voice sounded strong. I said, "I've sold the place, all the orchards, the cattle, the barns, everything. I talked to Mr. Gamble today. He'll close the deal on Monday. I only kept this house and the ten acres around it, that go down to the creek. Now I've got no cause to be worrying about drought and frost and insects. My daddy wouldn't want me to worry one bit.

"So I won't be needing any of you any longer, except Mr. Trice, of course. If you want to get on with the new owner of the orchards, talk to Mr. Trice. He'll put in a word for you. He'll stay on in charge of the grounds, here.

"And I've got your wages for this season. No need to come back on Monday. If you're staying in the cabins I expect you to be gone by dark tomorrow."

I called their names, each and every one, because Mr. Gamble wrote out the list for me, and the amounts, and I'd put the money in those soft-feeling vellum envelopes I found in Daddy's walnut desk. The paper felt so good in my hands, like a linen napkin, and I wrote on the outside, as carefully as I could, each man's name and the amount. I used Daddy's ink pen. I'd never touched it before that day, except to look at it. When I called out the names, each one of the men came up to the steps and nodded his head, polite as you please, and never said a word more than, "Thank you, Miss Fairchild." Some didn't even say that much. I couldn't watch to see them look into the envelopes because I was still reading the names, not until I read out Paul Wilson and Paul Wilson, Junior. Then I stood at the top of the steps and looked around at them, to see what they were doing. Not a one of them so much as glanced in my direction or said a word more, even when they opened those envelopes and saw there was nothing extra in there. They didn't even look at one another, just shuffled around in their dirty old shoes and put back on those sweaty hats and moved on, like a herd of cows. Henry Trice had been a ninny to worry that there'd be trouble. Not even old Blankenship so much as looked back at me.

After I called all the names I looked over at Henry Trice and he just stood real still, hat in his hand, peering down at the ground. The others started moving on down the road toward the bunkhouses, but he just stood there. When he finally looked up at me, it was the most peculiar gaze I've ever seen before or since, like I'd grown a third eye or something, like he was trying to look right through to my insides. He'd never looked at me direct like that before.

So I finally said to him, when he didn't open his mouth and just stood there staring at me in that strange way, "Henry . . . ," because I was thinking, he must be stunned to see how commanding I am, like Daddy. He must be shocked, thinking I'm so helpless and all, to see how I can handle myself. But he still just stood there and stared, until finally I took a step down off the porch and said, again, "Henry . . . ," thinking maybe he hadn't heard me the first time. And he looked at me and said, quiet, almost in a whisper, "Miss Fairchild . . . ," but that's all he got out. He shook his head, like he was trying to wake himself up, and turned around and followed the men back down the road without saying another thing to me. It didn't make a bit of sense.

I stood on the steps in the dark, thinking to myself that

this was nothing like what I'd expected. Ora was sleeping
here nights back then, before her Mama died and she had to
start tending her feeble-minded brother, James Earl. But
she was dead to this world that night, back in her room
sound asleep. She missed it all. So I sat in the rocker on
the porch awhile, thinking how proud Daddy would be, how
glad to know I'd finally taken over and started making decisions. Didn't he acquire all this land for me? What did I
know about running an orchard? I just rocked and rocked
in this very same chair. And I figured Henry Trice didn't
know what to say, seeing me learn to fire a pistol and take
over the place all in one day. I knew I'd caught him by surprise, and I was sure I'd get another letter from him. And I
did, the very next day.

> September 20, 1920
>
> Dear Miss Fairchild:
>   I am sorry you did what you did.
> James Hobsen and Walter Fitzgerald and
> Charles Blankenship have been with your
> father for about seventeen years apiece. All
> the other local men about the same. Except
> for young Moore, who's only been with us
> for three years, but his wife had a baby this
> spring, their second. Your father always
> prided himself on being fair with the men.
>   You hit us all a low punch when you
> said you'd sold off everything except the
> house and ten. I guess I figured you loved
> the orchards and farm the way Mr. Fairchild
> did. Nothing could have made him let them
> go, not me or you, either one. He loved them
> that much.
>   So now I can't stay on either. It
> wouldn't be right. I promised Mr. Fairchild
> I'd keep up the place and run it the way he'd
> want, but this changes everything. I could
> not stand myself if I stayed on after these
> men who have trusted me have been fired.

If you'd like I will ask around
Lovingston to find someone to come out and
keep the house up for you, to chop the wood,
tend to the grounds, and mend the house as
it needs. I owe your father that much. Ora
can see to the burial ground. I will be off the
place by the end of the week.

Miss Fairchild, I considered it a great
honor to work for a lady like you. But I just
don't know how to figure everything that
happened here this evening. It will nag at
me for a long time. I leave this place with a
sad heart.

Yours truly,
Henry Trice

He makes it sound like I did something wrong, like
Daddy wouldn't have wanted me to sell those trees and
cows and let those good-for-nothing hired hands go. Those
men were no concern of mine. What did Henry Trice know
of Daddy's wishes? What right did he have to chastise me?
Daddy wouldn't have cared two hat pins. He just wanted
me to be happy and safe and secure. Not worried about
money. And he thought he could trust Henry Trice to take
care of me. And he just ran off, first sign that I was in control he just ran off, like a scared little boy. He was no better than a hired hand himself.

Those men weren't worth a thought. They could pick
just as easily for the next owner. Wouldn't matter to them
so long as they got a noon meal and wages to go out and
drink up on Friday. I never so much as heard Daddy call
one of them by name, so why in the name of kingdom come
should Henry Trice act so self-righteous about me letting
them go?

He sure had me fooled. That's the last thing I figured
him for, self-righteous. This letter doesn't say a thing about
my hair, but I remember just as sure as I'm sitting here that
he said I had hair like a goddess. And I would've sworn it

was right here in this letter. Maybe there was one more letter. That's what it is. I must've misplaced it. Or else Ora's been snooping in my personal things. Maybe I burned it, 'cause it was so offensive. Vile. But I don't remember burning it. I forget so many things these days. Seems like I've read those words over and over. The first time, I turned blood red and about fainted, I was so shocked. Nobody ever talked to me like that before or since. Ora had to get me some apple brandy, I was so upset. I'm sure of it.

That's what it was, he said those things to me. He didn't write them. He came back up to this house the very next night. That's when he said those things about longing to touch me. And wanting to walk with me in the woods again, in the moonlight this time. He said those things right here on this porch, after the men had cleared out, while Ora was asleep. He was out of his head. Said he couldn't sleep for thinking about me. That's what it was. I had my long nightgown on, the one with the tiny pink embroidered roses all around the bodice. My hair was down my back, brushed shiny. I wonder whatever happened to that gown. Aunt Bunny made it for my hope chest. But I stood right up to him. I told him, I said, "Henry Trice, get off this place. Stop. Don't say another word. You disgrace yourself every time you open your mouth. And I don't ever want to see your face again." I fired him, that's what I did. He was worse than a hired hand, he was downright common.

Lord, it wears me out, thinking of him and all that carrying on. I could have sworn he wrote it all out in a letter, but he must've come back up to the house the next night. I've just confused it a bit. I feel like I could rest my eyes a minute. Rock a bit and rest my eyes.

I haven't heard a sound from Ora in the longest time. "Ora? You in there?" Well, she's probably snoring on the back porch, trying to make me think she's working. She barely gets the dusting done every day any more. I think I'll just close my eyes a bit. Woo, that last yawn made my eyes tear up. This heat gets to me. The air's so heavy today, I can hardly breathe. Not a breath of air.

The back porch. I'm out here on the porch. Not a stitch on. I'll just step in the tub. Yi. The water feels cool. I bet Ora put the tub back here so I could get a breeze. It feels so cool on my skin. She must be down in the garden. I'll just close my eyes and sink down and forget the heat. And I'll put on one of my soft summer dresses when I get out, that yellow one I got in the box Aunt Bunny sent. I love old-fashioned dresses. So ladylike. Lucy probably looked almost pretty in it when she was a girl. Dead Lucy. Dear dead dumb Lucy. She didn't look as pretty as me. My skin's so soft. White and soft. Where's the soap? I can never find the soap. I hope Ora set out some of that cologne I like. The gardenia. I'll need some more soon. None for Christmas this year. Nothing for Christmas this year. Just a card from Mr. Gamble. The water's so cool. Who's that in the corner? Ora? Who's that? I see you standing there. Speak up. I'll scream. Ora! Don't come any closer. I know who you are. I'll tell. Go away now. Don't come any closer. I have a pistol. I'll use it. How can I get out of this tub? I'll get my pistol. I've got to get up. He'll see me. That's what he wants. To see me. To touch me. He said so that night. I know who you are. Even with that shadow on your face I know who you are. I'd know you anywhere. Don't come any closer. If I get out of the tub he'll see me. Don't look. Go away. Stop. My God, you can't touch me. I'll scream. Get your hands away from me. Don't put your hands on my shoulder. I'll have you killed for this. Daddy! Help! I can't move. The water. I'm shaking all over. Don't make me stand up. Why can't anybody hear me scream? Why? Dear God, dear God in heaven, your hand is touching my breast. I can't stand it. That's what you always wanted, isn't it. To see me. To touch me. To touch me there. My God, I can't stand it. I can't breathe. I knew it. I'm going to scream just as loud as I can. I'll bite you. Don't turn my face. Let go of my face. Stop. Don't. I can see you. My God, stop! It's you!

"Miss Lottie, Miss Lottie, you're having that dream again. Wake up, Miss Lottie. Don't fret so. You're all in a sweat. A-glistenin in this heat. You've gotten yourself all worked up. No need hollerin for your daddy like that. Just calm yourself down now. I'll get you some water. Some nice fresh water."

Richmond
2:45 p.m.

Judy looked at the half-filled jelly jars, blocks of dark orange cheese, boxes of cereal and noodles, and cans of cat food on the counter. All week long she'd been trying to use up what she had. How could she still have all this left? She picked up a small half-used can of tuna and sniffed it. Smelled fishy to her; so how else is tuna supposed to smell? "Sophie, want a treat? Here kitty." The cat didn't come. It wasn't like her to stay away when Judy was in the kitchen. Usually she was right at her feet. "Come on, girl. Tuna. Kitty steak. Chicken of the sea." Still no sign of the cat. That's right, Judy thought. I shut her up in the closet while those men were here.

She walked into her bedroom. She could hear Sophie

94

crying to get out through the tiny crack she'd left for venti-
lation. "Sorry, Sophie. I didn't mean to torture you. Must
be hot as hell in there. I thought I gave you more air than
that. Come on." She opened the door and the cat bounded
down the hall. Judy followed her and set the can of tuna on
the floor by the sink, looking around for a bag to put the
other groceries in.

What had seemed like next to nothing earlier in the
morning was turning out to be more than she'd expected.
Wasn't that always the way? The old time/task formula.
Figure how long it will take, multiply by two, then add an
hour for error. Of course if you're in a hurry, double it. The
two men from Goodwill had to be told every move to make,
and then they moved like molasses on a winter's morning.
She'd expected them to be there half an hour, an hour at
most, and they'd stayed almost two. Now she had these
leftovers from the fridge and pantry to take to Mrs. C. Who
would want to talk. And she still had the kitchen floors and
counter to do. Well, she'd pack up the food, turn in the key,
get her deposit, and say her good-byes. She could check
those all off the list, then come back and finish up here. She
could give it all a "lick and a promise," as her mother used
to say when she did a job half-way; but she didn't want to
leave a mess, even if she was in a hurry. Call it supersti-
tious, but she wanted to walk away from a clean slate. She
could do everything and still get away by five. Be with
Drew by eight. Nine at the latest. No problem.

She found some brown grocery bags on the floor of the
pantry and started putting the groceries in while the cat ate,
singing to herself, "It takes two, baby, it takes two, baby, me
and you, it just takes two. . ." I'll just leave these left-overs
in the Tupperware, she decided. Mrs. C. is nuts over
Tupperware anyway, so she won't mind throwing out the
dribs and drabs if the bowls and lids are an extra-added
bonus. Besides, she'll probably get a curiosity-fix checking
out what I had for dinner all this week. Mostly stuff from a
can. She'll really tut-tut over that, especially since she
asked me over to eat a couple of times. Judy didn't like to

cook all that much, anyway, but this week she was particularly unimaginative, just ate what was fast and easy and fill-
ing while she ran errands and got ready for the sale. Drew
did most of the cooking when they were together. She
thought of the first dinner he cooked for the two of them at
his place. Grilled tuna steak. With fresh lemon sauce, and
asparagus, and sliced melon. It made her mouth water to
think of it. Maybe she ought to run get a burger. She had-
n't eaten since that pastry this morning next door. Nah.
Save the time. She looked at cold pork and beans in a pale
plastic container. Even Sophie wouldn't eat those, but they
wouldn't be bad with some cut-up hot dogs. She stuck them
in the bag.

She almost dropped a can of peas when she heard the
knock at the front door. Who the heck can that be, she wondered, leaning back and looking over her shoulder, the view
clear to the front screen. Mr. Toms, the mailman, was
standing there. Since she'd stopped her mail as of today she
couldn't imagine what he was doing at the door. He was a
sweet little man, but he ran a close second to Mrs. Calabash
in terms of nosiness about her personal life. Her mother
could rest in peace knowing they'd taken up where she'd
left off.

"Hey there, Mr. Toms. I didn't expect to see you today,"
she called as she walked to the door, opening the screen.

"I got the stop notice, Judy. But you just had this one
card. I thought I'd take a chance and bring it on, since you
were here Saturday when I came by. Thought it might be
important." He held out a postcard.

"Thanks." She took the picture postcard he handed her.
"Thanks a lot." It was an art reproduction. That Flemish
couple getting married. The one with the mirror in the
background, and the pregnant bride. Had to be from Drew.

"You moving close by?"

"Nope. Want some ice water?"

He stepped off the front stoop. "Got a thermos.
Wouldn't go out in Richmond in the summer without it.
Liable to be hot as Hades, if you'll excuse me saying so.
Well, good luck, Judy. Wherever you go."

"Thanks, Mr. Toms. Take it easy." He walked across the grass to Mrs. C's. The two of them would make her ears burn for sure.

She stood in the doorway while she read the message on back of the card. "You are cordially invited to the marriage of Giovanni Arnolfini and his lady love. Or, better still, Judy Marsh and Drew Carter. Whenever you say. Love always." That was it. Just "Love always." She stared at his handwriting, bold and clear. She ran her fingers across the message, wishing she could touch him instead. "I say, immediately if not sooner. That's what I say." She tucked the card in the back pocket of her cut-offs and headed for the kitchen. "Get your rear in gear, Judy." She started singing at the top of her lungs, "It takes two-ooo, baby, it takes two-ooo, baby . . ."

Nelson County
3:00 p.m.

"Spare the rod. Spare the rod. Spare the rod. Spare the rod." Clarence Winston walked down 606 toward Lovingston. Left and right. Left and right. Left and right. He was tired; he muttered, "Spare the rod," out loud, but not loud enough for anybody else to hear. Passersby rarely got close enough to Clarence to hear what he was saying anyway. Something about the way he looked, whether it was the snake and dragon tattoos winding down his muscled arms, or his scraggly black hair. (So what if he had a little bare spot on top. Wasn't nobody gonna say a thing about it. No siree.) Could be his beard—folks around here so dumb, they think anybody with a beard's one of them hippie-cowards. Or the grey-dirty jeans and T-shirt. Something kept people at a distance. Kept them from meeting his eyes. He wanted it that way.

"Spare the rod. Spare the rod." Some days it was,

"Holy Ghost, Holy Ghost." Left and right. Left and right. Clarence tried to recite one or the other all the way from Saunders Peach Orchards to McGritz. This afternoon as he said it, he was thinking about the waitress, Diane. Cock-sucking bitch, he thought. Ass-twitching cock-sucking bitch. She's asking for it. God's eternal damnation. Unless she's baptized. She's definitely asking for it. Gives me a boner just thinking about it. Damn her. Goddamn her to everlasting hell. But not for a few more weeks. Not until all the peaches are in. Then I'll head for the valley. The apples. Vengeance is mine. Goddamn right. Mine. Didn't that jerk-off Pastor Winn, Pastor John T. know-it-all Winn, didn't he say God's in all of us? At least a million fuckin times. Don't that mean me? Damn right it does. Vengeance is mine. Clarence son-of-the-Father Winston's. Couple more weeks. Then she's mine.

He kept up his pace, left and right, left and right, using the heel of his right hand to push down hard on the bulge in his crotch. "Spare the rod. Spare the rod." He was dying for a cigarette, but he'd have to stop saying it out loud if he smoked, and today he wanted to say it all the way. He really did. He was getting irritated. Two or three days he'd missed. Three. Yesterday he hadn't made it all the way to the restaurant, but it wasn't his fault. Damn hippie bikers tried to run him off the road. Think the road belongs to them. I'd a shot them if I'd had my gun, he thought. Pretty faces laughing, running me off the road. T-shirts all differ-ent colors, like girls. I'd a shot both of them. Like to have seen those pretty faces then. If there'd just been one, I'd a chased him. But two and a bike. That's too much. I know when to let it ride. Yes sir. I didn't spend all that time inside without learning when to let it ride. Only thing, those little pretty-faced assholes got away. Motherfuckers. And messed me up. I couldn't start over. If I hadn't a yelled at them I coulda probably kept on. But I had to at least yell, at least let them know they didn't scare me one bit. Not one fuckin bit. Laughing like that. I coulda taken them both. Easy. But they had the bike. I wouldn't a minded having that bike, come to think of it. Wouldn't have to walk. Nah. I wouldn't want to go to a gas station all the time. Call attention to myself. Or the bike. That's when they get you. That's when the stupid assholes who don't play it right find themselves back in the slammer. Nope, to hell with the bike. Who needs a piece-of-junk bike. "Spare the rod, spare the rod." Clarence shoved his hands in his pockets and walked on toward the restaurant, left and right, and toward Diane.

The air was so still and hot that he had dried perspiration rings on top of one another all the way down the sides of his shirt, with a soaking patch closest to his hairy armpits. The smell of the sun-baked asphalt hung in the air. Bitch better not look at me like I'm some kind of stinkin slimeball, he thought. Stare down at my hands while she's taking my order, like it'd make her sick to look me in the eye. Ain't she ever seen working hands before? Hands that serve the Lord? So who does she think she is, Grace Goddamn Kelly, waiting tables at McGritz? Little tobacco stain on my teeth, little dirt under my nails. So what? Ain't it all made by the hand of Almighty God? Wasn't he God's own son on earth? Better not act like she's too damn clean to wait on me. I know better. She ain't clean until she's been baptized. And I ain't baptized her yet. But I will.

Clarence could see the church back home just as clear as if it was sitting by the side of the road. First Church of Divine Holiness in Parkersburg, West Virginia. His daddy had lived by the book, and he raised Clarence, his only begotten son, by the book. He wasn't one of those nuts who spout scripture on Sunday and beats his kids with wires and burns them with cigarettes and shit like that, like a lot of the guys inside. No siree. He was a church-going man, a good man, one who made the family go to church twice on Sundays and once on Wednesdays, for family-night supper. Anything go wrong at that church, his daddy was up there fixing it. And he tithed every dollar he ever made. Was proud of saying, "I made part of this for my Lord." Even made Clarence give a penny of every dime of his allowance, soon as he started getting one. Of course he had to do his chores to earn it. What his daddy called Honest Labor. Mucking the stalls. Chopping the wood. Burning the trash. No sir, he wasn't one of those fathers who put their kids in scalding water if they caught 'em doing something nasty, or washed their mouths out with kerosene if they talked back. His daddy was a God-fearing man. He went by the book. The good book. He didn't even think about sparing the rod. Clarence do something wrong, he'd have to take down his britches, bend over, grab a hold of his ankles, and his daddy would whack him with an old metal curtain rod. Number of whacks depended on what he'd done. Something like skipping school, he only got a couple of whacks. But talking back to his mama, that was breaking a commandment, and he could count on at least twenty. Hard ones. For the Lord. Clarence learned early not to talk much. Too much mouth get you in trouble. Learned to keep his mouth shut and go about his business. The Lord's business.

Daddy blessed the food every meal, and read the Bible to Clarence and his mama every night before they went to bed. His mama would knit. He could almost hear those needles clack-clacking, hear her say, "Idle hands are the devil's temptation," when Daddy would look over his glasses at her. Sometimes he'd read for ten minutes, sometimes an hour, sometimes half the night. Claimed he was guided by the spirit within. He read right through the whole entire book. When he finished, when Clarence was about eleven, he started over. Clarence was gone before he finished a second time.

Mama didn't have much to say, though. Clarence never heard her raise her voice. Daddy would say, "A virtuous wife is a blessing, Doris, one of the Lord's own blessings. Keep in mind, the meek shall inherit the earth." She hung out the clothes, cooked the food, scrubbed the house clean, and knitted for the poor. She never complained; set on inheriting the earth, he guessed. Clarence wondered why he didn't have any brothers or sisters. He asked his mama once, and she said, "The Lord's will be done." When he asked his daddy the same thing, when they were out taking up hay one fall day when he was about ten, his old man said, "The Lord blessed us with you, Clarence, when your mother was late in life, like Sarah. Blessed be the Lord." And that was that.

Clarence's parents looked more like grandparents—he didn't have any of those—but he'd never thought too much about it as a boy, since he only saw other kids and their families at church and school events. His daddy was skinny as a fence rail, but his arms and legs were nothing but muscle. Even if he looked like a beanpole, he was strong as a mule. Strong as a damned mule. Clarence ought to know, better'n anybody. Funny, his daddy wore them little gold-wired spectacles when he read, but not when he was working, fixing something. Said his hands saw for him when he was working on a machine. It was a gift from God. Mama didn't have any shape at all, not like some of the other women at the church or the ones he saw on TV, when he sneaked a show. She didn't look a thing like Lassie's mama. Her clothes just hung like clothes on a line. She wore hose rolled at the knees, that bagged around her skinny ankles, and brown work shoes, whether she was going to church or not. No make-up, no siree. Not even to cover up the wine-stain birthmark on one cheek. And all he could remember her smelling of was Cornhusker's Lotion and whatever she'd just cooked. Not gussied up and wild-smelling like those whores and hussies he'd met when he went to Pittsburgh. Daddy was against those women who dressed gaudy and smelled like sin itself, to attract the attention of men. The devil's own temptress, he'd say. To sin in the mind is as bad as sinning with the body, he'd say. So to avoid sin and temptation Clarence came straight home from school every day to do his work. "Yield not to temptation," his father always spouted. So it was pretty much him, Daddy, Mama, and the Lord his whole growing up.

Except for Pastor Roberts. Sunday nights his daddy didn't read from the Book. Of course they'd heard the word just about all day and early evening, too, at church, but still he knew his daddy would've read at his regular time if it weren't for Pastor Roberts. Soon as they'd eaten their left-over Sunday supper, Daddy would turn on the TV—nobody ever dared turn it on but him, because of all the filthiness on it—and the three of them would sit on the sofa and watch the Oral Roberts Revival Hour. Sometimes Mama would have a pad and pencil, so she could copy out the Kraft cheese recipes that came on the commercials, but most of the time she just rubbed lotion into her hands and sat listening, like him and Daddy, or she'd knit. Pastor Roberts had a reading and a message every week before he did the healing. And the last prayer he'd invite the people at home to come up to their sets and be healed. "Go on up there and touch that TV and ask for forgiveness, Clarence," Daddy would say. The first time it happened—I couldn't a been more than seven or eight—I said, "But Daddy, I ain't done nothing. I ain't been sinning. Honest." He shoved me on up to the TV, and I prayed, and afterwards he made me take my pants down and he whacked me a lot of times. I lost count. Like to passed out. "Spare the rod, spoil the child," he kept repeating, while he whacked me, sort of like a beat to music, a hymn. "Children, obey thy parents." So I never talked back again after that when he made me stand up at the TV and ask for forgiveness at the closing prayer. I just shut my eyes, put my fingertips on that warm wood, and thought to myself, "Spare the rod. Spare the rod."

When Clarence went to high school he started having dreams at night. The first time it happened he got down on his knees and prayed until daylight. Somehow his daddy would know, he'd know for sure, and Clarence was positive he'd have to pay for his disgusting, sinful thoughts. But Daddy didn't say a word about it—Mama must not've told him about the nasty sheets—and he got so he'd dream that dream right often. And different girls from school and church would be in them—even his Sunday School teacher, a couple of times—would show up in those dreams. And he'd wake up, right as soon as it was over, and be all out of breath and damp, and he'd think to himself, "Spare the rod.

Spare the rod." His grades dropped off in school; teachers said he was smart, said he just wasn't trying, wasn't paying attention. He couldn't keep his mind on his work with all those girls giggling and carrying on around him. And when he got home he wouldn't be able to remember what he was doing. Couldn't concentrate. Daddy was on his back, seemed like, day and night.

At eighteen, he just took off. Wasn't any use hanging around. His old man was bound to find out about his filthy thoughts. He'd taken to buying magazines, but he didn't dare bring them to the house. Had to hide them in the woods. Finally, when the tension between him and his daddy seemed like it was bound to explode every minute they were in the same room, he headed out, headed for Morgantown. He knew he could find work there. And girls. Not silly high school girls, either. Working girls. "Spare the rod."

He'd gone straight to the Holiness Church in Morgantown. Hitched the whole way, loving every minute of it. "Go ye into the world, spreading the Lord's word." Daddy wouldn't understand. Of course he didn't give anybody his real name. Claimed to be an orphan. Called himself Denny. They let him do odd jobs around the church for food money until he got settled. Even sent him over to the college. One of the members was a janitor there. High up. Gave him a job working on the grounds crew. Nothing to it. At first, though, he couldn't believe how disgusting the students were. How they threw trash around like the world was one great big garbage can. And the girls. Hussies and whores, every last one of them. Twitching around making goo-goo eyes at every boy who walked past them. Except him. They didn't even seem to see him. He went to church regular, worked, read his Bible at night, and started sending Mama ten dollars a week when he was settled. Swore to himself he'd cleanse himself of evil thoughts. He didn't send an address, though. Didn't want his daddy coming after him, telling him he had to work at home, claiming he needed him. Wasn't Daddy stronger than two men half his age? Didn't Clarence know? "Spare the rod."

He did fine for about six months, too. But he knew something was missing. He'd still have the dream every few nights, and spend at least an hour at daybreak the morning after on his knees begging his Heavenly Father's forgiveness. But all around him he could see sin. Except in church. He'd hoped to meet some young woman who had dedicated her life to full-time Christian service. He prayed for her. They could serve the Lord as missionaries, taking His word into bars and pool halls and places that were like hell, right here on earth. But the only girls at the school were like the heathen girls back in Parkersburg, or like their mamas. He felt certain that when his intended came along he'd get a sign. And he did.

She was a college girl. But she wasn't like the rest. No siree. She ate a bag lunch outside the English building where he worked, even when it started getting cold. Folded her bag up and put it in her purse every day, threw her garbage in the cans. And her brown coat was like one his mama used to wear. It didn't have no waist. It just came straight down from the shoulders. That was the first thing he'd noticed. That and her blond hair, the same color as his favorite Sunday School teacher, Mrs. Emily Coggins. He knew she was the one before she even looked up. When she did look up she spoke to him, just as polite as you please. Not like those other snobbish too-good-to-give-him-the-time-of-day sluts. "Hello." With that smile of hers like one of God's own angels. The first few times, he just said "Hello," back. He didn't know what to say. He went home and prayed. Read Song of Solomon. All eight chapters. Over and over. "Behold, thou art fair, my love; behold, thou art fair."

"Spare the rod."

Clarence was dying for a cigarette—he chewed the whole time he was picking, to keep his hands free—but he hadn't missed a beat, and he was halfway there. He'd turned off 606 onto 29. Highway hotter'n fat frying in a pan, he thought. Hot enough to burn the top of his head, even if it was so late in the afternoon. The sun ought not be so hot this time of day, he thought. Need rain. Sweat poured off his forehead. His lips tasted salty. Made him even thirstier. I better never catch the son of a bitch who took my hat, he thought. Bet it's that scrawny kid who can hardly pick fruit for biting his nails. He's been over by me the last two days. Staring, like when he thinks I'm sleeping. Bet he's the one who lifted it while I was getting my shut-eye at lunch. He ain't been wearing a hat—all that long sissy hair. Who knows why he'd take it? Lot of the guys inside said they took things just for the fun of it. "Thou shalt not steal." Better not show up with it, that's all I've got to say. "Spare the rod. Spare the rod." He'd be there in less than a half hour. Then he could have a smoke. Two or three if he wanted, while he had a few cold ones in the bar.

He started talking to the girl after a while. She lived in the town there, in Morgantown, a townie. She was a committed Christian. Born again. Accepted the Lord when she was eleven. "Thou has dove's eyes within thy locks: thy hair is as a flock of goats." She didn't smoke or drink. She went to church regular. Read scripture daily. She was studying to be a teacher, to work with poor children back in the hills. Said she'd wanted to do that ever since she was a child herself. Ever since she'd learned that song, "Jesus loves the little children, all the children of the world; red and yellow, black and white, they are precious in his sight. Jesus loves the little children of the world." Her name was Louise. And Clarence fell in love with her. He loved her almost as much as his Savior. He started to dream about her in the dream. He prayed not to, but he did. But they only talked. For weeks. Until he followed her one evening.

"Spare the rod."

He'd stopped to get his paycheck, and he saw her coming out of the library. She was wearing her brown coat, holding her books tight against her chest, probably because it was cold. He wanted to ask her to eat supper with him at a restaurant. But he couldn't get up the nerve. So he just followed her, waiting to get up his courage. Only it turned out she was just like the others, he thought. Worse than the others. She was a slut, pretending to go about the Lord's work. He'd never forget what he'd seen with his own eyes. Made him throw up. Made his lunch come up in his throat just to think about it now.

Wonder if that nigger'll be in McGritz staring at me today. Staring at me with those black eyes of his, like two pissholes in the snow. I've a good mind to tell him to go on back to hell, even if he is a crip. Not fooling me. I knew as soon as I saw him he was the devil himself, the goddamn black devil himself. Didn't fool me none with his legs cut off just below his knees like that. First time I saw him, he made me all jumpy, even if he didn't say a word or look in my direction. Just sat there in that chair of his, drinking a beer, staring at the TV. Where's a cripple nigger like that get money for beer, I thought. Hard-working people paying for his beer, I'll bet. God-fearing people like my daddy. Then it come to me, he was probably a Vietnam vet. Probably got his legs blown off fighting the gooks. When I went in the big room to order my supper I asked Diane, "Who's the nigger in the bar? He leave his legs in Nam?" She laughed, like I was telling a damn joke. Laughed like a hen getting ready to lay an egg. When she got her breath back she said, "Craw-Dad? He ain't never been out of Nelson County, 'cept when he went to the hospital over in Charlottesville night he lost his legs. Craw-Dad in Vietnam? If that don't beat all." I could feel my face getting dark all over. What right did that slut have to laugh at me? That whoring slut, dressed in a dress two sizes too small for her, buttons popping on her stuck-out chest, skirt almost up to her twat. Hair bleached like a whore, a goddamn mother-fucking whore. Made up like some Jezebel, making every man in the place think sinful, lustful thoughts. Acted like a goody-goody that first night she waited on him. Asked what he wanted to eat, he said, "Don't matter. Four dollars' worth. Don't matter. It all turns to shit." Looked down at her pad, like she never heard the word before, like she don't go to the bathroom like the rest of us, like she was all embarrassed. She didn't fool me. What right did she have to laugh at me?

"Spare the rod. Spare the rod."

Clarence found out from Jack, the bartender, that Craw-Dad was a deaf mute. He was one of that litter of Shifletts, Jack said. Something wrong with most of them. None of them had good sense. Craw-Dad used to catch fish and craw-dads in Davis Creek, bring them to the cook at the restaurant, when he was no bigger than a milkcan. None of them Shifletts went to school. Didn't have enough sense. Nobody could remember his real name. Everybody just called him Craw-Dad. Night he lost his legs, he was drunk and fell asleep by the railroad tracks. Never even heard the train. Too drunk to feel it, I guess. Sliced off both his legs. Took him over to Charlottesvile. Tried to give him artificial legs; he was too dumb to learn how to use them. So they sent him back home in his chair. Collects a government check every month. Spends most of it on beer. Guess he eats what his mama cooks at home, though she must not be much of a cook, skinny as he is. How you reckon he does it? Reckon he just beats if off? Who'd want to do it with a dumb black nigger cripple, even if he does have government money.

Made Clarence think of those sisters inside. Goddamn perverts, do it with anything, including the guards. Sickos, doing unnatural acts. One-way ticket straight to hell, to everlasting perdition in hell.

Clarence remembered, once he got Jack going on the subject of Craw-Dad, he could hardly shut him up. He asked why the crip hadn't been there the first couple of nights of the picking season. Jack said he was probably sick. Got sick all the time. Didn't come in for weeks at a time. Used to pick, as a matter of fact, before he lost his legs and went on the dole. That night Clarence first saw him, he sat in his chair and looked at TV and acted half-dead, not paying any attention to anything but his beer and the television. Didn't even drink that much beer, just a mug or two.

Clarence was so hot, his mouth was so dry and salty, the thought of a beer almost made him stop and lick his lips. But he kept going. "Spare the rod, spare the rod." Left and right. He could just see the top of the sign over the next rise in the highway. He'd make it today, God willing and the creek don't rise, he thought.

Louise wasn't a bit better than Diane, he thought. Fact is, she was worse. He'd made a fool of himself. A complete and total fool. That evening, right at dusk, he'd followed her for about a mile, trying to get up his nerve to ask her to go eat supper with him. She just walked to those houses right off campus. He walked about a half block behind, up and down the hills, trying to get up his nerve. Praying. Praying for courage. Knowing in his heart she was sent to him from God. His beloved. He didn't pay a bit of attention to where they were going, just kept his eyes on her.

She came to one of the wood frame houses that butt right up to one another and went up some side steps. He heard her knock and go in. She must not live here, he thought. Else she wouldn't have knocked. He waited about ten minutes. I'll just stay here until she comes out again, he thought. She's probably just visiting a friend . But she didn't come out for ten more minutes, so he decided to sneak up the steps and peek in a window. I've never even seen her without her coat on, he thought. It had gotten dark enough so he didn't have to worry about anybody seeing him. People were always coming and going in Morgantown, anyway. College people. So he walked up the steps, slow and quiet, and sure enough there was a window right by the door. He could see curtains, but a light was shining through the middle, where they didn't meet. He stood real still for a minute, his heart beating fast. Then he peeked in. What he saw made him gag, made him gag and turn around and run down the steps as fast as he could go. He saw Louise, sitting on a sofa with her coat off, just kissing a man and running her hands all up and down his back. He was rubbing her, too. And he was black. Black as the night. Clarence barely got to the bottom of the steps before he threw up. Retched his guts. He kept on running, right out of town. Running as fast as he could.

"Spare the rod."

Clarence needed a drink bad. Thinking about Louise like that always made him sick to his stomach. Dizzy-headed. Made him wish he could've baptized her. Made him remember how tricky Satan is. Get thee behind me, Satan. That night he'd run until he couldn't run no more, then he started hitching to Parkersburg. Left all his stuff back in his room. Earthly possessions. He was going home where he belonged. It was cold that night, and he didn't get many rides. All he could think about was pounding that nigger's head. Made him remember the one and only time Daddy took him and Mama on a vacation. They went to Coney Island Beach. Drove all the way. Stayed in an efficiency just three blocks from the amusement park. He got burned all over, but he didn't care. Clarence couldn't have been more than five or six. He loved the sun and the waves and the colored lights at the park at night. He begged his daddy to take him on the rides, but he wouldn't. He'd walk him up there every night—Mama would lie down and rest—and play this one game called "Hit the Coon." This black clay head moving back and forth, his daddy throwing a ball as hard as he could trying to hit it. Clarence standing there, watching. He'd never forget that. That's what he wanted to do. Hit the coon. And hit Louise. Bash her head in, too. Send her to everlasting damnation, where she belonged. Long-tongued liar.

Hope that goddamn Craw-Dad's sick, Clarence thought as he kept his pace toward McGritz. I'm sick of looking at him. Sick of having him stare at me with those black eyes of his, those high and mighty eyes that say, "I dare you to mess with me, Mister Whitey Big Man." Don't he know I could take him out in under a minute, him scrawny like that, in a wheelchair. Don't he know I wouldn't even work up a sweat? All this civil rights shit gone to his uppity black head. Better watch himself, even if he is a crip. Get too smart with me, I'll take him out. Didn't I put plenty of them in their place on the inside. "Get thee behind me, Satan." He don't fool me. Not one bit.

"Spare the rod."

If he knew about that he wouldn't look at me, direct like that, like he's just waiting to mess in my shit. Plenty of them I put in their place. Messed up Pencil-Dick something awful. Put him in the infirmary over a week. But Slat-faced Sammy was the best. After him nobody messed in my shit, black or white. Shit, doing that Craw-Dad would be easier than doing a broad. He couldn't weigh as much as the last one, with half his legs gone and skinny as a straw. If he wasn't in a wheelchair, I'd a fixed him already, even if he is deaf and dumb. Don't nobody get away with staring at me like that. Don't matter if he's seen my face on a poster. He can't read. Too dumb to do anything about it. Still, he's got no right staring. Gives me the creeps.

Clarence headed up the last rise. He knew when he got to the top, the rest of the walk would be nothing, all downhill, right to the parking lot. Usually he didn't mind walking in the sun at all, but today, without his hat, he felt irritable. Hotter'n hell, he thought. Even smells hot, like when Mama was canning and had the kitchen all steamed. Looked like even them little blue flowers by the road needed a drink.

He'd hitched on back to Parkersburg. The prodigal. Only he'd been sending his mama money all the time, 'stead of wasting it. And he hadn't been sinning. He'd been going to church regular. Just those dreams. And Louise. Louise wasn't his fault. She was one of the devil's own disciples, sent to lead him astray. He wished he'd cleansed her from the earth: "And I heard another voice from heaven, saying, Come out of her, my people, that ye be not partakers of her sins, and that ye receive not of her plagues." He'd return to the fold. He'd help his daddy. He wouldn't stray again. That's what he figured.

Took him until morning to get there. Everything all quiet, nothing changed, just the way it was when he left.

Trash fire smoldering out by the barn. He could smell it. He went up to the door, walked right in the back door into the kitchen, like he'd only been gone overnight. Nobody in Parkersburg locked the back door. "I'm home," he'd called, thinking there'd be rejoicing and feasting and tears of great gladness.

His daddy came into the kitchen that morning in his longjohns. Like he was waiting. He stopped in the doorway and stared at Clarence like a stranger was in his midst. I'll never forget that look, he thought. I'll never forget the way he looked at me like he couldn't stand the sight of me. "Get out of here before you wake your mama," he said, real quiet-like. "Get on out of here now before you cause more trouble."

"Daddy, please forgive me," Clarence had said, exhausted, tears running down his stubbly cheeks. "You been getting the money, ain't you?"

"Your mama don't know nothing about that money. Sin money. You're no son of mine, you hear? The way you made that woman suffer. Took just about everything out of her when you run off. No sir, you're no son of mine." He moved over to the drawer where Mama kept the utensils, reached in and got out a butcher knife.

"Daddy, I ain't been sinning. Honest. I been working. Going to church." He'd taken a step toward his daddy and stopped when he saw the knife move up to belly-level.

Daddy just stared at him. "Spare the rod and spoil the child," he said. "God knows I tried to raise you right. But you were worthless. Wicked. Always were. Now get on out of here, before I have to hurt you. I won't have your mama suffer no more."

Clarence backed out the screen door and left, walking into the city. He'd gone to the Y, spent a few nights. Nobody there knew him. Called himself Denny. They took him for a drifter. He sneaked out to the home place every day, hid and watched them. Couldn't see any sign Daddy had told his mama. She just hung out clothes and swept the porches, like always. She did look skinnier, though, and it seemed like maybe her birthmark was darker than ever. He watched during the day and read The Revelation of St. John the Divine over and over at night. Memorized that one verse: "And he opened the bottomless pit; and there arose a smoke out of the pit, as the smoke of a great furnace; and the sun and the air were darkened by reason of the smoke of the pit." And he remembered from Sunday School: "Suffer the children to come unto me." Ain't we all God's children?, he thought.

Made him think of the fire. Of course he wasn't there, he didn't see it, but he could imagine the whole place in flames, like a trash fire, like a damn stinking trash fire. Wonder what they felt like, burning up like that. "Ashes to ashes." Pastor Winn said they'd just slept away. Said the smoke got them in their sleep, they never felt no pain. But how in hell did he know? You'd think God called him up on the damn telephone and told him. Wasn't a thing left but a few of Daddy's tools, and them all melted and bent to useless. Not a damn thing to show they'd even existed, except for me and all the carpentry work at the church. Didn't even own the house and land. Lived there for forty-some years, renting the whole time. "Do not lay up for yourselves treasures on earth," his daddy would say. "In my father's house are many mansions." Guess he's in one now.

"Spare the rod." Soon as he got to the door he could stop. He'd a done it. For the first time in days. He'd smoke a whole damn pack of Marlboros. And drink as many beers as he wanted. Who cared if that tramp Diane looked at him like he was something crawling on the earth. Her day would come. Damn soon, too. Wonder that scrawny kid didn't pass right out in the heat today. Looks like one of them nervous Nellies, one of them sweet britches, whimper if you look at them hard; ready enough to turn up their butts, though. He'd seen enough of that kind on the inside. Kid minded his own business, though. Kept right on in the heat, that disgusting ponytail wet as a nasty washrag. I'll give him that. He didn't quit, even if he did stop every few minutes, when he didn't think anybody was looking, and chew on those nasty nails of his. Chewed 'em down to the quick. Thought this heat would get to him, but he stuck it out. I'll give him that. Wonder if he's one of them draft dodgers. Wouldn't be a bit surprised.

Wonder if the crip'll be there today. Probably. Better not stare at me. I've a good mind to tip over that chair of his. Now that'd be a sight. He'd be scrambling around on the floor like a crab. See them craw-dads backin back. That'd be some sight. About makes me laugh thinking about it. I could say, "Reach on up and touch the television, crip. Touch the television and be healed." Watch him sprout legs and feet right there on the floor of the bar. Glory glory. That Diane'd look at me in a different way. Or two hooves. Maybe he'd grow hooves. That's a thought. Trying to tempt me, out here in this godforsaken wilderness. Peaches, though. Peaches instead of apples. Still, that old devil's a tricky fool. Could be a sign, a sign from God that it's time. Time for one of his own miracles here on earth. Time for another Holy Ghost. Can't no woman be a Father or a Son, no siree. But a Holy Ghost, now that's another think altogether. Thine is the power. Don't I know it. Amen.

"Spare the rod."

Inside I was known, I had respect, I was the man. Nobody'd think about staring at me like that nigger Craw-dad. Not unless he wanted a roughing-up. Some of those sickies got off on that. That's how they got their cookies. I didn't have to do it, though. Had my own trustees. Just like the boss-man. Never let any of those sweet boys next to me. Sin and perversion. Didn't Daddy warn me about sin and perversion and the everlasting flames time without number. I keep myself pure. Pure for the baptism. Pure so I can go home whenever I'm called, whenever he wants me, his only begotten son. Glory glory.

Clarence remembered the first time he'd made a Holy Ghost. She'd asked for it, too. Just like this Diane-bitch. He'd hardly been out of the slammer any time before his heavenly Father sent him about his business. Her dancing like that right in front of a crowd, a regular Salome, a damned mongrel bitch in heat. Hardly enough clothes to cover her privates. Skirt up to her ass. Mini-skirt, somebody said. Tight, too, like the skin on a sausage. And tits. Tits that wouldn't stop, stuffed into some black halter that showed half of them to anybody with eyes. She didn't mind poking them in her partner's face one bit. Just grinning the whole time, looking like she'd do it right there on the floor. I got a sign that time. That's how I knew it was time.

"Spare the rod."

That pathetic band was trying to sing that song about the whorehouse, the one about the house in New Orleans. And it came to me: she was sin incarnate. I saw that pock-faced scrawny singer closing his eyes, like he was praying, wailing out stuff about the ruin of many a poor boy, and God, I know I'm one. That's when it came to me. Just like it says in Ezekiel: "And they shall burn your houses and execute judgments upon you; I will make you stop playing the harlot, and you shall also give hire no more . . . So will I satisfy my fury on you." Thy will be done.

Nothing to it, waiting out in the parking lot for her to come out hanging all over that partner of hers. He'd already sinned, just dancing with her like that. Him and every other dick in there, just staring at her thinking about it. Wasn't nothing to hit him from behind, drunk as he was, and drag her on off to the Mustang. What ever happened to that Mustang? I liked that car. I really did. Couldn't have her hollerin like that, loud enough to raise the dead. Had to knock her out.

She looked real peaceful laying there. Came to me like a sign. She needed to be baptized, purified, and sent to heaven a Holy Ghost, pure as the day she was born. "Go and sin no more." Baptized with the blood and the water. People forget the blood part. Signed her with the sign of the cross. After. What was one more sin? Thinkin about it like that, all that time watchin her dance, might as well do it. Father forgive me for I have sinned. Then slit her throat just as easy as cuttin open a sweet potato, nothin to it. Lamb of

God. Signed her with the sign of the cross. Spit of the only begotten son, blood of her body, holy, holy, holy. Sent her to the father, a Holy Ghost. Praise the Lord. The Lord works in wondrous ways.

"Spare the rod."

He passed the Dairy De-Lite. Usually this time of day the parking lot was crawling with kids. Didn't even see a car today. Too hot. Kids were swimming in the river, or staying inside. Just another half mile or so and he'd be there. Couldn't hardly wait for the air conditioning. This heat would satisfy a snake on a rock. Idiots never got him for that. Never even so much as stopped him to ask him any questions. Probably didn't even find her until I was long gone, he thought. Daddy was right about Pittsburgh. That place is a regular Sodom and Gomorrah. Crawling with sinners, sluts like that one. Jerk she was with was probably too stupid to remember his own name, too drunk to know where he was. Don't matter. Law never came after him for that one. Or the other one, either. Just goes to show you. Nobody thinks twice about hussies. But a trooper. That's another story.

Wasn't no time at all after the fire, them niggers acting up in town. Not more'n a week after the double funeral for his mama and daddy. Pushing and shoving their way at the drugstore where they no more belonged than a bastard at a family reunion. They knew it, too. They weren't bad niggers. Just that NAACP come in town stirring them up. Bringing them smart-ass city niggers talking crazy, getting people all agitated. I didn't think twice about knocking them around. Putting them in their place. Didn't mean no harm. Just gotta show what's what. I was just in there buying cigarettes, minding my own business. Just made me mad. If the Lord wanted blacks and whites together he'd a made 'em that way. Plain as the nose on your face. Lord don't make mistakes. No sir. It's people that sins. Just got to me, seeing them sit there like that. Arrogant as you please and all. I wouldn't a hurt one of them bad. I knew most of them niggers. Known them all my life. Sheriff had no business sending in them state troopers. Wouldn't a been a thing to it if he'd let well enough alone. Them troopers coming in there with dogs and clubs and guns, things got way out of hand. Wouldn't nobody gotten locked up, just a few niggers pushed around, if them goddamn state troopers hadn't showed up. Getting up in my face pushing. I was just trying to get some room to breathe, that's all. I didn't even hit that trooper. Just pushed him out of my face. How'd I know he'd fall against the counter like that? Splat his head open? Wasn't my fault. Damn judge don't listen where police are concerned. One in a fucking million chances that trooper would get hurt. Much less die. No sir, judge gotta have an eye for an eye where a damn trooper is concerned.

Didn't bother me. Didn't bother me none. Had to learn to bide my time. Too hot-headed when I was young. And the damn brothers inside knew where I stood, that's for damn sure. Never gave me no trouble. Shit. Half the time they called one another nigger. Kept to themselves. None of this mixing of the races like mongrel dogs. Long as they knew where I stood I didn't have no trouble inside. Even one of my trustees was black as the ace of spades.

"Spare the rod."

Didn't have to have the sense God gave a goat to break out of that tin can, he thought. Bide my time, watch and see, learn the ropes, act like Mr. Kiss-ass Model Prisoner in front of the dumb-ass guards. I knew the Lord wanted me about His work. Knew when the time came I could walk out of there, like our Savior walked out of the wilderness. Took him forty days. Took me fourteen years. Wasn't I the son of my Heavenly Father? Hadn't Daddy said so, said I was his? Yes siree. No hurry. Knew when the time came I'd be outa there. Like Jesus and his days in the wilderness. No trouble at all setting up that kick-back with the kitchen suppliers. Easier than messing in mud. Day came I just rode out in their truck. Right out the back gate. Right by the guards' stupid noses. Walked away. Been walking ever since.

Clarence smiled as he walked up to the door of the restaurant, McGritz Family Restaurant and Lounge. No way they'll ever put me back in a fuckin cage. No way. The Lord's will be done, he thought, as he turned the knob to the wooden door. "Spare the rod." He'd said it all the way. Today was a day the Lord hath made, even if it was hotter'n holy hell. Couldn't wait to get out of this heat. Have a beer. Didn't Almighty Jesus change the water to wine? Nothing wrong with a few beers, long as he kept his body a temple to serve the Lord. And a smoke. He sure as hell was dying for a smoke. He'd sit. Relax. Make his plans for Diane. No need to rush. Had to wait for a sign. Still, he couldn't hardly wait to baptize her.

Davis Creek
4:00 p.m.

"Was that the clock striking four, Ora?"

"Believe so."

"Sit down a minute and quit that sweeping out here. There's no sense stirring up dust. Makes me feel right gritty all over. And don't go on any more with that foolishness about me moving into town, Ora, you hear. You might as well cut out all that talk about a home. I've got a home, so that's that. I'd just as soon die as sit around in a hospital with a bunch of old busybodies, poking their noses into my business. I don't want to hear another word about it."

"All's I'm saying, Miss Charlotte, is I don't know how much longer I can come up the hill here every day. What would you do if I couldn't come? How would you eat? Tell me that. You who's never touched a frying pan in all your born days. And not another living soul except James Earl even knows you still exist, and him without the sense God gave a pissant. What if I just up and died in my sleep one night, if my heart just wore out?"

117

"No need to put on the holy martyr act with me, Ora. A promise is a promise. Besides, you know good and well you and James Earl are remembered in my will. Didn't I tell you you'd get this gold-piece necklace? Isn't it my prized possession from Daddy? I'll never forget the day he put it around my neck and called me his treasure. So there's not a bit of need in this world for you to carry on so. You'll get what's coming to you soon enough."

"May the good Lord look out for you, Miss Charlotte. Your daddy never gave you that necklace."

"Not another word, Ora. I won't hear it."

"Turn your mama and your daddy both in their graves to hear you talk such nonsense. Time you left here, that's what I have to say. Past time."

"I can't leave this place. I've no intention. Daddy wouldn't hear of it. Nobody would tend to the family plot if I left here. Besides, doesn't James Earl like having some money of his own? Keep that in mind. And you're still strong as an ox. Even if you do act pitiful. Always have been."

"That's not the point, Miss Charlotte. You're just trying to make me get off the mark. When cold weather gets here I don't know if I can keep climbing this hill day in day out. My arthritis pains me an awful lot. Seems like more and more every day. It's nothin for James Earl to haul up the kerosene and chop the wood and climb up on the roof every now and again when it needs fixing. Nothin for him to turn up that little bit of garden in the spring and pick the apples and peaches in the yard either. He'd just as soon be doin that as sittin in front of the television all day. It's these old bones of mine that can't take this everlastin trudgin any more. Before I know it Sunday's come and gone and I have to start all over again."

"You ever pray for me at those holy-roller meetings you go to, Ora?"

"Ain't right, Miss Charlotte. Ain't right the way you mock the Lord. You oughta be ashamed."

"Well do you?"

"Course I prays for you. Every day. In meeting, too."

"What do you pray?"

"That you'll get some sense in your hard head. I ask the Lord Almighty to bring you down off this mountain. Put you in a home. Ask him to help me bring you to the light."

"I've told you not to be spreading my business around, Ora. If anybody comes up here after my money I'll have you to thank."

"That's not true and you know it. I never calls you by name. Never talks about you 'cept as my white lady. I knows my place. Always has."

"Ora, you're always singing to Jesus out there in the kitchen, asking him to help you tote your earthly burden. Why in this world are you trying to make up excuses to ease out of your sworn promise to my daddy? I have no intention of moving into town, and that's final. If you choose not to come it'll be on your conscience. I don't want to hear any more on the subject, you hear?"

"I hear all right, but that don't mean the day won't come when I can't do a thing about it. Ain't a person in the world would've taken care of you the way I have, promise or no promise, Miss Charlotte, and don't I know it like I know my own name? I'll never forget the night you like to died, when your appendix just about ruptured and you out of your head with fever and pain. It's a wonder we didn't both go to our reward that night."

"I wish I'd been in my right mind when you drove the car into town, Ora. That's one sight I cannot begin to imagine."

"I tell you, those fifteen miles might just as well have been five hundred. And me not even knowing how to back the thing out of the drive, much less go forward. If it hadn't been for the Dear Lord, you can bet we'd both have been called home that night. I'll never understand how we made it. Don't tell me the Lord don't work in mysterious ways. Don't I know better?"

"That car was Daddy's pride, it surely was. Imagine it running after sitting all that time. And the keys still hanging in the kitchen where Henry Trice left them. I swore after spending those three weeks in that hospital I'd never set foot in one of those places again. That damned fool Dr. James like to killed me, remember? After he cut me open and took the appendix out, he had to cut me open again two days later and clean up his mess. I was hot as a coal fire and all swelled up like a blow-toad. He said it was 'cause I like to ruptured, but I know good and well it was 'cause he was no-account, half-drunk all the time. Daddy had no respect for him at all. I like to died 'cause he barely had the sense God gave a goat. Of course James Earl was a sight to behold driving me home in that car. Sitting up tall with his elbow propped up on the window, looking for all the world like a swell. That's the last time I remember him with good sense, before he had his accident. Well, what will be will be. I didn't have any choice but to sell that car, but I sure was sorry to see it go."

"Well if you got sick now, Miss Charlotte, how you reckon we'd get you to town? James Earl half-witted, can't talk right, me all crippled up with the arthritis half the time, and not another living soul in this county even knows you're alive? I just wish you'd think of that. Not a cent of that money you've got hidden all around this place would do you a bit of good if you got sick and I wasn't around to help."

"You've no business talking about my money, no business at all."

"Now don't go pretending like I haven't tried to reason with you, Miss Charlotte. That's all I'm saying. Don't say I haven't warned you. See now, I've got everything laid out for your supper, and I'm going to leave early so I can get ready for the meeting tonight. You shouldn't need a thing. I've put the back windows down 'cause it smells like rain, but if you get too hot you ought to be able to raise them in your room about halfway, and you'll catch a breeze. Phew, I swan, fanning with this apron don't do a thing but stir up the hot air."

"You cleaned out my chamber pot, didn't you?"

"Don't you always ask me if I did and don't I always tell you I did? Both of them, the one downstairs and the one up under your bed. You're about the only person I know who don't use an indoor bathroom. It's a shame you had the electricity turned off. I still can't understand why you stopped paying the electric bill. Doing without lights don't bother me a bit, but it sure is nice to have running water and a toilet. Yes ma'am."

"No point in throwing good money away when a privy does just as well. Daddy wouldn't want me to be wasteful. He was a thrifty man, that's for sure. It was one thing when he was practicing law and running the farms, but when all it's doing is going out and there's no money coming in, I can't be too careful. No sir. I ought to figure how much I've saved the last fifteen years or so by doing without electricity and the water pump. Maybe I'll do that tonight. I just don't like to go out back in the dark, you know. Too many people sneaking around here after dark. Don't shake your head at me like that, you know good and well who I mean."

"Miss Charlotte, there's not a bit of truth in that, no ma'am, not a word of truth. Now if you'd come on into town and live in the home, you could have company at night, and TV, and a proper bathroom, and you wouldn't get so jumpy after dark."

"My gracious, I only saw television that one time, when I was in the hospital, and if that wasn't the biggest bunch of foolishness I've ever laid eyes on. I'd rather sit and look over Daddy's old books and snapshots any day. . . I swear, I don't remember seeing so many birds this early in the afternoon. . . Look over there. In the willow. They're all over the trees. Hear those sparrows just too-weeing to one another? And the starlings? There's nothing uglier than a starling. What you reckon that clatter is all about?"

"James Earl was something wild this morning, grabbing onto me. I'd guess we're in for an electrical storm to fare thee well. I'd best get going, 'fore I get caught in it and drenched to the skin. Anything else you need before I go?"

"Did you leave me some fresh water? Seems like I can't get enough to drink in this heat."

"In the pitcher in there on the kitchen counter. And I filled the pitcher up by your bed, too."

"Look there in the front hall, Ora. Don't you have a umbrella you left a while back? Look in the drawer there by the stairs. I think you left some of those fold-up rain hats in those little plastic cases. Remember, you got about five of them when the big IGA opened a few years back."

"Thank you, Miss Charlotte. I'll see you in the morning. You be sure and eat something, now, you hear? Corn bread and cobbler are underneath the napkin on the table. There's a bit of ham left in the ice box, but you better eat it tonight. The ice is all gone. James Earl will have to bring a block up tomorrow or the next day."

"Ora, you could sleep over. Like you used to before your mama died. You and James Earl could come on up here to stay. He could have that back storeroom off the kitchen porch. I don't think that would be improper. He'd be like a handy man. And you could have your old room. Then you wouldn't have to worry about the walking."

"You know I can't do that, Miss Charlotte. I need to be around my people, even if you don't. Good night now. I'll be sure and include you in my prayers."

"I don't want Henry Trice bothering me tonight, Ora. He just won't get off the place."

"Now, Miss Charlotte. He's not gonna bother you and you know it. Mr. Henry was never anything but a perfect gentlemen, so you don't have to worry one second about him. He's probably been long in his grave. Let him be, you hear?"

"I don't care what you say, Ora. I know he's out there, and he's after more than my money, you can bet on that."

"That man never did you a minute's harm, Miss Charlotte. He was 'bout the most politest white man I've ever known. I don't know where you get these fool-headed notions about him, but there's not a word of truth in them. Ain't nobody around here seen him since you sold the place and fired the men. No sir, nobody's laid eyes on him since that night. So there's no sense frettin yourself about a bunch of foolishness. Why don't you let me take that necklace on up now, Miss Charlotte, 'fore you forget about it and sleep with it on. That chain's mighty delicate, you know. More than seventy years old now, way I reckon it. You'd have a fit if you broke it. "

"You know as well as I do the chain's not that old, Ora. Daddy gave it to me on my eighteenth birthday. So it's just a little over fifty years old. Why in the world you say such stupid things I will never understand, unless it's to provoke me. Don't worry about it, I'll take it off myself when I get good and ready."

"Miss Charlotte, I don't like the way you twist things. Lying is the devil's own trick, sure as the world. Your daddy gave that necklace to Miz Alice for their first wedding anniversary, Cinchy told me, and after she died he always kept it on his dresser. You've got no call to make up such things about it, no call at all."

"I want you to be here on time tomorrow, Ora. I start the day on the wrong foot when my breakfast isn't on time, you know that. You're sure the clock's all right now?"

"Sure as I can be, Miss Charlotte. Ain't you heard it strike yourself all day long? I'll just get my things out in the kitchen and be going on now."

"Wait a minute, Ora. Let me go in and get some money for you. Buy James Earl some ice cream tonight, you hear? And bring me a little something sweet when you come tomorrow. A Hershey Bar or Almond Joy. Just wait one minute while I find some change. . . And bring another one of those magazines with the good stories in them. You know the ones I like, the ones with those true-life stories."

"Don't I know? That all, Miss Charlotte?"

"Be on time tomorrow, you hear?"

"Are you going to Scarborough Fair—parsley sage rosemary and thyme," Judy Marsh sang to the empty back stoop as she propped the screen open with her rear, hoisted the last bag of garbage up with both arms, and headed for the cans in the alley back of the duplex. "Remember me to the one who lives there—He once was a true love of mine," she continued in full voice as she walked down the brick path to the fence. She smiled, imagining Drew in the Dustin Hoffman role, dragging her, laughing uncontrollably, to the back of some bus. That's exactly how Drew made her feel: happy, set free from convention, like there was nobody in the entire world except the two of them, like they didn't have a single solitary person to answer to except one another. If she squinted she could imagine herself as the Ben-guy's girl friend—what was her name? Eleanor? Elaine?—looking out the rear window of the bus, hair flowing about her face. She could hardly wait to get in the car and take off. This was it. All she had to do was give Sophie her pill, shower and change, put the last few things in the trunk, and drive to Lexington. She'd be with Drew in a matter of hours. She dropped the bag in the trash can, saying "Da-Dah," banged the lid on, and turned back toward the house just in time to see an orange streak head into the Nandina bushes at the side of the yard.

"Sophie? Here, girl. Come on." She crouched down and walked slowly toward the bushes, not daring to act upset. The cat freaked at her own shadow. Damn. She could kick herself. Leave it to Sophie to find a way to wriggle out of the crack in the closet door. "Here, kitty kitty." Madame Queen could put on a pout that would last for hours if she sensed Judy was about to do something drastic that she would consider beneath her feline dignity. And Judy definitely was intending a drastic maneuver: drug her, take her in the car, drive to Drew's where aged, finicky

Sophie would be forced to share space with two frisky female kitties. Judy got down on her hands and knees, peered under the dark bushes, feeling the cool mulch in the flower border. "Sophie? Want a treat? I've got a treat for you." The dank earth smelled like chrysanthemums after they've sat in water a day too long.

Judy stood up, brushed off her knees. "Damn." Guess I'll finish loading the car, she thought. Take my shower. Change. Stay busy. She's bound to be back by then. What's the good of pouting if no one's around to watch? Judy was walking up the two steps of the back porch when Mrs. Calabash opened her matching door and came out on her twin stoop, shoulders drooping. Looking every inch the helpless widow.

"Well, now, Judy. I thought I heard your screen door bang. Why don't you come over for a glass of iced tea? I cut some mint from the yard this afternoon. It'll cool you off in this heat. All that packing." She peered at Judy over her bifocals with her lips stretched out in a fake, nervous-looking smile. Judy knew iced tea and heat weren't the point. "Haven't taken off yet?" She stood, both arms crossed over her bib apron, strands of her grey hair trickling out of her bun. Judy, in her cut-off jeans and tank top, long brown hair in a ponytail, looked cool despite the record-breaking heat. She couldn't help smiling. Here she stood; it was pretty obvious she hadn't left.

"Thanks, Mrs. Calabash. Sounds great. But I'm trying to get away before it gets dark. You know how I hate driving in the dark." Judy opened her own screen, but Mrs. C. didn't budge. She felt a little embarrassed leaving her neighbor out there, since she was so clearly anxious for company. Judy was just as anxious to get going, though. "Listen, Sophie just ran off. Her nose is pushed out of joint because of all the commotion, people in and out this week-end at the yard sale. She still hasn't gotten over Mother dying, you know, and leaving her behind with me. And now this. Anyway, if you see her would you open my screen and holler in? I'm going to take a shower. Okay?"

"Sure, Judy." The older woman opened her screen, too, looking at Judy as if she were wearing pasties and a G-string. "You wearing that?"

Busybody. No. I'm wearing feathers. "I kept out a dress."

"Oh. Good. Well. Need any help?"

"Thanks. I've only got a few little things to throw in the car now. Otherwise, the place is spic and span." Judy was a better housekeeper than Mrs. C. anyway. She wasn't worried about that. She was only fretted about catching the cat and getting on the road. The sooner the better. She waved and walked inside, leaving Mrs. Calabash standing in her doorway.

The kitchen was no cooler than the yard. The little brown envelope with Sophie's pill was conspicuous on the otherwise bare, clean counter. Judy had intended to give it to the cat as soon as she'd thrown out the garbage, and now the beast had taken off. She couldn't leave without her. No way. Her mother had gotten Sophie as a little fur ball of a kitten, had her for ten years, every day of which she'd treated her like the Queen of Sheba, and Judy had inherited her two months earlier. Other than Judy, Sophie was the last of the family. Of course, she could leave without the cat; she could ask Mrs. Calabash to look out for her and call when she showed up. Mrs. C. would like nothing better. But Judy was determined her landlady wasn't going to know where she was going, what her plans were. Call it silly, she wanted this move to be a clean break, an infinitely fresh start. With a little luck, still, if she could round up Sophie, in a few hours the cat would be sniffing around, getting used to her new territory. And Judy would be with Drew.

She looked into the living room at the small pile next to the front door. Guess I might as well finish putting the rest of the things in the car, she thought, as she picked up the owl and lugged it out the front door. Mr. Huffman had picked it up like it was a lunch bag the night he gave it to her; she counted the steps to her Chevy parked at the end of

the walk, "Eleven, twelve, thirteen, fourteen, down you go."
She sat the owl on the back seat, shook out her arms and
hands, and walked back to the living room. No sense standing around twiddling my thumbs, she thought. That won't
get the cat back any faster. Walking up to the small stack of
things by the front door she bent over and snapped on the
transistor radio. Lines of that Kris Kristofferson song she
liked so much filled the empty room: "Nothing short of
dying, half as lonesome as the sound, of the sleeping city
sidewalks, Sunday morning coming down." No more lonesome Sunday mornings for her. She picked up the portable
sewing machine, walked back out the front door again to
her car. She pulled the trunk key from her pocket—she'd
already made about six trips with her clothes on hangers,
stacking them on the back seat, so the owl was pretty much
the last thing she could get inside—and used her right hand
to open the trunk. Just a few suitcases in there, a folder of
legal papers, and the emergency first-aid kit Drew gave her
when she started driving back and forth to Lexington.
Plenty of room for her sewing machine and the small card-
board box still in the house. She walked back and picked it
up. "Fragile" written neatly on the front, in school teacher
printing. Hers. Only those four juice glasses inside. The
matched set she'd kept when she cleaned out the family's
house this summer. Her hands had started shaking when
she found them in her mother's kitchen cabinet; she'd for-
gotten about them. Her parents had plenty of things worth
more money, and she didn't have any trouble selling or giving away the lifetime of stuff they'd stockpiled. But she
hadn't been able to part with these glasses. She walked out,
put the box in the trunk beside her sewing machine, shut the
trunk, and went back into the empty living room.

"The best laid plans of mice and men . . .," she sighed
as she sat down on her pillow to rest a minute before taking
her shower. This heat was exhausting. News blasted from
the radio; something about troop movements in Vietnam.
She only half listened, saturated with death and protest and
politics. She leaned back against the white walls, thinking

of her life in this apartment. Her cocoon. When the weatherman started speaking, she listened: a storm front, left over from Hurricane Camille, heading toward western Virginia, vicinity of the Blue Ridge mountains. "Thanks a lot, Sophie." She dreaded driving in the rain in the dark, but she wasn't about to let a little bad weather keep her away another night. Nope, no way. She'd wasted enough time already, especially the two weeks it took her to make up her mind.

She stood, stretched and walked toward the bathroom. She'd get her shower, fix her face and hair, by then Sophie was bound to be back. Walking from empty room to empty room, Judy thought about her four years in the apartment. Now it was as if she'd never lived there at all. No whispers or echoes, just the slap, slap, slap of her red sling-back sandals on the waxed wood floors. Just white walls and doors and clean, clear windows. Funny how it looked like anybody could've lived there. But it had been hers; she'd been free here; alone and free for the first time in her life. She'd had so much fun going to yard sales and thrift shops, picking the furnishings. And she'd had just as much fun this weekend selling those same things to people who wanted them. That one couple couldn't believe she was willing to sell the maple kitchen set for twenty-five dollars. But she wanted them to have it. They looked so pleased counting out their money together. Funny she didn't feel attached to the place itself. Really, it had been like a holding pen, holding her as she got to know herself and what she wanted in life, holding her for right now, this decision, this move. It was perfect for her when she needed it, but that was all behind her now. It wasn't a place or things she needed anymore. She could travel light.

Walking into the bathroom, she picked up her brush from the vanity, pulled out the hairholder and started brushing her dark brown hair. She'd put it up that morning because of the heat. It had been years since she'd worn it in a ponytail. Funny how it made her look so much younger, more like a teenager than a thirty-seven-year-old school teacher. Just that one little thing. She brushed the long thick waves of hair, thinking she looked more like the young gal in The Graduate with it down. Only hers wasn't stick straight like Ali McGraw's. Wait a sec, wasn't the daughter/bride Katharine Ross? Wondering, thinking Drew would remember, Judy noticed her stomach churning, making noises like a garbage disposal. She should've eaten, but she hadn't wanted to take the time. Not after she'd cleaned the fridge. She would've had to go out. Stepping out of her cut-offs, pulling her T-shirt over her head, she looked in the mirror. Not bad for her age. Good firm boobs. Flat tummy. All this running around the past couple of weeks had helped her lose a few pounds, too. Five-five, a hundred forty-some pounds, she wasn't fat, but she was a little chunky. She'd fought being plumpish all her life, but in the last few years, without Allen around to "pinch an inch" and taunt her, she'd stopped worrying about it. Especially since she'd started going out with Drew. Not bad at all.

She turned on the hot water, let it run, put her hands under the spigot. Her older sister Meredith had been the beauty. The one with the to-die-for body, the killer blond hair, and the dimple in the right place, on her chin. Like Daddy's. Judy's was on her right cheek. Natch. It was funny how things worked out. All those years she'd been jealous as hell of her older sister; now things like who had a dimple where seemed ridiculous. She wished Merry were around, wished she could get to know her, and they could go out to lunch together and talk. Trade love stories. She turned on the cold, pulled the shower adjustment on and let the water spray while she took off her bra and underpants. Stepping into the tub, she let the water run over her, cool her, let it ease the stress in her muscles.

Her daddy had always said she needed somebody to light a fire under her tail to get her going; wouldn't he have been stunned to see her in action this past week? No wonder her muscles were all tensed up. She'd run around like a poodle in heat. Now she had no choice but to wait for Sophie. The warm water soothed her worries about time, about driving in the mountains.

Funny how it was Drew who'd lit the fire, Drew who was so gentle, who never seemed to be in a hurry for any reason. He never even complained about how long it took her to get ready to go out. That time he'd washed her hair.

"Can I come in?"

"Sure." Soaking in the bathtub at his apartment, Judy felt somewhat self-conscious about Drew seeing her. It wasn't the same as when they were making love. She felt more exposed. He'd sat down on the edge of the tub, trim in his undershorts. She liked that he was short and slender. His clear blue eyes behind his glasses smiled at her.

"How's about I wash your hair for you. Would you like that?"

"Okay." She'd turned her back to him, her neck somewhat stiff.

"Hey, loosen up. Okay?" He'd rubbed the shampoo in and used his long fingers to rub the suds into her scalp. Circling round and round. Eventually, she'd laid her head back against his thigh, completely relaxed. "You have the prettiest hair. And I love the way it smells." She'd almost fallen asleep as he massaged her, rubbed his lathery hands over her shoulders and head.

"Here, lean back against my arm." And he'd rinsed her hair by pouring warm water over it from a coffee can. Cans and cans full of warm water.

When they spent the weekend together, they stayed at Drew's, away from Mrs. C's telescope eyes. His apartment was a haven, an eyrie. On the second floor of one of those old Lexington clapboard houses, it was cluttered with plants, instruments, books, music stands, album covers. It always looked as if someone left the room a moment before and was bound to be back any second. Music echoed, either from his flute, guitar, piano, or stereo. The tall windows let in streams of sunlight in the daytime, the stars and moon at night. She couldn't see the stars clearly like that from her windows in Richmond. She could burrow in there, feel safe, welcome, at ease. She was dying to be there.

Stepping from the tub, she reached for one of the large

bath towels she'd kept out, knowing she'd need this shower after she cleaned the apartment, before she got in the car. She sat on the edge of the tub and squeezed her hair with the towel, wishing Drew were doing it for her. She'd sold or given away almost everything. Like her memories, she didn't need most of the things from her past. Drew had dishes, furniture, most of the same records she had; he'd lived alone his entire adult life, and he was only months away from forty. His things would be her things. She didn't need the things in this apartment anymore.

Using the towel to squeeze water from her hair, she sang, "Bali Hai will call you, any night, any day; Here am I, your special island, come away, come away." She loved that song. She'd gone to see "South Pacific" with Drew, the second run at Loew's. He couldn't believe she'd never seen it before. He'd held her hand for the first time when the native woman was singing "Bali Hai." She understood that kind of longing now, knew she wanted to get to Drew's that night. As soon as she could. She wished she could beam herself there, avoid this one last drive altogether. At least it was only one-way this trip.

Standing, Judy kicked the dirty clothes and towels into a pile. Her red sundress was hanging on the back of the door, Drew's favorite. The one she wore the night he asked her to marry him. The one she was going to put on to surprise him. She started brushing out her damp hair. She never used a blow drier or hot rollers. She liked her hair natural, fluffy. She stood still and listened a moment, but she couldn't hear the cat meowing at the back door. Old Sophie would definitely be mad at Judy when she came back. Rattling around in her cosmetics case, Judy found deodorant, Shalimar, toothpaste and her toothbrush. She could barely hear the radio, hear the Roger Miller song they were playing over and over these days. She knew it by heart, though: "Freedom's just another word for nothing left to lose." These past few weeks those lines kept playing in her head while she was deciding whether to marry Drew or not. If she chose freedom it was true, she wouldn't have anything to lose. Same old same old. But she wouldn't have Drew. And if she chose Drew? That had been the question that had hung her up, made her wonder if she'd be able to marry again. The modern woman's "I love him, I love him not," she thought.

Damn, Sophie. Judy put the finishing touches on her make-up. She didn't wear much, just enough to make her brown eyes and clear skin and dimple stand out. "Accentuate the positive," her mother used to say at least twenty times a day. Staring at herself in the mirror, Judy could see she was good looking; not great looking, but good looking enough. Still, she was reticent and shy when she first met someone; she took her time getting close to people. She didn't have one of those bubbly ultra-confident personalities that lure people, guys and girls, make them call you up and ask if you want to do something on the spur of the moment. Merry had the personality; guys called and came by honking their horns for her all hours of day or night. Judy could imagine one of her high school classmates pointing to her own picture in the yearbook years later and saying, "I don't remember her. I'd swear I've never seen her before in my life." She pretty much stayed to herself in high school and college. She rubbed her lips together, liking the feel of the lip gloss sliding over them. What difference did any of that make today? Drew liked her just the way she was. And she liked herself.

Turning from the mirror, she reached down for the bundle of damp clothes. Everything was soggy. She tied the dirty clothes up in one of the towels, snapped her cosmetics case shut, and went through the living room and out the front door to stash them in the floor of the back seat of her car. That was it. Everything was packed and ready. She was just three hours away—three and a half at most if she stopped for food—from Drew. She looked all around, up and down the sidewalk, but she didn't see any sign of Sophie. She called without much enthusiasm, "Here, Sophie. Here, kitty. Come on back. Please." The cat rarely went out front anyway. Car noises scared her to death.

Crazy neurotic cat still wasn't used to the switch from Roanoke to Richmond. Not likely she'd be out front.

Going back into the living room, Judy could hear the Stones blasting from the radio. She sang along, "Baby, the last time, I don't kno-ow." In just that few minutes she was hot again. Her hair was bound to frizz. She didn't like it *too* fluffy; made her look like a cross between Janis Joplin and Abbie Hoffman. She looked at her watch; it was a little after six, and still as hot as it had been at noon. Not a breath of breeze. She walked to the back door, called, "Here, Sophie. Come on, girl. Come get some water. You're bound to be thirsty," willing Sophie to come back.

Maybe she should call Drew. He didn't know when she was coming, didn't even know for sure that she *was* coming, so he wouldn't be checking his watch and worrying. He'd be practicing the flute or playing guitar, maybe sitting at the desk under the window getting ready for his fall classes, or maybe just drinking iced tea and listening to records. Still, if she could just hear his voice, hear him say, "I'll be here waiting for you." But her phone was disconnected, and she would have to go next door, and Mrs. Calabash—who would've been tickled pink—would've made herself conveniently busy within hearing distance, humming to herself while moving the knickknacks around on the mahogany shelf near the phone. She kept a dustcloth in her apron pocket; Judy was certain it was a prop for just such opportunities. So she decided not to call. She thought of her mother's favorite saying: "Make the best of a bad situation." Considering her wretched life, it's no wonder that was her philosophy, Judy thought as she stared out the screen. "Here, Sophie. Come on, kitty. Here, dammit."

She stepped out onto the back stoop, sat down at the top of the steps and stared all around the yard. Her dress had lost its starch, felt damp already as it laid against her thighs. The air was a kind of humid haze; her roses drooped. The Peace and Tropicanna she'd planted herself, a couple of springs ago. They needed water. She would miss them. She'd have to plant some more at Drew's this fall. The

Richmond heat and humidity, the anxiety to make the cat appear, like when she was a kid trying to make the minutes pass on Christmas Eve, put her in a kind of trance. She looked through the heavy air, toward the Nandina bushes. They seemed to waver, like ghosts. No sign of Sophie. She was beginning to feel nervous, irritable, off-balance: the way Allen had made her feel, there at the end. She hated that feeling. Luckily, it didn't happen too much anymore.

Mrs. Calabash's air conditioner buzzed and dripped, buzzed and dripped. The Allen memories were hanging around in her mind today, wavering like the heat auras around those bushes. She thought: play them in your mind this one last time, leave them here in this empty apartment. They have nothing to do with you any more. No room for them at Drew's.

She leaned her cheek on her fist and thought of the fluke when she first met Allen Crandall. A blind date. She never went on blind dates. She smiled thinking of how young and stupid she had been: she'd been blind all right, blind to what a user he was. But she had gone. And Allen Crandall had been handsome, no doubt about that: tall, muscular, sandy-haired. Sort of a Mickey Mantle look-alike. He'd been smart, self-confident and, that first night, charming. He talked a lot—she realized, later, he was talking mostly to his pal Mike who'd arranged the date—and opened doors and asked her to dance the slow songs. They drank rum and Cokes and laughed and kept interrupting one another and singing along with the juke box, and the whole evening seemed perfect. It was the best date she'd ever had. Even if, later, she could never remember a single thing Allen said directly to her the entire evening.

After they'd been seeing one another for a while he would drive to Roanoke to watch the Sunday afternoon football game with her father. She would sit in the den and do needlework while the two of them talked and watched the game. It all seemed homey and cozy to her at the time. It was the most comfortable she'd ever been with her father since Meredith had died, drowning in the quarry when she was supposed to be at the spring formal her senior year in high school. Most of the time it had seemed like Daddy could hardly stand to be in the same room with her. He was rarely home, anyway, he was so busy selling houses. Those afternoons her mother would cook a roast, they'd eat at halftime, she'd wash the dishes, and Allen would leave to go back to Richmond after the game was over. He'd kiss her at the back door, and she'd taste his cigarettes, his cherry-cobbler-and-beer breath, and something indefinable, desirable. Nothing like kisses from the boys in high school. She'd always been embarrassed for them and herself fumbling around in the front seat of a car. When she'd come back into the den after saying good-bye, her father would say, "Allen's quite a fine young man. Can't imagine why he bothers driving all the way down here for a meal and a game. Sharp as a tack, too. Bet he'll make a fortune in law." And he'd shake his head as though the whole thing bewildered him, and read the Sunday paper.

The first time she went away with Allen for the weekend, to D.C., she knew what would happen and she wanted it to happen. Despite the fact her mother had told her, at least a million times, "Keep yourself pure for your husband. No decent man wants used goods," Judy knew if she wanted to keep seeing him she'd have to meet his needs. Besides, she wanted more than kissing, herself, at the end of an evening. The only surprise was that Allen turned out to be about as romantic in bed as those high school boys had been in the front seat of a car. When she climbed in the dark bed beside him he didn't speak, just unbuttoned her soft cotton gown and climbed on top of her and pushed himself into her. She'd grabbed his bare back with her fingernails she'd been so surprised by how much it hurt; he must've mistaken this for passion, because he started thrusting fast, and in seconds he stopped and rolled off her. She had laid still, eyes open, waiting for some reassuring word from him, some acknowledgement he'd gotten carried away, some promise that next time would be different. All she heard was his steady breathing. Quietly, not wanting to wake him, she'd gone into the bathroom and showered, running the water as hot as she could stand it. After it started to cool she sat on the edge of the tub and dried herself with the rough hotel towel, trying to sort her feelings. She'd have to offer herself more, not lie there like some high school virgin. She'd made him ill-at-ease. That was it. She crawled, naked, back in bed beside him, wanting to do better. That's what she did the next morning. They never talked about that first time. He'd chosen her. She needed to be there for him.

And she had been, throughout their eight-year marriage. She'd cooked, entertained, done the "don't worry about me; work as late as you need to" routine. She hadn't flipped out when she found the paralegal's grey kid flats in the trunk of Allen's BMW; she hadn't lost it when he moved his things out, or when he petitioned for divorce. But the night the divorce was final, when she was by herself in their three-level glass-and-stone dream house with the realization that this was it, her father was right, she wasn't woman enough for someone like Allen Crandall, that night she'd lost it. She couldn't sleep. She took a pill. Then another one. And, at some point toward morning, she took a lot of pills. Only thing was, she didn't think to call and tell her ride not to pick her up at the usual time, and her principal got worried. She could hear him clearly: "Judy would never be absent without letting us know." They broke in, got her to the hospital in time. In time for what? She'd always heard of pumping a person's stomach. She thought it meant pumping stuff out, not pumping stuff in. Gross black stuff. For hours. Until she gagged and threw up so much she thought she was dead and in hell. That's how it felt. Until she realized it was worse than that, she was alive. At the time, she'd wondered: for what? She couldn't figure it. Now she knew, thank heaven: for herself, for her second chance at life, for Drew.

Drew. She opened her eyes, sat up and looked around. "Sophie?" There she sat by the back screen, her pink tongue hanging out, panting like her heater was on high.

Judy had never seen her pant before. God, it was hot as hell. She felt like panting herself. "Poor kitty. Am I glad to see you." She picked her up, the cat drooping in her arms like dirty laundry, and walked into the kitchen with her. "Where's your dish?" she said as she looked around the empty kitchen for a moment, before remembering she'd packed it in the car earlier. "Okay, girl, sit here." She put the stunned cat down on the counter.

Sophie looked at her as if to say, "Have you lost your mind? The counter? This is definitely forbidden territory." Judy put the stopper in the stainless steel sink, turned on the cool water and let it run while she petted Sophie's back. "Never mind. We won't tell Mrs. C." Sophie leaned over, put her head down toward the water and started to drink quietly. Judy liked that about cats; they never ate or drank like they were desperate.

She picked up the tan envelope to read the directions: "Administer tablet a half hour before departure. Place in back of animal's throat. Hold mouth closed until animal swallows." Right, Judy thought. I'll just say, "Swallow, Sophie." No problem. Sounds like a two-person job to me. Wish I had a stun gun. "Guess neither one of us is going to like this much, girl. This isn't going to be a bit of fun." She put the single white tablet on the counter. It looked harmless, smaller than an aspirin, but she couldn't imagine Sophie swallowing it. "Okay, let's get this over. You don't want me to go get Mrs. Calabash, do you?" She wanted to do it by herself, be on her way with no more interruptions or intrusions. Waiting for the cat to drink her fill, she noticed she was thirsty, too, and cupped her hands under the faucet. "I could drink a gallon of Mrs. C.'s mint tea about now, girl." She got a palmful of water and then splashed more on her flushed face. Sophie stopped drinking, stared at her. "Beg your pardon, Madame. You're right. We're breaking all the rules."

Face dripping, Judy reached for the cat and held her in her arms the way she did every day, Sophie's light body nestled in the bend of her left elbow, Judy's hand resting against the cat's chest. Their hearts beat against one another, ba-bump, ba-bump. With her right hand Judy petted the exhausted cat's head to reassure her. "You're not going to like this one bit. But hey, que sera, sera. I didn't like you running away, either, you know?" She grabbed Sophie's front paws in her left hand, tightened the pressure on her body, and reached for the pill. While Sophie wiggled and hissed and growled low in her throat, Judy shoved the pill into her mouth and circled her right hand around the cat's face to keep her from spitting the tablet out. "So swallow, okay?" Sophie's orange eyes looked desperate. Judy held her like that for a couple of minutes, her hand moving back and forth with the movements of the cat's wriggling head, waiting to be sure she would be forced to swallow. "Sorry, old girl. Calm down. Almost done."

She bent over and almost threw the frantic animal toward the doorway to the hall. Sophie ran into the empty living room, tail twitching, looking all around. "Nowhere to hide, girl," Judy said. The outraged cat looked back over her shoulder at Judy with a "How dare you" look on her face, then walked to the pillow next to the wall and started licking her front paws. Probably wants to get the danger off them, Judy thought. She's not gagging so she must have swallowed the damned tablet. Thank goodness.

Judy walked down the hall herself and sat on the cool floor beside the cat, reaching over to pet her behind the ears. "You're not long for the land of the conscious now, Sophie. Might as well not fight the feeling. That pill's supposed to be a whammy; it's all she wrote." Sophie continued to lick herself, chest, sides, everywhere Judy had touched, her tail flicking every few moments. Judy got the message: Sophie wasn't about to forgive and forget right away. She'd have to wait a while for the medicine to work; she wasn't about to drive in bad weather, in the mountains, after dark, worrying whether her freaked-out cat was going to jump on her head any minute or not. On the radio, the weatherman droned on about the storm front moving in. "Come on, girl. Go to sleep. Let's get on the road."

Waiting for the medicine to take effect, Judy reached for her purse, pulled out her compact and lipstick and started primping. As she looked in the small oval mirror she thought, okay, without the frizz, a few pounds lighter, you could be Natalie Wood's sister; not bad. Drew says, "You're plenty pretty." She liked that. Putting the make-up back in her straw pocketbook she touched the envelope that contained her scribble-scrabble copy of the letter she'd written Drew three weeks earlier, and the telegram he'd sent back in reply. She had written and re-written that letter, trying to get every word just right. She pulled them out, read them both over, which made her that much more anxious to get going. Hers was in pencil, full of scratched-out words, crumpled, hard to read. She could make it out without any difficulty, though, since she'd practically memorized it:

July 25

Drew —

Please believe that I love you. I'm just too scared to go ahead with our plans. Not because of you. Because of me. I thought I'd put all the Allen mess behind me. But the closer it gets to the date we planned to tell your folks, the more scared I get. I've started thinking the old bad thoughts about myself. I can't stand that.

I guess what I'm saying is, I need more time. Please give me a month alone to get my head on straight and sort my feelings about myself out. If you haven't heard from me by August 25, it's over. If I do call—and I want that more than anything— you'll know that I've faced down my demons, so to speak, and we can get on with our lives, no big question marks left. No matter what, I'll never stop loving you. I'm just afraid I'd ruin it if we got married. I'm afraid I'd be a bad wife. I still hear Allen's voice in my head telling me that over and over. Damn him. I can't let him ruin any more of my life. I've got to make it stop, once and for all. But I have to do that by myself.

Believe me. The weekend with you at the Homestead was the happiest I've ever been. You made me feel loved. I couldn't stand it if it didn't work.

All my love,

Judy

His telegram was not nearly as long, or as confused, or as messy; she'd been careful to fold it exactly the way it arrived, originally, each time she read it. It said:

UNDERSTAND COMPLETELY AND RESPECT
YOUR WISHES
STOP WILL BE WAITING FOR YOUR CALL
STOP LOVE ALWAYS
STOP DREW STOP

Judy had thought that telegram was Drew in a nutshell. Confident. To the point. Caring. More worried about her feelings than his own. And he loved her enough to respect what she said. No pressure. No guilt trip. No man had ever done that. Not her father. Certainly not Allen. The telegram helped her realize how lucky she was to be with Drew, how different he was from any other man she'd known, convinced her that trusting him wouldn't be like playing Russian roulette with her feelings again. Damn, Sophie. She looked at the groggy cat, who looked back at her with heavy-lidded, offended orange eyes. "Okay, Sophie-girl. How about giving me a break? Just once today. Go to sleep, and before you know it you'll be in your new home." And I will, too, she thought. Finally. She rubbed the dazed cat between her ears, felt her relax.

Judy looked down at the cat, whose eyes were closed, whose long Creamsicle fur was rising and falling. She lifted her gently. Her breathing didn't change. "So this is it, girl. We're on our way." She picked up Sophie, who was like a jumbo noodle in her arms, stood and put the limp cat over her shoulder. "Rain or no rain, we're on our way." The hands on her watch pointed to six thirty-five. Not bad, she thought. Still close to two hours of daylight. Ought to get me over the mountain. She glanced around the room, but didn't see a thing that would indicate anyone had lived there. Just her pillow, transistor radio, and pocketbook. Things a visitor would bring. She turned off the radio, stuck it in her bag, reached for the pillow and purse with her free hand. As she opened the door, a blast of muggy air hit her in the face, but that didn't bother her a bit. "Are you going to Scarborough Fair?" she hummed. Finally, she was getting in the car to leave. She could almost feel Drew's hand on her cheek, see the pleased smile on his face, hear his steady voice saying, "Judy. I knew you'd come."

Massie's Mill
6:00 p.m.

Daniel placed his white paper napkin in his lap the way Miz Malory taught him, bent his head and muttered, "Thank you for the food. Amen." Saying grace made him feel goofy, but he didn't like to act disrespectful, not to Miz Malory. Even if he was in an awful hurry to get going. Besides, she had fixed him a nice supper. No sense letting it go to waste. He shoved a forkful of the hot cheesy casserole into his mouth, chewed, started talking where he'd left off when he sat down.

"I told this guy exactly what you said. That I wanted to get on permanent, and that you'd speak for me, just to call. He looked at me like I was dirty or smelled bad, you know what I'm saying?" The boy gobbled mouthful after mouthful of the food, eating like it was the first time he'd eaten in a week.

The older woman sat without touching her food, her hands folded above her plate, her elbows resting on the arms of the chair. She wasn't the sort of woman who wore make-up to her own supper table; her plain face was clear, clean; it looked like she'd never plucked her brown bushy eyebrows. They matched her short bushy hair, the kind of unnatural hair that grown women have after they've been going to the beauty parlor once a week for the last twenty years. Still, while he couldn't picture her as a girl, Miz Malory had an easy-going face that Daniel liked, the kind more like people his age than grown people. Grown people usually gave him annoyed looks, or don't-bother-me-kid looks. Not Miz Malory. She looked right into his face when he said something; he liked the way her brown eyes stared into his eyes like she was telling him she was interested in what he had to say. Those eyes hadn't had a mean look in them since he'd started rooming at her place over six weeks ago. Now they had a worried look. "I don't understand Harley Haney acting like that. He's got boys of his own. It don't make a bit of sense to me." She picked up her spoon, started tapping it on the red plastic placemat. "Let me open the back door and get some air in here. If this storm don't break pretty soon, I'm going to faint dead away." She walked to the kitchen door and opened it while Daniel kept on eating. "Ought to pick up one of them fans at the IGA. I saw they had them on the end of summer sale." She sat again.

"That guy asked for my draft card. I told him I wadn't old enough for the draft yet. Asked for my birth certificate. Told him I didn't have one. Said, you ain't from around here are you? I said, No sir, I ain't. That's when he told me to wait out in the hall. I could see him in there making calls on the phone, but I couldn't hear what he was saying. I thought he was calling you." Daniel reached for the Pyrex dish and used the serving spoon to put another large gooey portion of noodles and peas and hot dog on his plate.

"Take your time, Daniel. You're not going to a fire. There's plenty where that came from." She sat back down, wiped her forehead with the napkin beside her plate. "Here. Have some rolls and butter. They're brown-and-serve. Like you like." She passed a wicker basket of bread to Daniel, and then a glass dish with a round of pale yellow creamery butter on it. "He never called here. Least, if he did I didn't hear the phone ring. And I was never too far from the kitchen all afternoon, except when I was taking in the clothes. What time you say this was?"

"You remember when I left? Right after I got my shower? I went straight there. Couldn't a been much later than 4:30. Maybe quarter to five."

"No. He never called. Who you reckon he was calling?"

"If it was the draft board or the social services it won't be no time at all until my dad shows up here. You can go to the bank on it." Daniel stuffed a whole buttered roll into his mouth. He hadn't gotten completely used to eating at a table, with someone keeping him company. Back home, he mostly ate in front of the television, usually straight from the pot or the frozen dinner foil.

"I don't think so, Daniel. Why would he do that? I've never known him to be the least bit involved with politics. You don't look that old anyway. Besides, don't nobody around here pay a bit of attention to that Vietnam mess. It just don't make any sense." She seemed to notice what she was doing for the first time, stopped tapping with the spoon and picked up her fork and took a bite of her food.

"Man, back in Norfolk that's all they talk about. Anybody with long hair they take for a draft dodger. I'll have to clear out. Much as I want to stay, ain't nothing in this world could make me go back to Norfolk and my daddy now."

"Help yourself, Daniel. Have some more casserole." She stood and took her own plate, the food hardly touched, to the counter. She looked at Daniel sitting alone at the oak farm table. That table was big enough to seat eight people, ten in a crunch, but right now nobody was in the huge country kitchen except the two of them. "Miss Malory's—Rooms—Light Breakfast Included," the sign out front read. Daniel had been there most of the summer, and nobody else had stopped in, nobody except Miz Malory's own relatives from Charlottesville who came over for Sunday afternoon chicken dinner every few weeks. Not much traffic through Nelson County. Not even a stoplight. He wondered how Miz Malory made it on her own. She put her hands under her apron, stood at the counter looking at him, her forehead wrinkled.

"Maybe he was making some other call that didn't have a thing in this world to do with you. Maybe he was just conducting business, something he had to do before five o'clock. Or calling home to say he'd be a little late."

Daniel wiped cheese from his mouth and moustache fuzz with his crumpled napkin. "He called me back into his office in about five minutes. Seemed like an hour, but I noticed when I was going in that the wall clock said five, so it couldn't have been more than five minutes. Said he'd have to ask around, talk to you, talk to Saunders. Saunders don't know me from a hole in the floor." He split open another roll, buttered it. "Said he'd call me here tomorrow night, let me know if he had anything. What I figure is he's gonna send the MP's after me. He thinks I'm one of them hippie draft dodgers. I could tell by the way he treated me. Sneery like. I'll bet you anything it was because of my hair."

Miz Malory sat back down in the ladder-back chair catty-cornered from the boy. "Well suppose he does. You aren't registered. How you figure that'll put your daddy on your trail? It don't add up, Danny. You're jumping at shadows."

She was staring at him now with those eyes that were like two little bitty magic eight-balls, eyes that usually had answers to his questions instead of the other way around. He chewed the roll, swallowed before he answered. "Don't you see? If they don't find no draft number, they'll probably call the juvenile services. And the social services will have it down that I'm a runaway. And they'll call my daddy. And he'll be out here before you can say Bo Diddley. I was dumb as rain to use my real name."

Sitting up straight in the chair, still staring directly into his eyes, Miz Malory spoke: "So what if he does come? We'll sit down and have a talk. Just like we're talking now. I'll fix a nice meal. I'll tell him you're welcome to stay here with me as long as you like. That we have an arrangement."

He could tell that she was serious. She didn't tell jokes. She laughed like all get out looking at the shows, like "Lucy" and "Jackie Gleason." And at his jokes. But she didn't tell jokes herself. He knew how ridiculous her idea was, much as he liked to think it might work, much as he wanted to stay on here. "You don't know my daddy, Miz Malory. Much as he don't want me around, I'm all the family he's got. Besides, he'd want me to go back to take care of unfinished business, so to speak."

Her eyes snapped. "Pardon me for saying, but that's the most ridiculous thing I've ever heard. Either he wants you around or he don't."

"We're flesh and blood. That's how he always puts it. Flesh and blood. Ain't nothing stronger."

"Danny, you tell me you ran away because your daddy didn't have nothing to do with you, didn't even provide for you, never paid any attention to you except to punish you, and now you say he wouldn't let you stay on here if it didn't cost him a plug nickel? I hate to sound dumb, but it just don't add up." She reached for his empty plate. "You finished?" The casserole dish was half empty.

"I'm stuffed. Thanks. You know that's my favorite." He sat back in his chair.

Putting the dish on the drainboard, she walked to the stove and picked up another glass dish sitting between the burners. "Ready for some peach pie, or do you want to wait until later, while we're looking at TV?"

"Now, please." He put his napkin on the table, looked at her. "I told you, Miz Malory. I'm leaving right after supper. I'm not kidding."

She sat, putting the pie plate down on her placemat. "Danny, please let's talk this thing over some more. You can't just keep running every time you think your daddy might find out where you are. You've gotta face up to this thing, whatever it is. I know there's something you're not telling me. Something about this so-called 'unfinished business.'" She looked at him hard, her lips in a line.

He hadn't told her about the stealing. He hadn't told her about Buzzy, and that robbery where the old man got beat up. He didn't want her to think less of him, and he was afraid if she found out he broke into cars and every now and then an apartment—when nobody was home, of course— she'd be ashamed of him. Maybe even think he deserved to be sent back to his daddy. For the first time, he felt ashamed of himself. "In another year or so I'll be eighteen. Then it won't matter. I just gotta stay outa his way until then."

"Danny, then you'll have to register for the draft. You might have to go into the Army. You'll excuse me for say-ing, but I can't imagine you in the Army." Even though he'd put on about ten pounds since he'd been with her, he was still the size of a bamboo pole. "Maybe you ought to stay put. Go back to school, even. You could stay here, work part-time on the weekends. They don't make people go in if they're still in school. Why don't you just face up to him?"

Daniel never had a grandmother, but the thought struck him while she was talking that Miz Malory was like Aunt Bea on "The Andy Griffith Show." Soft and squooshy-looking, but hard as nails when it got down to trouble with her kin. He figured that was what a grandmother must be like. His daddy never introduced him to any relatives. Said he didn't have any himself, and the ones on his mother's side weren't worth knowing. More trouble than they were worth, was the way he put it. Just hit him up for money if he kept in touch. So it had only been the two of them, far back as Danny could remember.

"I got into a little trouble back home, Miz Malory. Nothing big. Honest. But the way my daddy sees it, me getting in trouble is the same as him getting in trouble. See?

So if I don't come back and face up to it, it leaves a bad mark by his name. He's big on pride. Standing up like a man. That and the Navy. Don't mess around with his name or the Navy, you know what I mean? That's what he's worried about. Ain't me he's worried about at all."

"I get your drift. You say this trouble isn't anything big, Danny. But you left, so if you ask me it must be right sizable. Big enough to make you run away once. And big enough to make you run away again. That is, if you take off tonight." She stood, reached into the glass-doored cabinet over the counter for a bowl. All the dishes had these little raised red apples going around the edges. Daniel really liked those matched dishes.

"I didn't do anything all that bad. Honest. One of my friends got into some bad trouble. And Daddy thought I was in on it. But I wasn't. I swear to God."

She scooped the warm fruit and crust into the bowl. "No need to bring the Lord into this. You want ice cream?"

"Yes please." He wasn't lying, but he knew the more he tried to avoid telling her about it the more she'd think he was lying. "I swear to you I wasn't even with Buzzy the night it happened."

She put the bowl down, got up and went to the refrigerator and reached into the freezer for the container of ice cream. Walking back to the table, she spoke slowly, "I never heard you mention any friend named Buzzy before. Some people judge you by the company you keep. You ever heard that?"

"Buzzy was all right. That ain't fair, Miz Malory. You sound like Daddy now. Buzzy wasn't all that bad."

She spooned the cool ice cream onto the warm pie. It started to melt almost as soon as it touched the fruit. "Sounds like this Buzzy wasn't as good a friend as you wanted him to be if he dragged you into trouble." She passed the dish over, looking Danny in the face.

He looked down at his apple-shaped placemat as he started to eat his dessert. "He had his troubles. But he wasn't all bad."

"So how did you get in trouble, Danny? Why don't you tell me about it."

He ate for a few minutes without answering. She sat, her arms resting on the arms of the chair, waiting for him to eat, waiting for him to make up his mind whether to tell her what happened back in Norfolk or not. He kept spooning the food into his mouth without looking up. Finally, after the last bite, he pushed the dish away from him. "That was mighty good. Thanks."

"You're welcome. It's nice to have somebody around here to cook for. Thanks for bringing the peaches home."

"They don't care, long as we get them from off the ground. Ain't stealing." They both sat still. "He started talking to me in shop. That was all. Asked me where I lived, you know, stuff like that."

She sat listening.

"Then we started meeting after school. Hanging out at the service station a couple of blocks away. Just talking."

"How long ago was this, Danny?"

"Oh, sometime around Thanksgiving. I remember, 'cause neither of us had nothing to do all that weekend. Daddy was busy at the base. He just left me some money and some frozen dinners. And Buzzy said his parents didn't pay any attention to the holidays either. So we just hung out. Usually I tried to be in by eight or nine, but Daddy was working a back-to-back shift, so we stayed out all night. Buzzy got some beer. I don't know where he got it. Honest. And he'd think up all this stuff for us to do. Like going over to the school and checking out the buses. Seeing if any were unlocked. He had all these ideas for stuff to do."

Miz Malory started running her fingers around the edges of the placemat. Daniel thought, I didn't mean to tell her about the beer. I know she don't approve of drinking. I shouldn't have told her the part about the beer. Maybe I shouldn't tell her any of this. But she just sat there waiting.

"Buzzy was cool. Real independent, you know? I brought him home once or twice, but Daddy didn't like him. Said he had trouble written all over him. Daddy never did like for me to bring anybody in the house, though. Said it just made more mess for him to clean up. So mostly me and Buzzy just hung out at the service station."

"Still don't sound to me like a reason to run away, Danny." She kept on walking her fingers around the edge of the placemat while she stared at his face.

"No ma'am." He could tell she was ready to wait him out. "See, the police came by one night. Right after school was out. Said there'd been a break-in the weekend before. Not too far from where we lived. They'd picked up Buzzy. This old guy was beat up pretty bad. He said there were a couple of other guys with Buzzy. Police thought I might be one of them."

Miz Malory stopped fretting with the placemat. "Were you?"

"No ma'am. I swear I wasn't."

"My mama always said 'A guilty horse flinches.' If you didn't have anything to do with it, why'd you run?"

"Daddy told the police he'd bring me in for questioning. After they left, he locked me in my room, didn't give me a chance to explain. He had me guilty from the minute the police hit the porch. Told me, he said, 'I told you that Buzzy was nothing but trouble.' He'd been working that weekend, and Buzzy had been over all Saturday afternoon. But I stayed home Saturday night when it happened. Honest. I didn't even know about it until the police showed up."

"So you took off that night? Reckon your daddy figures you were in on it. Reckon he's plenty mad at you for leaving, making him look bad to the law."

"Yes ma'am. That's about it." He stood to put his bowl and spoon in the sink.

"I'll get that, Danny. Keep your seat a minute. Let's see if we can figure this thing out."

He sat back down. "Don't see as there's any figuring to it, Miz Malory. I'll be looking over my shoulder, ready to jump out of my skin, if I stick around here now. Like I said, that man at the hatchery didn't like me a bit. And Daddy would turn me over to the police in a heartbeat."

The phone in the hall rang. "Just a minute. I'll be right back." She left the kitchen, but he could easily hear every word she was saying. He looked around the room, wanting to listen but not wanting to seem rude. Wood floors. He'd never seen wood floors in a kitchen. He sure liked this house, with all the little plaques hanging around, like the one saying "Bless This Mess." He bit his nails, tapped the fingers of his other hand on the table, but he couldn't help but listen.

"Hello. . . . Pretty good, thanks. And you? . . . The boy and I were just talking about you, Harley. . . . He told me that. Said he got the clear impression you weren't going to be giving him any work." She sat down in the chair beside the telephone table, leaned forward in the doorway and mouthed "Harley Haney, from the hatchery," so Daniel could read her lips. He already knew who it was. Maybe he'd been shooting at shadows after all.

"That's right. Been here six weeks. No trouble whatsoever. Been working regular out at Saunders. . . . Well of course he ain't from around here. . . . Now Harley, you know I haven't seen any driver's license or anything like that. I've never troubled about that. I'll take down my sign before I start doing business like that.. . . Well I can see that, what with the social security and all. Uh huh."

She's gonna get me the job, he thought. I'm not gonna have to leave after all. I can go on back upstairs and unpack my knapsack. Daniel leaned over so he could see her through the doorway and smiled, lifting his hand to flash a V for peace *and* victory, until he saw the strained look on Miz Malory's face. He stopped, feeling foolish.

"I still don't see that as any reason to call the police. What law has he broken? I tell you he's not one of them draft evaders. . . I just know, sure as I'm sitting here. You can look at his face and see he ain't eighteen. . . . I don't see what this has to do with your boys, Harl. . . . I see. Well, thanks for calling anyway. . . . Will you leave it to me, if I promise to get him to call his father? . . . You have my word on it. . . . Haven't I known you since you lost your front teeth? Don't insult us both. . . . If I say I'll do it, it's as good as done and you know it. . . . So this is just between us? . . . . Thanks for calling. . . . You, too. Give my best to Dorcas. Bye."

Daniel could tell she'd hung up, but she didn't get up from the chair right away. He waited at the table, chewing his nails, knowing it was bad news but still not wanting to hear her say it. He knew it, anyway. Knew he'd have to move on, or be looking over his shoulder for his daddy. This time he'd go farther away, so far he wouldn't have to give it a thought. Maybe Canada. He sure didn't like the cold, though. He'd heard about a rock festival up in New York somewhere. Near some farm. Maybe he'd hitch there, see if he could find the place, get work. Bound to be a lot of people like him around that place.

"Miz Malory?" He didn't want her feeling bad about this. She'd been nicer to him than anybody. Much nicer than those baby-sitters who used to watch the soaps all day and tell him to stay out of their hair. "Miz Malory? I could hear what you were saying. I could pretty well get the gist of it."

She walked back to the table, stood beside it with her fingertips on the wood. "I'm sorry as I can be, Danny. I'm afraid this is mostly my fault. I'd a never sent you over there if I'd had any idea Harley would act this way. He's just as hot as he can be over this thing. You'd think somebody came in and robbed him. He's that upset. One good thing, I got him to let me take care of it."

He could tell she was upset, the way her voice was low and all the words sounded the same. Seemed like she was gonna cry. He didn't think he could take that. "I heard what you said. I ain't gonna call my daddy, Miz Malory. I don't mean to make a liar out of you, and I guess if you need to call that man back and tell him you can do what you have to do, but I ain't gonna call. Ain't going back there. Ain't even thinking about it."

She reached over and rubbed his hair, pulled a long strand out of his face. "I just said I'd get you to call, Danny. I never said I'd make you talk to him. You go on and dial.

I'll just go in the other room and get you a little cash I've got on hand."

Well if that don't beat all, he thought. He rubbed his hands on his thighs and stood up, knocking against her. "Yes ma'am. I'll do that." He went to the phone and dialed his number, wondering what he'd do if his daddy answered. He was probably at the base. Still, he didn't even want to hear his voice. But the phone rang and rang, and after about ten rings he hung up, relieved. He yelled down the hall, "I called him. Nobody home. You got many tricks like that one, Miz Malory?"

She called back from her bedroom, "Don't you worry about it. Woman on her own has to know how to take care of herself."

Wonder what time it is, he thought. It's still light out. Couldn't be too late. He was back in the kitchen in three steps, and took a quick look at the tea kettle clock over the refrigerator. 6:37. Plenty of time to get out on the road, catch a ride with one of the truck drivers. He'd be in Pennsylvania by ten if he got a ride pretty quick. Twenty-nine was always crawling with trucks this time of day. Truckers like company. He shouldn't have any trouble.

Maybe this won't be so bad after all, he thought. Maybe I can get work in one of them factories. I hear they pay bet-ter'n around here. Other guys come up with these fake IDs. Buzzy had one. Maybe I can get me one. "I'm gonna go up and get my knapsack, Miz Malory. I'll be back down in just a minute."

"Let me pack you some sandwiches, Danny. It won't take me a minute. Do you have a flashlight?"

"No ma'am," he yelled, as he hustled up the steps, two-by-two. "I don't reckon I'll be needing one though. I shouldn't have any trouble getting a ride." He walked into his room. That's what he'd begun to call it. His room. The Army green knapsack was on the bed, and he grabbed it. But he stopped and looked around one last time, made a pic-ture in his mind. The single bed. The little table by it with a souvenir lamp made to look like a cactus. The plaid blanket at the foot of the bed he'd used when nights got cool. The bookcase painted dark blue. He'd always intended to try to read one of those books. But he'd just gotten in the habit of looking at television with Miz Malory evenings. She seemed to like the company. He liked this room a lot. He could see the big pines from his window, see one of them blue mountains on a clear morning. He sure hated to leave. He opened the wooden candy box on the table by the bed and took out the cash he'd been saving. Hoping to take Audrey out one of these days. Keep his eyes open for a used car. Stuffing the money into his jeans pocket, he took one last quick look around and headed for the steps again at a run.

"What do I owe you, Miz Malory? I paid up through the weekend, didn't I? How about today? You want me to pay for the rest of the week?" His voice was all breathless. He needed to be gone.

She was waiting at the foot of the steps with a flashlight and an envelope. "What's the rush? Stay tonight. Get started in the morning. I don't like you starting out this late. It's supposed to rain. We're supposed to have an electrical storm."

"Don't you worry about me. I won't be on 29 ten minutes before I get picked up. I never have any trouble getting a ride. See this honest face?" He made a big fake smile. "Besides, it's easier to get a ride at night."

"Seriously. Why don't you wait?"

"What if that guy decides to call anyway? I want to be long gone if he does."

"I guess you've got your reasons. But I sure hate to see you go, especially like this. Here, take this flashlight. There's some money in the envelope. Not much, but maybe it'll come in handy."

Daniel reached for the flashlight and held his other hand up like he was a traffic policeman, "Hold on, there. I owe you. Thanks, but I can't take any of your money."

"Don't be silly. Here, take it. I wouldn't be able to sleep tonight if you don't. Make it a birthday present."

"My birthday ain't till December."

"What difference does it make? This here's a present. You won't be around in December." She stuck the envelope in the pocket of his T-shirt. "You better wear a jacket. Gets cold nights out here."

"Not tonight it won't. Cool air will feel good. I don't know what to say."

"Thanks will do fine. Will you send me a postcard sometime, maybe come back to visit once you get settled?"

"Soon's I get me a car and a job I'll come back and take you out for a steak supper. What do you think of that?"

"Can't chew steak too good with these choppers. But I wouldn't mind going out to supper with you. I'll look forward to that. Let me fix you something to eat later, all right?"

"No ma'am. I'll stop and get some potted meat and Pepsis and crackers if I need anything. Besides, you know truckers. They stop at all the best places. I won't need any food. I better hit the road. Before it gets too much later."

They'd just been standing in the front hall. Daniel didn't really want to leave, and Miz Malory didn't really want him to go. She reached up and smoothed the hair out of his face again. "You make something of yourself, Daniel, you hear? You got plenty of sense. Whatever you did back there at home, put it behind you, okay?"

"Yes ma'am. I will. I ain't one for writing letters, but I'll be back one of these days. I promise." He picked up his knapsack and slung it over his left shoulder. He reached to open the door and stopped with his hand on the knob. "Miz Malory, do you happen to know a girl about my age named Audrey? A real pretty girl, with long brown hair 'bout down to her waist? Plays in the band at the high school?"

Miz Malory crossed her arms and thought a minute. "Well, she might be one of the Fix girls. I know the twins are Marlene and Darlene. They keep the nursery at church sometimes. Seems to me like the next girl to them in age is named Audrey. I'm pretty sure she is. Why?"

"Nothing. If you see her, just tell her hey for me, will

154

you? Tell her I was the one who left her the note. She'll know what you're talking about."

"I'll do that, Daniel. You take care of yourself, you hear?" She patted him on the shoulder as he opened the door.

"You, too, Miz Malory. Thanks for everything. Don't take any wooden nickels."

Daniel went down the front steps of the clapboard house, looking back over his shoulder at Miz Malory standing in the front door. He could smell the rain in the air. It was getting cooler. Too bad he didn't have a jacket after all. Turning for one last look, he waved goodbye and headed toward 29.

Davis Creek
8:00 p.m.

I don't like Ora singing that song she heard on the radio. "Hush, hush, Sweet Charlotte," she sings. I know she does it to irritate me. It's not a bit respectful. She's gotten too big for her britches these last few years. Probably thinks I'm about to die and she'll get my money. Well, she can think again. Even if I was to pass in my sleep she'll never get a bit of my money. Don't I give her plenty every week? And extra like I did tonight? And the very clothes off my back, when I get tired of them. Or they're too snug.

Maybe I'll write out another will tonight. I wish I could see her face when she cleans this place after I'm gone and finds all the wills I've left around. And none with dates. I read about that in one of those detective stories, how they found one will with one date and then when they found another one with a later date the wife was done out of all the money. Well, I didn't put any date at all on any of mine. My favorite is the one where I said, "I, Charlotte Fairchild, being of sound mind and body, leave the ten acres, the house, and all its contents to Elvis Presley, so long as he remains married to Priscilla and continues to be a loving father to his precious baby daughter." I'd like to see their greedy faces when they find that one. Then there's the one for St. George's, Daddy's church. They tried to stick their noses in my business right after he died. If there's one thing I can't stand, it's a busybody. That's why I stopped going. That one should really stick in their craw. It says I leave everything to St. George's Episcopal Church if they promise never to serve communion to Negroes, and if they do, then everything would become the property of Oak Hill Baptist. You can bet for sure the Baptists won't let the nigras in. Not those do-gooders. That's what I'll do tonight, I'll write another will. And I'll leave everything to James Earl, if he agrees to never live in the house itself, and to take care of the cemetery and the clock and keep everything as Daddy left it. Course the courts would never let James Earl inherit, since he's feeble-minded, and they might give it to Ora anyway, so maybe I'd better not write that one. Or maybe I should write one to Ora, and then she'd get so excited until she found all the others. I wonder if she'd lie for the property, take a chance of burning in everlasting hell by destroying all the other wills except the one leaving everything to her. That's something to think about. Whew. It's close in here.

Too hot to go upstairs, even. I'll get a glass of water and soak my teeth down here. Maybe I'll just light a lamp and sit here in the parlor and look at these letters again. I'll just open this back window here. Smell that rain. The storm's bound to break any minute now.

I know Ora was trying to irritate me when she sang that song, 'cause she usually sings hymns while she's cleaning. "Jesus calls us, o'er the tumult, of our life's wild restless seas, Day by day his sweet voice calls us, saying, Christian, follow me." If I've heard that once, I've heard it a million times. Daddy liked "A Mighty Fortress Is Our God." They played that at his funeral. Remember that, Ora? Da da da da-de-da da-ah de dah.

I ought to go on up and put on a gown, but it's so blamed hot I don't have the energy. Ora was right, these Bermuda shorts are right comfortable, especially with this elastic around the waist. I ought to give her some money to get me another pair. I ought to count my money, but I don't feel like taking it out. I'll bet anything she's been in it. I know she knows where it is. Some of it. How'd she find the money to pay the doctor that time? Maybe I told her. It's been so long ago. And me out of my head with a fever. Maybe I told her, then moved it. Maybe Henry Trice is the one who sneaked in here and took some of it. What did I do with the money I got for the car? Maybe he took that. Course Henry Trice didn't take it. He was long gone. What am I thinking about? But he does hang around here. He doesn't think I know. But I hear him at night, scritch scratching on the screens. He never did get over me. That's for sure.

I've got to get him off my mind, before I get upset. Doesn't take much in this heat. Still like this, my nerves get agitated. So what if I did go down there that night. Nobody knows. Ora can't know. She was sound asleep. Snoring. Daddy was cold in his grave. He can't know. No matter what Ora says about life everlasting. Henry Trice stared at the gun, and looked at me with those sad eyes. Doe eyes.

I'll read one of Daddy's books. That always settles me. Daddy used to read out loud to me, as far back as I can remember. Sometimes we'd take turns. We'd laugh so hard when we read that one about communicating with the dead. I know right where it is. Whoo, it's almost too hot to stand up. Kerosene smells awful strong without the air moving. Here it is, right on the shelf where he always kept it: *Can the Living Talk with the Dead?* by J. F. Rutherford. I remember, somebody from the Bible Society came round selling it. Daddy never did buy anything from leeches like that, said they were an insult to decent Christian people, but he said the title of this one was too appealing to let pass: *Can the Living Talk with the Dead?* Said the young fella who sold it had a face covered with purple pimples. Said if he'd been talking to the dead, he wasn't such a convincing spokesman for the practice. Daddy bought it anyway, and said later it was worth every penny he paid. He would read Mr. Psychic's part, and change voices for Lightbearer's voice. I always got to be Newday. I loved that part where I said, "Oh, there is no doubt about it; the proof has been brought to me by men who saw him drop, pierced with an enemy ball. If only I could have spoken to him once before he departed." I had quite a flair for the dramatic; Daddy always said so. But it wouldn't have been proper for me to do more than read at home with Daddy. It wouldn't have been my place. Lord knows I'd never do anything common like that. Not a Fairchild. Daddy would turn over in his grave.

I would read Newday's conclusion, then Daddy would tell me why Mr. Psychic and his argument for talking to the dead would win in a court of law. He'd laugh when I'd linger over that last part; where is it now? Here it is: "And all this testimony presented here on behalf of or by Mr. Psychic, even as claimed by him, is based upon the theory that there is no death; and since this theory is supported only by Satan's falsehood, I reject it most emphatically." I'd draw that part out, just to please Daddy. He'd say, "Well, now, Newday, I found Satan a very convincing witness. Very convincing indeed." And we'd laugh. Yes, indeed, this book was worth every penny he paid.

I want to look at the photographs. Right here on the shelf. When did the leather get so cracked? Chair feels good. Think I'll sleep right here. Don't feel like going up those stairs in this heat. Too hot up there anyway. That lemon oil Ora got for the lamps is light smelling. Cuts the kerosene smell some. Too expensive to use by itself, though. Daddy's handwriting is perfect, with the date and all under each snapshot. Such a fine, lovely hand. Everything about him was lovely. I can see him sitting at his desk, just as plain as day, writing with his black ink pen. He always used that. It's still over there on the desk. Haven't had any ink in years. My hand always looked clumsy compared to his. I wouldn't feel right using his pen, unless it was for business. I just like to hold it. I guess a will counts. I could get Ora to get some ink. That'd be right funny. Daddy would get a laugh out of that.

Mama's wedding picture. I can hardly remember her at all. She stayed in her room all the time. I hate to go in there now. Makes me think of her sitting there at that window with that pained look on her face. I never could understand that look. Married to Daddy and all. Seems like she couldn't help but smile. Her face kinda looks that way here, but not quite so unhappy as right before she died. I can't remember her ever having a smile on her face. Daddy was so lively, so witty. I don't see why he ever married her. I look more like him. Got his body build, even though I didn't get his height. Oh I was slim in my time, but never puny-looking like her. She looks frail, even in this picture. Cinchy said the baby boy took after her. Weak little old thing. Didn't bother me a bit when he died. Just cried all the time anyway. Nothing to act so maudlin about. Didn't seem to bother Daddy a bit. He just went off to work the day after the funeral, same as ever. Why in the world he let her name that scrawny runt after him, him so strong and handsome, I'll never know. Wasn't a thing like him. Took after her completely. Probably felt sorry for the two of them. And she stayed in that room from then on. Cinchy used to give me looks when I played upstairs, tell me to be still, not to bother Miss Alice Elizabeth. What difference did it make? There's not even a picture of that baby in here. No wonder. He wasn't a thing to look at. Ugly as a worm, if you ask me, all red and wrinkled and scrawny. Daddy said I was a beautiful baby. These pictures of me at six months, just as round and happy as you please. "Charlotte, July, 1900." No wonder he loved me best. Who could blame him?

I love this picture of him standing by his first car. Tall and handsome with his dark grey suit neat as a pin. He always was slim. But then he never got to be near as old as I am. And he didn't have to eat Ora's cooking. When he was in his coffin he looked exactly like this picture. Just as slim. Not an ounce of fat. He wouldn't believe this weight

I've put on. We looked so elegant, the two of us together. Him so handsome, me so petite and pretty. We made a picture. I wish I had a picture of the two of us together. Never saw him mussed, not ever. Even in the evening when he took his coat off, his shirt would look starched and fresh, like he'd just put it on. This picture of him in front of his law office is how I remember him. Here he is with Bunny and Lucy in front of the home place. They're all laughing like Daddy just told one of his funny stories. I'll bet he did. They were crazy about him. Everybody was. And this one in front of the Fairchild Acres sign. He was a striking man. No doubt about that.

This picture of me at Chatham Hall looks a tiny bit like Mother. Just a bit. Around the mouth. Daddy's written, "Charlotte, Chatham Hall, November, 1915." I've got that sad look on my face like her. I was sad. I wanted to come home so badly. I even lied and said I missed Ora. Ora was better than living with all those girls. They were plain boisterous. And nosy. At least I could tell Ora to shut up and leave me alone. That roommate of mine from Richmond who spread all her clothes and books and paints all over the room, and acted hurt when I told her I wasn't used to living like that. Such clutter. Disarray. She must've had twenty brothers and sisters, and she wanted to act like I was one of them. Sounded to me as if they lived like savages, even if they did have a fancy home in some come-lately part of Richmond. So what? Why in the world would I want to live in a room with her? So when I read and did my work and wrote letters home they started ignoring me. I heard whispers that I was a snob, thought I was better than they were. Well, to tell the truth, I did. Wasn't Daddy the best lawyer in Nelson County? Didn't I live on Fairchild Acres? Hadn't the Fairchilds been in Virginia ever since there was a Virginia? If playing field hockey with them and screeching in the dining hall every time some boy's name was mentioned was some kind of sign I was just like the rest of them, they could forget it. I wasn't. I couldn't believe it when Daddy sent me back the second fall. As soon as he saw how sick I got, though, he let me come home. Too sick to go to classes, or even leave my room. I couldn't stand being away from him. And I wasn't, ever again, until those damned heart attacks. Him still so young and handsome. It doesn't make a grain of sense. And people like Ora and James Earl still walking around, neither one of them worth his little finger. Life is so unpredictable. So unfair.

I never did get to his grave today. I'll go tomorrow for sure. The heat just saps my energy. I can see it in my mind's eye, though. That grey marble headstone, carved with peach blossoms, and his name the biggest thing written on it, David Lloyd Fairchild. Underneath that, Husband, Lawyer, Beloved Father. 1878 - 1920. Then, in script, "Love Always." It comforts me to go there. I should've gone today. Maybe I wouldn't have had that awful dream. I ought to walk some, to keep my feet from swelling so. I could pick the gentians he loved and put them in the urn, with some fresh water. Like his eyes. I guess I could put some in Mother's, too: Alice Elizabeth Weatherby Fairchild. 1880 - 1913. At Peace. Daddy chose that sentiment. It always struck me as perfect. We never talked about her much after she died, or before that, really. He'd go up to see her every evening after supper. Stayed too long to suit me. But they always had the door shut. And I never heard a sound coming from the room. Then Cinchy would go up to get her ready for bed, and I'd go in and kiss her cheek. And she'd kiss my cheek, but it would be like a little kitten breathed on my skin. Not like a kiss at all. She'd be tucked in bed, with her hair braided and her face smelling like lavender soap. It's funny, I can remember her smell better than her features. Ora didn't even know her. So after a while it was like she hadn't even been here. I told Ora to give her clothes to the church, the things Aunt Bunny and Aunt Lucy didn't take. Daddy made me take her silver dresser set, but I didn't really want it. Said she'd want me to have it. I wonder what made him think that? I always wished it had my initials twined together in the fancy letters instead of hers. I'd squint my eyes to make the letters blur and pretend they were mine. And Cinchy would glare at me. There was no point in keeping her around, even though Ora wasn't much of a cook. I didn't like the looks she gave me and Daddy. She hardly spoke, unless one of us made her. I guess she went on back to Charleston. I never heard.

There's the clock. Six, seven, eight, nine. Nine o'clock. Or thereabouts. It unnerves me to think it might be off. It kept perfect time all those years. It's Ora's fault. I think I will write another will. I'll leave everything to Ora, if she'll move up here. But she'd have to sleep in her old room, not upstairs. And James Earl would have to sleep in the workshop. And they'd have to keep Daddy's room and desk and books just as he left them. I'll write that out. I'd love to see her horse face when she found it. That old frizzy black hair of hers would probably stand on end. I wonder why her hair hasn't turned grey at all, and mine completely white. Her eyes would bulge out, that's for sure. Maybe I wrote one like that a few years ago. I just can't remember. I know I thought about it. Well, I'll write another one, after I rest just a bit. I can't stand to get up again. I'll do it later.

I'd like some corn bread in sweet milk, but I don't feel like taking the lamp out to the kitchen and fixing it. Damn that Ora. If she'd just stay up here all the time; that's really what Daddy meant when he made her promise to take care of me. I've gotten too old to be here all alone like this. Where's my gun? What happened to it? Where'd I put it? It's so hard remembering what I did when I came back here to the house that night. I was so agitated. I'm sure I've used it since then. I didn't want to wake Ora. And I didn't want her to see me with the gun. In my nightgown, all dirty. I was upset. How dare him treat me that way? Say those things? I had no intention of firing the gun. I never intended that. I only took it with me 'cause it was so late and I was afraid one of the men was sneaking around after he'd had some time to think of me firing them all. I didn't intend to hurt Henry Trice. But the way he acted. I've never been so insulted in my life, before or since. When he looked me in the eye and said, "Miss Charlotte, it's not proper for you to be down here at night. Let me get you a jacket. I'll see you back to the house."

"But, Henry, I came down here to meet you. I thought maybe you'd want to talk. About how things will be from now on, with the hands gone."

"Didn't you get my note? I haven't been able to sleep. Last night or tonight. I can't believe what you did. I just can't get it straight in my head." He walked around in circles, and wouldn't look me in the eye. He kept looking at his feet. I'd never known him to do that before. He always stood so straight.

"Henry, I know it was a surprise. I meant to surprise you. Don't you see how perfect it was? Daddy would be so proud of me." That's when it happened. When I touched his sleeve with my hand and he jumped back like he'd been bitten by a spider.

"Miss Charlotte. You've got to go back to the house."

"Henry, I came to see you." And I put my hand on his face. And I stood on my tiptoes. And he froze. He looked at me then. But he looked at me like I was crazy. Or a leper. Stunned, like. Disgusted. Scared. "How dare you!" I stepped back and raised the gun. I didn't aim it or anything. It was merely a reflex. He had no right to look at me that way.

"You've got no right to take liberties with me like that, Henry Trice," and I fired the gun. I didn't mean to. It hit him, too, up on the shoulder. It knocked him down. I remember him sitting down hard in the path, grabbing his shoulder with his hand, then looking at me so strangely. Like I was a monster of some sort. And what he said. It was unforgivable.

"Your father would be ashamed. I'm glad he's dead, so he can't see you like this." Doe eyes. Blood on his fingers. He turned away from me and looked at his shoulder and tried to get up. That's when I shot him again. And again.

I sat down in the road myself, after, and shook. I could hardly hold onto the gun. How had I shot him? I could hardly even hold the gun. It had been his fault. He shouldn't have said those things. He shouldn't have tried to grab me like that. That's what he did, tried to grab me. That's when he said those things about my hair. Tried to take liberties. I had no choice. A lady alone. I had to shoot him.

I waited for one of the men to come, or Ora. But nobody came. I don't know how long I sat there with Henry Trice's body before I realized nobody had heard the gunshots. Or if they had, they hadn't paid any attention. So I had to do something with Henry Trice. He wasn't moving. It took me over an hour to drag him to the smokehouse. We hadn't used it for years. Then I thought, what if the animals smell him? Ora never comes down here, and the men will be gone. But what if animals come around? She'll come down here to check it out.

I went back up to his cabin and got all his stuff—he'd packed most of it anyway—and I went to the barn and got some lime; the men used it in the compost. And I went back to the smokehouse and looked at him one last time, all sprawled out in the pit there, so pathetic-looking. Helpless. He shouldn't have said those things. Dragging that body was the most taxing thing I've ever done. It was like trying to move a croaker sack full of river rocks. Seemed like I was pulling in one direction and he was pulling in the other. I'd go a little ways, then have to stop and catch my breath. And I'd start shaking. Thinking about buzzards. All that blood. It took forever. Or what seemed like forever. And afterwards I came back up to the house and just sat on the porch until the sun came up. I didn't have the energy or the desire to go inside and wash. I was so dirty I looked like I'd been rolling in one of the fields. My white lawn gown was streaked with dirt, just streaked, and my hair was tangled. My feet looked like a field hand's. He had no right to treat me like that. To talk to me like that. No right at all.

When Ora woke up and came out on the porch, she almost fainted. I swear her face turned white.

"Miss Charlotte, what in the world happened to you? Just look at you. Oh, Lord, what's wrong?" She sat down beside me on the steps, put her arms around me like I was a child. Her hands felt like the lining of Mama's fur coat. I couldn't remember her ever doing that.

"I went to the cemetery to see Daddy. I fell asleep. Henry Trice came down there. Ora, you wouldn't believe what he tried to do. It shames me to talk about it." I put my head in my lap.

She stood up, put her hand over her mouth. Her eyes got as big as silver dollars. She reached for my shoulder. "Come in here, Miss Charlotte. Let me clean you up. Let me go for the sheriff. Do you need to go to the hospital? Dear Lord, what's this world coming to?"

"I'll be all right. Just help me upstairs. I can clean myself up. Don't you dare go after the sheriff. Or Mr. Gamble either. I couldn't look them in the eye if they knew. He's long gone now, I'm sure of it. I told him I'd tell. Please just help me upstairs. And bring me some water."

What did I do with the gun? I just can't picture it. Maybe I threw it down the hole in the smokehouse. That doesn't seem right. I know I brought it back to the porch. I've had it since. But I didn't have it when Ora came out there. I know she never saw it. She never said anything about it. And she would've. Just like she started asking me all those questions about Henry Trice a few days later.

"He seemed like such a nice man to me. Always polite. Never stepping over his bounds. You know what I mean? Your daddy thought a lot of him. And he always was a good judge of character. You said so yourself. He must've been out of his head to do something horrible like that. Just crazy out of his head. Had he been drinking? That'll do it. Did you smell liquor? I just can't imagine Mr. Henry trying to take advantage of you. I can't imagine it."

And she'd look at me with those shock-wide, staring eyes, asking a question without asking it. "I don't want to talk about it, Ora. Ever again. You hear me. He may have fooled you, but he was no gentleman. Breeding will out. Daddy always did say. Henry Trice was no gentleman. I don't want to hear his name again, do you hear me?"

If she'd seen the gun she would have said something about it. She never could keep a thing to herself. And those years when the kids would drive up here in their cars and shine the lights on the front of the house and yell out those obscene things. Mean things. And then cut off the lights and sit there doing God knows what. Seems like I had the gun then. I'm sure of it. I'd look out in the morning and see beer bottles and liquor bottles and other disgusting things. I'd send Ora out there to clean up even before she fixed my breakfast. Enough to take my appetite. But they stopped coming after a while. After the road washed out. I asked her then, I said, "Do you know where that gun is, the one Henry Trice taught me to shoot?" And she'd look at me like she didn't know what I was talking about. So I know she didn't find it somewhere. I just wish I knew what I did with it. For the longest time I worried somebody would come up here looking for him, or come up here after me. I remember for nights I looked for the bullets. Went out there with a lantern after Ora fell asleep. I never did find them. Or did I? Maybe I just imagined it. What happened to the bullets? I didn't dare talk to Ora about it. She'd preach. The wages of sin. What did I do with that gun? I was still out of my head with grief over Daddy.

What in the world is all this thinking about Henry Trice tonight? Has he been sneaking around here again, trying to get to me? I always did think he crawled up out of that smokehouse and sneaked up to the house and tried to get in. Soon as he got his strength back I know he came for me. I could hear him. He's probably out there tonight. I don't care what Ora says. I know he's still after me. He made me shoot him, with all that dirty talk. He didn't dare go to the sheriff himself. I'd have been forced to say how he tried to rape me, me with no daddy to protect me, just a nigra girl here on the place. Who would they believe? Henry Trice or me? A Fairchild? I'm sure he tried to get what he came for. I hear him sneaking around, whether Ora believes me or not.

Imagine, Ora reproaching me for selling the orchards. I wanted to slap her face. Turned out I was right. Wasn't many years before that fruit tree disease came through here and wiped out just about all the trees. Wiped out that man who bought the land, that's for certain. Henry and Ora were wrong. Dead wrong. Last thing I needed was trying to run a business. I didn't have a head for it. Daddy wouldn't have wanted it.

I need to put my feet up. I can smell the rain in the air. And my ankles ache like the dickens from the swelling. I can't make it up the stairs tonight. I'll just sit here and put my feet up and doze. I won't put on a gown. That way if Henry comes I'll be dressed, and he won't get ideas in his head. If he says anything about the gun, I'll tell him his memory's playing tricks. That's all it is. I better use the pot. I guess Ora left it out on the back porch.

Woo, look at that lightning. It lights up the whole room, like midday. Don't even need an oil lamp. I can see the porch just like at noon. That's a relief. Drank a lot of water today, in all this heat. I don't want the rain to start up while I'm out here. But I can smell it, strong as can be. We're gonna have a big rain, that's for sure. Where's that pitcher of water she left? Wish I'd brought a lantern along. Goodness me, that lightning flash was even brighter than the last one. I see the pitcher over there on the kitchen table, with a glass. Let me put my teeth in the glass. I hear the rain now, pounding. Funny it would start off so hard. I'll just leave my teeth in here, go lay down on the divan in the front room.

It's too hot for a sheet even. Feels good to get off my feet. Always did sleep good when it rained. Lord, I'm tired. Tired as can be. Sure wish I had a candy bar. I like a little something sweet at night. Ora'll bring one tomorrow. Should've told her to get a few. I'll give her money for a box of Hershey's tomorrow. That way I can have one whenever I want it.

Lovingston
9:30 p.m.

"Wake up, Aimee. We're going to get off for supper. Stevie and Stell are hungry." Helen, barely awake herself, shook her youngest, whose thumb was sucked so far into her mouth that it seemed to grow from there. Aimee continued to lean on Helen's shoulder, as if she'd been drugged. Helen smoothed her blond hair out of her face. "Come on, hon. We need to get something to eat. Get the bags and stuff, would you, kids? I'm going to have to pick Aimee up."

She staggered to stand. Had she been dreaming? She was groggy, a little disoriented, like when you wake up from having a baby. She hadn't realized how exhausted she was. Stevie and Estelle reached to the overhead rack of the Trailways bus while Helen struggled to get both arms underneath Aimee so she could lift her. Aimee was the one of her children who never took naps. Who never went to sleep without her Silky in one hand and her other thumb in her mouth. Aimee who seemed to always be watching the family, saying little. Now she was dead asleep.

Helen had picked out Covington when they got to the bus station in Richmond. It was in the mountains. A bus was leaving in half an hour. She'd never heard Joe so much as mention it; maybe he didn't even know it existed. Her boss, Tom Graham, was from Covington. One of his old high school buddies was the Purchasing Agent at West Virginia Paper, so he kept an account with Tom at the store. She'd heard him say times without number what a great place it was to grow up. So she figured it was as good as anywhere for the time being. Helen had hoped that they could go all the way without getting off to eat, so they could get there in time to get settled in a motel for the night before it got too late. But these local buses took forever, stopping at practically every out-of-the-way crossroads, and the older kids were about to starve. It had been a long time since McDonald's. She was famished herself.

"How long before the next bus, sir?" The driver looked at Helen, who was holding her sleepy daughter like a sack of flour.

"Be along in about an hour, hour and a half. Just wait right there at Loafer's Corner. The store. Pretty good food at the Inn. Not too expensive, either. I think they serve until ten. By the way, heard on the radio earlier today that they're due for some weather here tonight. Big storm. You might think about stopping here."

Estelle whispered to Stevie, "Over my dead body. Hicksville, U. S. A."

"Thanks," Helen said, as she and the children stepped down. The door wooshed behind her and the bus pulled away, leaving a trail of hot gas fumes. It was still as hot as it had been at noon. And just as muggy. She could smell rain in the air, though. A storm would be such a relief. Funny how you forget all about the weather when you're riding in air conditioning, Helen thought. Aimee stirred in her arms.

"Mama? Mama? Are we there?" She rubbed her eyes and wiggled to stand.

"Not quite, honey." Relieved, Helen helped the child stand. "We're somewhere called Lovingston. Don't you just love that name? We need to get something to eat. Then we'll catch the next bus to Covington. Maybe I can call ahead and get us a room. Okay?"

"I'm not hungry, Mama. But I've got to go to the bathroom. Bad."

The sidewalk in front of the grocery store was wooden, and a bench the size of an old church pew sat up against the frame wall. Dim lights were on inside the store, and Helen could make out a few of the hand-written signs in the window: "No Drinking In Here"; "No Cridet, No Return"; "Giant Tomato Contest: Last Year's Winner: 4 lbs., 4 oz." Despite the fact that the street was deserted Helen got the impression that Lovingston was a safe place; I'll bet nobody's had her purse snatched here in the history of the town, she thought. Joe wouldn't like this place a bit, though. Too down at the heel.

Helen looked up the dim street. She could see a neon sign that said Lovingston Inn about a half a block up, across the street. Feeling a bit wobbly from the hours on the bus, her lack of lunch, and the deep sleep, she stretched and pointed. "That's where we'll eat. What do you think? You can use the bathroom there, Aimee. All right?"

"I certainly hope you don't plan to stay here for the night," Estelle said, before Aimee could answer.

The three travel-tired children picked up their bags and stood waiting for Helen to tell them what to do. The street was as dark as pitch. No streetlights. But the front window of the inn looked friendly enough. The driver said it wasn't too expensive. Helen was beginning to have second thoughts about this trip. The children looked exhausted. And here they were, out in the middle of nowhere. On their way to nowhere. It was only because it was dark and they were all tired, she told herself. Tomorrow morning, when the sun was shining and they were fresh, it would seem like an adventure again. Helen took her bag from Stevie's left hand. "Come on, kids. Let's cross the street. Doesn't seem to be too much traffic."

"Funny, Mom. Truly funny." Estelle rolled her eyes.

They trudged in a straight line the few steps to the white clapboard inn. The dining room was fairly empty, but the lights were still on. Helen opened the door that was glass halfway up, with about a dozen little panes, and a bell sounded. A blond woman about Helen's age, wearing a little plaid apron around her waist, came up to them, holding menus in her hand. "You all want something to eat? Or just drinks? We don't have a lot of choices left." She didn't seem anxious for them to sit down. Probably had been on her feet all day, Helen thought.

"We'd like some supper, please, if that's all right."

"Sure. Right this way. I think we've still got some meat loaf. And you can always get a sandwich. Hey, leave those suitcases there by the door. Nobody's gonna bother them."

A dark-haired attractive woman in a red sundress stood at the counter, tap-tapping her bill on the glass top. "Could

I pay this, please? I'm in a bit of a hurry." She smiled at Aimee, despite her obvious impatience.

"Be with you in a minute." The waitress led Helen and the two older children to the table. The antsy lady spoke quietly to Aimee, who lingered. All Helen could make out was something about "a cat" and "sleep."

"Come on, hon," Helen signaled. Her tired little girl, thumb still in her mouth, joined the rest of her family. All four sat down at a table with a clean plaid cloth that matched the waitress' apron. Even weary as they were, the solid squareness the four of them made at their places pleased Helen. Five wouldn't fit. Glad they'd come, reviving somewhat, she took the offered menus.

"Can I get you anything to drink while you make up your minds?" The waitress probably wanted to hurry things up, Helen figured, since it looked like they were her last customers. No doubt she needed to get home to her own family, put her own feet up.

"Would you bring me some coffee? No cream." She looked back at her children, who were staring around the room. "What do you all want to drink?"

"Can we get sodas, Mama?" Estelle asked.

"Sure, why not, we're on vacation. Bring them each a Pepsi, please."

"We just have Coke. That be all right?"

"Fine." She left to get the drinks, and Helen passed out a menu to each child, even Aimee. She couldn't read much, but Helen figured she'd want to be treated like the others. They all relaxed in their chairs and looked over the single large sheet that was divided into Breakfast, Lunch, and Dinner choices.

"I think she said they had meat loaf today on special. Get whatever you want."

Stevie spoke up. "Mom, it says $3.95 each for the Daily Dinner Special. Is that too much? If it is, I'll just get a grilled cheese. I don't mind."

"Don't be ridiculous. You love meat loaf. It's one of your favorites. At least mine is. And, like I said, we're on vacation. Get what you want. I know you're starving."

"If we get the meat loaf can we still get dessert?" Estelle wanted to know.

"Sure. No kidding, get what you want. I don't know how much longer we'll have to ride the bus tonight. I'd say another couple hours at least. And the driver said it wouldn't be here until about eleven. So you might as well enjoy your dinner." She smiled, wanting to put them at ease despite her own niggling doubts. "Like I told you, I've got plenty of money."

The waitress brought their drinks and took their orders. Estelle spoke up first and asked for meat loaf with mashed potatoes and gravy and applesauce. The other two said they'd have the same, so Helen ordered that, too. It was easier than trying to make up her mind. She'd made up her mind enough for one day.

When their waitress had gone back into the kitchen Estelle looked at her mother and said, "Do you think we ought to call him?"

That child is psychic, Helen thought. How does she know what's been nagging at me? Can she read my mind? Nobody had mentioned Joe since the taxi picked them up at home. Now Stell was saying exactly what she had festering about him in the back of her thoughts. Helen took a long sip of her coffee. It was good. Fresh perked. "I don't know. Let me think about it."

"I don't think so," Stevie jumped in. "You left him a note, didn't you? You told him we were on vacation, didn't you? So why look for trouble. He can't bother us now. As soon as you call him he's gonna start ordering you around, Mama. Then what would happen? I don't want you to call him. I really don't."

"Stevie, I said let me think about it, all right? I'm a little discombobulated right now. Let's eat, okay?" The waitress came back with a tray with four plates of food, family-style, and a basket of rolls.

As she served the dinners she asked, "Anybody want spoon bread? I forgot to ask."

None of the children said a thing; Helen realized they'd

probably never heard of spoon bread. So she answered: "This is fine. Rolls are perfect. Thank you." She picked up her fork.

"Y'all ain't from around here, are you?" The waitress stepped back from the table, propping her empty tray against her hip.

"No, we're on vacation." The children stared at Helen as she answered, not one of them yet eating, though Stevie had a fork of potatoes almost to his mouth.

"Storm's coming. Better be careful on the roads. They can be right tricky at night. Dark as a tomb. Especially if you don't know your way around. And it's raining. Twenty-nine's not too bad, though."

"Thank you. We'll probably order some dessert, if that's all right."

"Sure, enjoy your dinner. Just holler if you need anything." She went back to a table by the kitchen door, flopped into a chair, and lit a cigarette.

"She thinks you're driving, Mama. Why didn't you tell her we're waiting for the next bus? We ARE catching the bus, aren't we?" Estelle looked directly at Helen, her eyes like two warning flashers.

"What difference does it make, tell me that? What business is it of hers? Eat your dinner." The day was wearing on Helen. They ate for a few minutes without talking. Helen was glad for the quiet, but worried that the sudden change had been too hard on the kids. Too much for all of them, really. Stevie reached for a roll and met her look and smiled. The girls kept their faces near their plates, eating like starving hobos. Helen ate. The meatloaf was dry, but catsup-y tasting. The mashed potatoes were real. Lumps and all. But they were hot. It took them all no more than five minutes to clean their plates.

The blond waitress stubbed her cigarette and walked to their table. "Who wants some dessert? We've still got some cobbler. Apple or peach. Homemade."

Helen looked at each face. The three shook their heads no slowly. "No dessert? Not even ice cream?" She looked at Estelle, who made it a point of honor to always order dessert on the rare occasions they went out. She shook her head no again. "That's it, then. Just the check."

"You can pay me up at the cash register." The waitress started toward the front, and looked back over her shoulder at them, "Hear that rain? It's coming down like cats and dogs. Maybe it'll get some air moving. Tomorrow ought to be nice. A pretty day always follows a heavy rain."

Helen paid the bill and handed the waitress two dollars extra. She saw some postcards of the Nelson County Courthouse by the mints and cigarettes. She reached toward them, then changed her mind. What would she say to him? Besides, why let him know where they were? He'll probably think she was at her sister's in Baltimore. He'd never guess Covington. "Get your suitcases. Aimee, you can walk, now. Just hold my hand. Good night," she yelled to the waitress, who was already pulling down the shades.

When she opened the door, Helen was stunned by the force of the rain. It was coming down in buckets. She could hardly see a step in front of her. It was like they were stepping into a wall of water. "Wait a minute. Let me get my bearings." The children didn't move. They just stood under the overhang clutching their bags. Even Estelle didn't say a word. "We're gonna get soaked to the skin. I can see the light across the street, there, by the store. Just barely. Let's all hold hands. I don't see any cars. We'll just have to make a run for it. It'll be dry there. The bus'll be along pretty quick, now."

"Mama," Estelle whined, hesitant to step out into the rain.

"Well, what do you want me to do? Come on." Helen reached for Aimee's hand.

They stepped out from under the awning and started to edge across the sidewalk to the street. The force of the rain was so strong that they all had to lean forward in the direction of the store. Holding hands, they moved slowly, like people playing that game where everybody's blindfolded and someone leads them around the playground. They were drenched after the first few steps.

"Mama, I'm scared," Aimee screamed. Aimee, who never complained. Helen was scared, too. She held Aimee's tiny fingers tightly. The water running over them made their hands slippery and cold.

"Just hold onto me. Stevie, have you got Stell's hand? Take it, you hear. Can you see the light?"

"Yes ma'am. We're right here."

They kept leaning forward, step by slow step, until they reached the three wooden steps up to the sidewalk on the opposite side of the street. Crossing the street, which was about twenty feet wide, had felt like crossing twenty miles. Helen had to grab a post and hold onto it and pull Aimee up. She yelled: "Three steps. Remember? Stevie? Stell? Three steps up." They all lifted their soaking feet up onto the wooden walkway and pushed forward a few more steps to the bench. Helen pulled Aimee onto her lap, and the other two collapsed on either side of her, dropping their suitcases to the sidewalk.

They sat, huddled together, trembling. Helen couldn't hear a thing except the rain. No cars. No insects. No voices. The neon light up the street flashed out. They were left in total darkness. Hadn't the store's lights been on? She was feeling confused, scared, but she didn't want the children to know. Aimee was shivering against her.

"The bus ought to be along any minute. Rain won't keep one of those big old Trailways off the road. Just keep a lookout for the lights." Helen tried to sound more confident than she felt.

"Mama, I can't see a thing. It's not like in my room at night. It's like that time Stell closed me up in the closet by accident. I'm scared." Aimee shoved against her, hard, pushing her little body as close as it would go.

"My new shoes are ruined. Why don't you call somebody? Why don't you do something? What if the bus doesn't stop?" Stell's critical voice had a sharp edge to it. She didn't need Stell going haywire.

"Shut up, Estelle." Stevie's voice sounded calm, thank goodness. "I'm going to get some help, Mama. I'll just find my way back to that Inn. Somebody's bound to be there still. It's only been a few minutes. It's just across the street and down half a block. It shouldn't be any trouble to find. I don't mind getting wet. I'm already soaked to the skin."

"No you won't. You stay right here. The bus is bound to be here any minute. I won't have you going off in the dark like that, in a strange place. Just sit down. I mean it." Helen was afraid her voice was sounding a little hysterical. She couldn't help but be scared. Wouldn't Joe think this was a riot—her out here with the kids, God knows where in the country, scared to death of the dark and the rain. He'd get a big kick out of it all right. Tell her it served her right for going off half-cocked.

Stevie stood up. "I'm going to get some help. Or call somebody. Or something. Daddy would expect me to do something."

Helen groped her hand toward his voice, catching the sleeve of his shirt. "Please, honey, just wait a few more minutes."

But he was gone. Already swallowed in the dark. "I'll be right back." She could barely hear him above the rain's roar. "Don't worry. I'll bring somebody." He slipped into the night. Helen couldn't hear his voice or his footsteps at all.

"Stevie? Answer me. Are you all right?" Helen yelled, but the rain was so loud she could hardly hear her own words.

Panicked, her mind raced: I must be losing it. "The bus'll be here in a minute and we'll climb on and laugh at how silly we were to be scared." Damn. I forgot to call ahead for a motel room. Guess we'll have a little bit more trouble before we're in bed. Joe would laugh so hard at me. I won't tell him. But Stell is bound to. She won't be able to resist.

"Stevie?" Aimee was sitting up, her back tensed. "Stevie? Answer me. You're scaring me. Come back. Please." She sat that way for almost a minute, then collapsed against Helen again. She started sucking her thumb. "Mama. I wish I had Silky. Would you get it for me?"

Double damn, Helen thought. I must've left it on the last bus. When I was trying to carry Aimee and my purse. "I can't get it right now, hon. I can't see. I'm sorry. Just cuddle up against me. Everything will be fine. I promise."

They sat there without speaking, waiting.

Finally, "Mama, the water's up around my feet. Honest." Helen could feel it swirling around her ankles, too, but she hadn't wanted to mention it, hoping her imagination was overreacting. Estelle leaned hard against her other side. She could feel the water soaking her shoes. It seemed powerful, like a waterfall. Or a wave at the ocean. Not like a rain puddle. Not like that at all.

"Let's just wait for Steve to send help, okay? We'll get the bus, get dry. We'll laugh about this tomorrow. I promise." Helen hugged her two daughters. "Just hold onto me. Tight as you can. Everything will be fine. You want me to sing 'Beautiful Dreamer'?" Neither girl answered. She couldn't bring herself to sing anyway. Her throat was too closed up. She started counting to herself, wondering how far she'd get before Stevie came back or the bus arrived.

"Did I tell you? The bill for the shoes today came to thirty-five dollars. Even. No cents. Isn't that something? It never happens. I knew it was a special day when that happened. Did I tell you?"

Neither of the girls said a word. Probably they hadn't even heard her. They sat, huddled against Helen, the rain beating down on the overhang. She hugged them both hard, waiting for something to happen, waiting for this to be over.

Davis Creek
9:45 p.m.

Daniel held onto a peach tree with a trunk about as big around as he was. Rain pounded all around him, and the ground was so slippery he had a hard time getting his footing. I shoulda done what I planned to do and caught a ride before this rain started, he thought. I never even heard of rain like this. I never felt this wet, even in the shower. Not even body surfin. Soaked to the bone. I sure never been this wet with my clothes on. I can hardly get my breath, the rain's so thick. Creek sure is making a racket. Sounds more like the Atlantic Ocean than Davis Creek.

Some bright idea this was, trying to find that old lady's house at night. Once he got out on the road, he figured this was the last chance he'd get to check the place out, maybe find something worth a lot of money. Or even some money. Maybe even a diamond ring. Daniel had hiked in about an hour before the rain started, climbing up the hillside most of the time, trying to remember what Miz Malory told him about where the place was. Searching for the old peach orchard. Once he'd thought he'd seen something faint, like a light, but he got turned around, didn't see anything but dark and trees.

Now you gotta find it, dummy, or else find somewhere else to get in out of this weather. I can't even see any headlights. Can't remember which direction the highway is. I wouldn't be able to tell up from down if it wasn't for the rain. This flashlight is about as useful as tits on a tailpipe. Having a helluva time holding onto it with these slippery fingers. Feel right foolish holding onto this tree, but I'm afraid I'd slide right down the hill if I let go. The tree's bark was rough, started to hurt his hands, calloused as they were from picking.

Wouldn't Pauley-B get a kick out of this? He told me to stay away from haunted houses. No such thing as ghosts. Still, he'd say "I told you so," if he could see me now.

Didn't count on a storm like this, though. Rain like this can't last more'n five or ten minutes more. Just gotta wait it out. Gotta hold on until it lets up, then try to find somewhere dry to sleep. At least a cave. Maybe in the morning I can find the house. It's bound to be around here somewhere. I couldn't be far off.

He'd gotten the bright idea, while he was heading for 29 to catch a ride, to try to find the rich old lady's house. There was bound to be stuff in there, even if the relatives had carted off most of the furniture and stuff. Or maybe she'd just died and nobody knew it, and she was still there dead, just a pile of bones. A skeleton couldn't hurt you. And maybe there'd be some jewelry, or silver, or even money hidden away somewhere. He wasn't in any rush, he figured. He could take his time and search. He sure as hell wasn't punching a clock. Old people hid money in the craziest places. Maybe the relatives didn't even look in the right places. So he planned to have a look around, see what he could find.

Maybe I better turn off the flashlight, save the batteries, he thought. Wasn't doing him a bit of good anyway. Then the lightning flashed, and all he could see all around was trees. Nothing but little dried up peach trees. He couldn't even see a path or a road. How in hell did I get up here? I swear I came up a path. Took a dirt road off the highway, thought it was some truck road, then saw this dirt path, figured somebody must've been using it so it had to go somewhere. Now I can't even see that.

At least he felt safe under this tree, even if it was just a scrawny half-dead peach tree. Didn't even have any fruit. Ain't that what they said in school, get under a tree during a storm. Or was it don't get under a tree during a storm? He was getting confused. This pounding rain would get anybody confused. Probably even confuse that guy who picked peaches with him, the one who looked like such a tough hombre. Pauley-B shouldn't a lifted his hat today. He was just asking for trouble. I'd hate to be around when the guy figures out who took it.

I shoulda taken a ride. I woulda been long gone by now. Been in some truck stop in Pennsylvania having a burger and fries. Man, I shouldn't a come up here. Hasn't stealing stuff already gotten you in enough trouble? How many times before you figure it out? Still, taking stuff from some dead old lady's broken-down house ain't exactly stealing. But if I'd gone on like I planned I wouldn't be in this fix.

Hanging onto the tree, Daniel wished he was back in his room at Miz Malory's. Or looking at television with her, having another dish of that peach pie. He sure could get himself in some fixes. His daddy was right about that. No more stealing after this one. No looting. He was gonna get a job, get a car, get himself together. Like Miz Malory said, he had plenty of sense. Just had to start using it.

The lightning flashed again, bright as day. Suddenly he heard a roar so loud he jumped and dropped his flashlight. At the same instant he lost his footing, slipped and lost his hold on the tree trunk. He was swimming in mud.

Man, what's happening? Sliding out of control, unable to grab onto anything, he felt a flash in his mind, like when you get an electric shock. Sounds like the mountain's falling down, he thought. Sounds like the whole damn mountain's falling down.

Nelson County
10:00 p.m.

Clarence sat alone in the corner of the tiny bar. Only room for a couple of tables and four stools. Dark, too, except for the light from the TV and the neon Budweiser sign. Last hour or so he could hear the rain pounding on the roof. Wouldn't be so hot picking tomorrow, he figured. Or maybe they wouldn't pick at all.

He didn't mind the dark, but he didn't like being closed in; he came two or three nights a week, anyway, to check out Diane, get a fix on her comings and goings. Much as he didn't like people to notice him, he had to come and watch her, so he'd be ready when the time came to baptize her. The Lord never said it would be easy. Take up thy cross and follow me. She definitely would not be as easy as the other two. Even if she'd gotten used to seeing him, and didn't act so all-fired superior any more, she still had a lot more grit than the other two. So he put up with the lack of leg room and fresh air in order to do his duty, fulfill his earthly mission.

Jack and Diane both pretty well knew him by now, but he wasn't worried about Jack. He could smell a rat, and Jack was all right. Probably seen his troubles, too, if Clarence's guess was right. Like most bartenders, he was more ears than eyes. And Diane wouldn't be around to run her mouth much longer. Besides, he'd checked out the post office in Lovingston one day. They didn't even have any federal posters up. Enough crooks and crazies in Virginia to keep the cops busy, he figured. They didn't have too much occasion to worry about escaped cons from West Virginia. Probably hadn't had a felony here in this hick town in ten years. Probably never had a killing, a sacrifice. They were in for a surprise, that was for sure.

McGritz hardly ever got full on a week night. Around supper time they'd be pretty busy, but the bar didn't fill up except on Fridays and Saturdays. These people around here were like the people in Parkersburg, Clarence thought. Most of the men stuck close to home during the week. Usually the crip was here, though, taking up space with that chair of his and pouring the government's money down his throat. But he hadn't been in tonight. Too damn sweet. The rain might melt him. Make him sick. He could use a bath, though. Probably hadn't had one in a month of Sundays. Clarence washed in the creek every morning before he started walking to the orchards. Made him feel clean, to face the day the Lord hath made. Cleanliness is next to godliness. It's for sure the crip ain't no neighbor to the Lord, stinking filthy as he is. Makes me sick to think about it.

Clarence lifted his mug to his lips. The bar didn't have any windows, but from where he was sitting he could see into the restaurant, and the windows in there would light up bright as day every few minutes. Didn't hear any thunder, just this lightning. Raining hard as thunderation, Clarence noticed. Must've been like this when Noah gathered the animals two by two. Wouldn't mind having a goddamned ark to get back to the cave. Shit. The rain would feel good after all this heat. Little rain ever hurt nobody. And the cave stayed dry as a match. They'd never put him in a cage again. No sirree.

The Lord takes care of his own. Consider the birds. Clarence had all he needed, moving around from crop to crop. A bedroll, a few changes of shirts and jeans, a jacket for the night chill. Move from place to place, wipe the dust from your feet, have no fear for what you shall eat or drink. The earth is the Lord's and the fullness thereof. Been doing it for years. People like Saunders pissed him off. Acting like those peaches were his. Like he owned all those damned frigging acres of peach trees. The Lord would tend to Saunders in his own good time. Probably have a stroke or a heart attack or have his guts eaten away by cancer. Getting fat off the land. Render to Caesar what is Caesar's. Saunders would get his. That wasn't Clarence's problem. He was sent to save Diane. Save her from her tempting, lustful ways. Purify her in the name of the Father, the Son, and make her a Holy Ghost.

He could see her sitting in the dining room smoking and talking to the other waitress, Thelma. Skirt hiked up above her knees, shameless. Hadn't nobody been in for a good while, not since the rain started pouring. Cool as a cucumber. Didn't seem like nothing much got to her. That night he'd left the note on her car. She just read it and laughed, put it in her purse. Didn't seem to bother her a bit. Probably used to men talking to her like she was a Jezebel. Probably got off on it. Some women did. Probably more than let on.

Yeah, a couple of truckers had been in there drinking

heavy and running their mouths that night. She'd come in on her break and sat down at the bar. She never did that. Not once since he'd been coming. All he could figure that night was she wanted to twitch her ass around them two truckers. Come on to them. Tease them. That's what she was. A goddamn cock-teaser. Both of them talking a bunch of filth, showing off. And she was just sucking up to it. It was disgusting to watch. One of them leaned over to her and asked her where she'd recommend spending the night hereabouts. She just laughed, said there weren't no motels in Nelson County, they'd have to head on down 29 to Amherst, if they were going South. He whispered something I couldn't hear, and she laughed like a sailor and shook her head. Looked him right in the face, just as brazen as you please. And the guy had said, "You can't blame a man for tryin," and finished off his mug and asked for another one. Other guy just laughed to beat the band, pointed his thumb at his buddy and said "He's paying for this round." Diane twitched on back into the dining room, acting like she was a homecoming queen or something.

I couldn't help putting that note on her car, hiding back behind the dumpster to see what she'd do. See if she'd scream or run back inside to get Jack. She read it and laughed, though. Put it in her purse. Probably showed it to Thelma the next night. He'd made it filthy. Something like "To the lady who can't sit her fat ass down and give the time of day to anybody. Shithead. Just because you look like an asshole don't give you the right to act like one. May the fleas from a dozen camels infest your pussy, if they haven't already. P. S. Your mother's a bitch like you for not teaching you any manners." Something like that. Didn't seem to bother her one bit. We'll see how she acts when I go to baptize her, though. We'll see if she'll laugh then.

Clarence drank his beer and thought about how easy it was going to be. I'll just wait in the back of her car, he thought. I'll get down on the floor in the back of her Pinto and wait till she leaves. There ain't any lights out back, and she acts like she's walking around in broad daylight when she leaves here after work. Don't seem to worry her a bit to go out there alone. Her mama should've taught her to watch out for strangers. She'll probably just get in and drive off. Won't ever think about checking in back. She never does. But some women can smell trouble. Just like a man can smell a bitch in heat. Don't matter. Even if she does, I'll have the knife ready. Tell her to drive on or I'll cut her. She's so brazen she'll probably think she can get away from me. Vengeance is mine. Won't be hard. Not as easy as the last one, but he didn't mind a little struggle. Didn't Jacob struggle with the angel all night? Nope, wouldn't be as easy as the last one.

Clarence was working a concert. Working as a guard. That's where he got his USHER hat. Some of them teenagers get so drunk they'd start talking big, starting fights. He'd have to put them out. So the day of the concert the guys who sponsored it would pick up a few tough-looking locals, to stand up front and keep people away from the band. Show some muscle to the hopped-up hippies. It was easy picking up work at concerts. One-night stands, between one crop and the other. This band seemed to be working the women up into a frenzy even more than most. Some guy old enough to be their daddy was singing, too. It was disgusting to watch. But he hadn't even thought about a baptism until the show was about over. Until the encore, in fact. Everybody sweating and screaming and jumping up and down. Women busting out of those halters and T-shirts. No underwear. Like heathens. Might as well have nothing on. Jeans cut off up to their asses. Jumping up and down screaming and squirming. And that guy comes back out and starts singing about "Brother Love's Traveling Salvation Show." If that didn't beat all. And this ugly-looking girl bumps up against me. Falls on me. Drunk as could be. Couldn't a been older than fifteen, sixteen. Had no business drinking. Had pimples all over her face and crossed eyes. And she just fell all over me laughing. And when I went to stand her up she rubbed right up against me. Put her hand right in my crotch. And I knew she was the one. I saw the light, just like Paul on the road to Tarsus. Took her right into the woods there. She could hardly wait to get her clothes off. Gave herself to me, like she couldn't get enough. Moaning, begging for more. Breath so thick with liquor I could've cut it with a knife. She must've been high on drugs, too. Hash or something. Because she wanted more and more. Moaning like that. When I said, "Say, take my life and let it be," she just said it, "Anything you want, just don't stop," she said. And when I said, "Say, thy will be done," she just said it, "Thy will be done," pushing up against me like nothing would ever satisfy her. She was the one, all right. I said, "I don't like doing this, but I've got to do it to save your everlasting soul." She just laughed low in her throat, "God, you're good," she said. Didn't even know what happened when I signed her with the sign of the cross. Eyes just bulged out. Holy, holy, holy. Happened so fast I almost forgot to spit in her face. The Lord works in wondrous ways. After it was over I didn't go to pick up my money or anything. Crowd still screaming, band still playing, that guy singing on. Just walked out of the woods, walked off to the highway, walked away. Never looked back.

No, Diane wouldn't be that easy. But she was definitely the one. The crip was a sign, clear as the other two. Tonight couldn't be the night, 'cause he wasn't here. But he'd be back. And Clarence would know the right time. The Lord would send him a sign. He'd learned to be patient, bide his time. Time was something he had plenty of.

When the lights went out, Diane and Thelma screamed. Clarence sat still; his eyes were used to the dark, because of being in the cave at night. He'd learned to stay still as a cat, watch, let his eyes get used to the dark. Before a minute went by, Jack had some candles lit on the bar and Diane and Thelma came in, bumping into tables and chairs on the way, giggling. The lightning lit up the front room, but the candles made it seem like a church service of some sort in the bar. Rain hammered the roof.

"Don't you think we better lock up and go on home, Jack? Ain't nobody coming in tonight." Diane giggled while she spoke, nervous-like, taking one of the candles from the bar and holding it up to her face. She was smiling, like a kid on a scavenger hunt. "Business ain't exactly booming." She laughed and nudged Thelma.

"Yeah, might as well. Let me just check the kitchen. You all stay in here." He took a candle with him and walked back through the door to the restaurant.

"OH!" Thelma jumped a mile when she saw Clarence in the shadows in the corner. Diane just laughed.

"You scared me half to death. I thought I was seeing a ghost or something," Thelma said. He couldn't see her face too clear, but he knew it was homely. She had a mouth like a horse, with about a million teeth as big as a picket fence. But her shape wasn't bad. Not as good as Diane's. But not bad.

"Afraid of your shadow, or a little rain? Or both?" Clarence grinned, but there was no humor in his face. He lit a cigarette, and the match showed his smile.

Diane, she was the show-no-fear type. "I'm just glad we got some rain. We sure needed it. Say, mister, you want a ride home? I've got my car outside. Looks like weather for ducks out there. Either that or fish." She giggled the whole time she spoke, cocky brazen edge to her voice. But he won't fooled. The storm had scared her shitless, so she wanted a escort. Or was she pulling some Good Samaritan number? She and Thelma leaned their shoulders together and laughed like them silly grade-school girls that always made fun behind his back. The front room lit up again, but still no thunder cracked.

Clarence about jumped up out of his chair, but he didn't make a move. A muscle in his cheek twitched, but other than that he was still as a corpse. He could do it. Just that easy. Do it tonight. Of course, Thelma was right there. She'd heard everything. But he could do it and go. Head for the apples early. Or go on down South. Pick oranges. But Craw-Dad wasn't here. He hadn't gotten a sign. He'd have to wait for a sign from his Heavenly Father. Suddenly, he laughed out loud. He laughed so hard he leaned over the table, and the two women started laughing with him.

"Hey, some other time, okay? I'll take a rain check." And he kept on laughing. The women sat down at his table and laughed until tears ran down their faces.

Jack came back, with a flashlight in his hand. "What's so damn funny?"

"Nothing, Jack. Nothing, really." Diane stood up. "Let me get my pocketbook and we'll go, okay?"

Thelma followed her out of the room.

"I'll finish cleaning up tomorrow. It looks pretty rough out there. We better get a move on."

Clarence sucked down the last few gulps of his beer and put a few dollars on the table.

"On the house tonight, bub," said Jack, as he walked behind the bar, took off his apron, and hung it on a peg.

"Thanks. See you in the funny papers." Clarence crumpled his dollars in his pocket and headed for the front door. He hollered back into the kitchen to Diane, "Don't forget that rain check, now. Blessed be the tie that binds."

He opened the front door, and the blast from the rain knocked him off balance. Laughing, thinking about baptizing Diane, he steadied himself and pushed forward into it, saying to himself, "A little rain never hurt nobody."

U.S. 29
Outside Lovingston
10:15 p.m.

Judy eased the car to the edge of the road, took her sweaty hands off the steering wheel, and wiped them on her dress. The last twenty minutes had been hell. She must have gone no more than five miles since she left the restaurant back in Lovingston. She turned off the engine, relieved to be stopped, even if it was pitch black outside. Her headlights weren't doing her much good anyway. Rain drummed on the roof. When she'd left the restaurant it had barely been coming down. Now it was like somebody had opened a giant fire hydrant; the force was that strong. Her heart was keeping time with it. Times like this, a person needed a car radio.

She turned to look in the backseat. She couldn't see a thing, not even her mound of clothes. She stretched her hand into the dark, felt fabric, touched around until she felt fur. Sophie was still as a stone, asleep on top of her clothes. Her coat was soft and her breathing was easy, regular. Judy realized that her own was fast, like she'd just run from the car to her front door. Only she hadn't gone anywhere.

Damn. Why hadn't she called Drew back at that restaurant? She'd thought about it while she was gulping down the day's special. She hadn't wanted to stop, but she was so hungry and thirsty she figured she'd take a few minutes. That way she could freshen up in the bathroom, eat a bit, and be on her way in less than a half hour. Which she had done. Which was why she hadn't called. She figured she had no more than an hour until she got there. Only now it was raining like it was the end of the world. That wasn't funny. Noah took the animals two by two. Never again by flood. It wasn't funny at all. She was more upset than she realized. Damn Sophie. She should've left this afternoon, like she had planned.

Everything was black as tar. She had to touch the window to tell where the inside stopped and the outside began. She couldn't even see the road, now that she'd turned off her lights. It was like being inside a carwash. She hated that feeling. It made her claustrophobic. Don't panic. "Hello darkness my old friend; I've come to talk to you again," she sang inside her head, trying to soothe herself. What could Drew do anyway? She would just wait. Wasn't she a world-class expert at waiting? Drew always took route 60 all the way from Lexington to Richmond, but she had her own way: 6 west to 29, 29 south to Amherst, 60 west to Lexington. She was a nervous Nelly at the wheel, always had been. She hated 60; it was like a death trap, with all those trucks whizzing by doing sixty or better. She preferred 6; it was less travelled, more scenic; she could stop at Scottsville or Lovingston to eat; she didn't have to worry that much about traffic until she hit 60, and by then it was pretty rural. It didn't add more than five miles to the trip, and her peace of mind was worth that. Only now she realized that 29 was practically deserted. Well, she'd never have to worry about that again; Drew would drive them back and forth to the symphony from now on. She wouldn't be out alone in a storm with a drugged cat ever again.

Her eyes were getting slightly used to the dark. Like when she was a little girl, and she'd lain in bed waiting to be able to see. Only then, usually, the moon and stars would be out. The goblins would gradually turn into doors and chairs. This must be more like being lost in a cave. Without a flashlight. She could barely make out the fuzzy outlines of the dash, the seat. She picked up the limp cat, put her on her lap, petted her back. "You wouldn't like this rain a bit, girl." Sophie was still in noodle-dom. But it felt good to hold her. Trembling, Judy longed to be relaxed, be at Drew's drinking a glass of wine, listening to music, her feet in his lap. That woman who came into the restaurant when she was paying her check; she was probably safe inside the restaurant, safe and relaxed. She was probably still there, right this minute. With those three kids. That little one looked like a Renoir child. Or a Mary Cassatt. Staring at me, her finger in her mouth, until I'd said, "Do you like cats? I've got my cat out in the car. She's knocked out. Sound asleep." Just for something to say. A cherub. That's what she looked like. They were probably sitting around eating dessert by candlelight this very minute. Would she and Drew have children? They hadn't talked about it. Time to talk about that later. She wasn't exactly an antique.

Lightning flashed. No noise, just a flash of light, like someone turned on a spot for an instant. She started, blinked, and it was gone. Behind her eyes she saw the outline of Afton mountain. The afterimage. Like an echo without any sound. No way she'd try to drive over Afton in this pounding rain.

I'll wait, she thought. When that happens again I'll be ready. Maybe I'm close to a house and I don't even know it. The power must be out. I don't remember lightning without thunder. This is too crazy. That must be why it's so dark. No power. If there's a house, I'll drive to it. I could do that. Real slow. Straight ahead. And I'll make a run for the door. Maybe the phone won't be out. That happens a lot. The power always goes out first. Especially in the mountains. I wonder why. Or is it the other way around?

The lightning flashed again. This time she could see an opening up ahead through the curtain of water. She'd never seen rain like this. Never even imagined it. It was like waves at the beach, like being tumbled by the waves, losing a sense of where she was. She'd hated that as a child. The car trembled with the weight of the rain. She trembled. She'd seen an open space, a parking lot. She wasn't sure. It didn't seem like a yard. No bushes or trees. She strained her eyes, to be ready. Her neck was like a rock. Why is it the things you want, really want, never come easy, she thought. Why is it Allen fell into my lap, and now I'm practically going through doom and disaster to get to Drew? Life's weird. Really weird.

This time she could make out a building in the flash. And she was sure it had a parking lot. Maybe it was a service station. Or a restaurant. What else would be out here in the middle of nowhere? In that case, probably nobody would be there. Not after nine o'clock during the middle of the week out here in the sticks. But what if there was a pay phone in the parking lot? Most country places had pay phones somewhere outside. She'd drive right up to it, get out, call Drew, let him know she was stuck. She just wanted to hear his voice. He'd be worried as hell, but she needed to hear his voice. He'd want to know. She didn't want him to come after her. She'd just tell him she'd stay in the car, in the parking lot, until the rain let up. To wait up for her. That she loved him. She felt in her pocketbook for her change purse. She had plenty of dimes. No problem. She'd just tell the operator to reverse the charges.

This time, in the flash, she screamed. She screamed and screamed, only she couldn't hear herself for the pounding rain. She'd seen a man, a man with a beard. He'd been close to the car, but he didn't look like he saw it. He was pushing into the rain, in a crouch, almost. He looked like he was concentrating on keeping his balance. Should she honk her horn? Offer him a ride? Fellow man-in-need. Good Samaritan. Something about him made Judy tremble even more, though. Frightened her.

Sophie didn't move. Shaking, Judy picked the cat up and lifted her onto the pile of clothes in the back.

Hands sweating, she felt for the ignition, turned the key to start the engine, checked the doors to be sure they were locked. When she turned on the headlights no one was there. The bearded man had disappeared into the dark. All she could see was sheets and sheets of rain. Slowly, Judy pushed down on the accelerator, eased the car into first and headed for the parking lot, praying the restaurant had a pay phone, praying it would work.

August 20, 1969
Davis Creek
2:00 a.m.

I'm wet. I'm in the water. That dream. Don't look at me. Don't look at me. I'm not dressed. It wouldn't be proper. Stay away. Don't touch me. I need to get out of this water. It's too cold. Ora didn't make it hot enough. I need to get out. Go away. You've no business bothering me now. I need my privacy. I need to get dressed.

"Ora. Come here right this minute, Ora. I need a towel. You didn't leave me a towel."

It's too dark. I don't remember it dark like this. I can't see a thing. I know he's over there in the corner, though, staring at me. Waiting for me to stand up.

"Ora. OR-A. I need you. I can't see. I need something to cover me up. I told you he was here staring at me. OR-A."

If I could see I could get my bearings. The lightning. My clothes are wet. I have on wet clothes. Bermudas. The lightning's not in my dream. It's daytime. How could it be lightning? And the rain's pouring. I heard the clock. I've never heard the clock in my dream before, either. What's going on?

"Ora. Help me. Something's wrong."

I've got on wet clothes. My legs are cold. It doesn't make any sense. I need to stand up. I need to find Ora. The rain's so loud she can't hear me. Why is it wet here in the front room? Why is it dark and then light? What's going on? I've got to wake up. I don't like this. It's confusing me. I'll shut my eyes. Then I'll open them, and I'll be awake.

There. I still can't see. That lightning flash. There's water all over the place. It's almost to the top of the legs on Daddy's desk. I've got to get up and get his books. The album. Some of them must be wet already. He'd be furious. What's going on? The rain's so loud I can hardly think. I can't swim. I've got to get out of here. Why is water in here? I'll go upstairs. What about Daddy's pen? His books? Daddy, what should I do? Tell me. Where's Ora? Why isn't she here to help me? She promised. I can't swim. I never learned. I just went to the edge of the water, up to my waist. The Piney's usually so low all I do is wade. I never learned. There was no need to learn. Mama couldn't swim. I remember Daddy saying that. What difference did it make? She never even walked down to the river, that I remember.

I've got to get out to the front hall, go upstairs, lay down in my bed. Then it'll go away. That's it. It's bound to be a bad dream. Why am I so cold? Hold on to the sofa. Wait for a lightning flash. That's it. Grab onto the desk. Now the door frame. Wait here. The water's so heavy. I never remember it heavy like this in my dream before. And it's pushing me. How can it be pushing me? The clock. I've got to go back for the clock.

"Ora. Get the clock. It's too heavy for me. You get it, you hear. And bring it upstairs. I knew you made a mistake when you didn't wind it. It wasn't mine to do. GET IT RIGHT NOW, ORA. IT'S YOURS TO TAKE CARE OF. BRING IT UPSTAIRS. GET JAMES EARL TO HELP YOU. HE'S STRONG AS AN OX. QUIT ACTING LIKE YOU CAN'T HEAR ME. I KNOW YOU CAN."

Rest a minute here against the door. Hold on. I ought to get my teeth. I don't think I can make it to the kitchen and back. Reach for the stairs. My Lord the water's strong. There. I've got the bannister. Pull. Pull. I can hardly feel the steps. Pull up with your arms. I can't be awake, but it feels like I'm awake.

There. It's dry now. I must be halfway up. I can't see a thing. I can't hear a thing but the rain and the water. But the steps feel dry. These wet clothes weigh a ton. I've got to get upstairs and get them off and lie down. I must be getting sick. Getting a fever. That's what it is. I'll lie down and wait for the sun. Ora will know what to do. She'll give me something for the fever and go into town and get somebody. I'm too old to stay out here alone. She'll have to come and stay now, now that I'm sick.

Maybe I'm having a heart attack. Daddy said he got cold all over. That's what he said about the first one. He got cold all over, and it was hard to move. And hard to breathe. But why am I wet? Did I soil myself? The noise. I hear the rain and the water all around me, like thunder. Maybe it is thunder.

There. I can see the top of the stairs. That lightning is just like daylight. I've never seen anything like it. Maybe it really is a storm. The weather was so peculiar yesterday. That's all it is. Just a storm. Ora will have a mess to clean up tomorrow. I've never seen water this high. Daddy said, build on the high ground, and you won't have to worry.

Phew, it took all my energy just to get up here to the top of the steps. Rest a minute. I'll just rest a minute, then go on into my room and lie down. Maybe I have a fever. I'm imagining all this. I just need to get into the bed. When Ora gets here she'll take care of me. I've been sweating. That's why these clothes are so wet and cold. It's the fever. I hardly have any energy left. Daddy's room is closer. I'll just go in there and rest. Ora will be here by eight. She promised. I just need to sleep. That's all. This is the strangest dream I've ever had. Fever dream.

There. The lightning. I can make it to Daddy's door. It's hard to breathe. I feel like I'm under water. This all seems too real. But it can't be. My mind's playing tricks. I've got to get in bed. Hold onto the dresser. That's it. Grab the cedar chest. Alice Elizabeth's. Hope chest. Sit down a minute. That's it. I don't think I can go another step. Catch your breath. O.K. Grab the bedpost. Pull around. Just let go. Fall.

This bed smells so good. It doesn't smell all damp. It's so close in here, though. It's hard to breathe. I've got to sleep, get rid of this fever. I need some aspirin, but I'd never get to the medicine cabinet in this dark. No more energy. I'll close my eyes. I can smell Daddy's tobacco. Can the living talk to the dead? Daddy? Henry? Can they? Talk to me. I'm scared. The rain's so loud. Talk to me, Daddy. Ora will be here soon. Mr. Psychic was right. You don't have to fix me a big breakfast, Ora. Just bring me some aspirin. And some water. I need some water to drink. I can't stand this dream. The lightning. Even with my eyes closed I see the lightning. How can that be?

"Daddy? How can that be?"

Afterword

A historical marker along U.S. 29 near Lovingston, Virginia, reads:

On August 20, 1969, torrential rains, following remnants of Hurricane Camille, devastated this area. A rainfall in excess of 25 inches largely within a five-hour period swept away or buried many miles of roads, over 100 bridges and over 900 buildings. 114 people died and 37 remain missing. The damage totaled more than $100,000,000 and Virginia was declared a disaster area.

Virginia Historic Landmarks Commission

8 Flood Victims Still Nameless
by Jay Strafford
Richmond News Leader
August 20, 1976

©*Richmond Times-Dispatch,* used with permission

Woods Mill—Seven years later, a lone marker along U.S. 29 here is the only visible reminder of the hurricane disaster that struck this Nelson County community.

But in Richmond are eight other, starker reminders: the containers that hold the cremated remains of eight still unidentified victims of massive flooding, triggered by remnants of Hurricane Camille, that devastated parts of Nelson and Rockbridge Counties on August 20, 1969.

* * * * *

"We've never got any answers," about the identities of the eight victims, said Thomas Jordan, an official with the Virginia Department of Health's anatomical division. "And as time goes by, the probability decreases to the point that no one really expects any."

195

The individual containers are stored away from view in the anatomical division's offices. For the past two years, officials say, there have been no inquiries about the nameless dead except an occasional question from reporters.

* * * * *

Herbert Sharman, an employee of the state medical examiner's office in Roanoke, described the eight victims as follows:

- A girl, 6 to 8 years old, weighing 60 pounds, 3 feet 10, blond.
- A man in his late 50s, muscular and stocky (about 215-220 pounds), 5 feet 11, balding with black hair. He chewed tobacco.
- A woman in her late 40s or early 50s, 150-160 pounds.
- A woman in her late 30s, 140-145 pounds, light brown hair, 5 feet 5, very well-groomed.
- A girl about 10, 70-80 pounds, 4 feet 7, long blonde wavy hair.
- A youth about 17, 155 pounds, 5 feet 9, blue eyes, moderately long brown straight hair, a sparse blond moustache. He bit his fingernails.
- A boy 12 to 14, 125-130 pounds, 5 feet 4, long dark brown hair.
- A woman about 70, 140-150 pounds, 5 feet 2, long white hair and no teeth. She had had her appendix removed and bore three scars on her abdomen. She was wearing a blue-checked shirt and green Bermuda shorts.

The ashes will be kept until 25 years after the flood [1994], in case identities are ever discovered, Sharman said.

Author's Note: 114 people died in the disaster; 37 remain missing; none of the descriptions of the missing match the descriptions of the eight "nameless."

Eight Hurricane Camille victims still unidentified after 20 years
by Meg Hibbert
Nelson County Times
August 17, 1989

Why has no one missed them enough in 20 years to find them?

The people could have been anyone's grandmother, aunt and uncle and four young cousins, on their way to a summer family reunion. Twenty years later they are still waiting for that family which has never come for them.

The remains of eight unnamed, unclaimed persons found in Nelson County after Hurricane Camille now rest —perhaps uneasily—in Richmond.

Mystery surrounds them. Who are they? Why were they in Nelson County? Why has no one missed them enough in 20 years to find them?

Their bodies were cremated and the ashes sent to the state repository after a nationwide attempt to identify them failed.

The eight might have been Nelson County residents, but it is unlikely. In a county of approximately 10,000 at the time of the flood, most people knew their neighbors' haunts and habits. They did not match descriptions of the 32 Nelson people missing as of that autumn, and no one in the county reported these eight missing.

Although they are unnamed, they are not completely anonymous. Autopsies and dental examinations done during body identification procedures after the flood revealed some—but not enough—about the unclaimed eight.

According to the records, the "Camille family," for want of a better name, is made up of three children, a teenaged boy, a grandmotherly-aged woman, a man and woman in boy, a grandmotherly-aged woman, a man and woman in their 50s and a younger woman in her mid-30s who probably had not borne a child. All are white, and the children, teenager and younger woman had blonde or light brown hair.

The man was stocky and muscular, balding with only a rim of black hair. His death papers state his teeth were ground-down and deeply-stained brown like those of a tobacco chewer.

Identical stomach contents showed at least three of the group shared their last meal together, according to Lovingston Dentist George Criswell, who assisted in body identification after the flood.

Except for dental observations made at the time and distributed to more than 10,000 dentists across the nation during the identity search, little more is known about the "Camille family" who were united in death and anonymity, if not in life.

Were these unknown eight on a family outing, camping along one of the county's creeks when the wall of water swept out of the sky? Could they have been Woodstock-bound hippies, on their way to the now-legendary rock festival in New York state?

Perhaps no one will ever know. But their existence in the medical records, in the vault in Richmond, and in the memories of those who worked in the flood aftermath is a kind of haunting—the last known Camille victims are still unnamed, and unclaimed.